HAVE FUN IN BURMA

ROSALIE METRO

HAVE FUN IN
BURMA

A NOVEL

NIU PRESS / DEKALB, IL

This is a work of fiction. All characters are products of the author's imagination, and any resemblance to persons living or dead is entirely coincidental.

This work may not be translated without consent of the author and NIU Press.

Northern Illinois University Press, DeKalb 60115
© 2018 by Rosalie Metro
All rights reserved
Printed in the United States of America
27 26 25 24 23 22 21 20 19 18   2 3 4 5
978-0-87580-777-5 (paper)
978-1-60909-236-8 (e-book)
Book and cover design by Yuni Dorr

Library of Congress Cataloging-in-Publication Data
is available online at http://catalog.loc.gov

He who looks outward dreams. He who looks inward awakes.
—CARL JUNG

CONTENTS

A NOVEL

A DREAM

I dreamed Burma before I saw it with my eyes. The golden spire of a pagoda glittered against the blue-black sky, and a full moon hung above it. I was moving around the spire like a planet in orbit, but very slowly. A voice that came from everywhere, from deep in my own throat, said *stay here*.

A month later, I heard the same words in my mind as I craned from the window of a decrepit taxi ferrying me past the Shwedagon Pagoda. Hearing the voice again was even more uncanny than seeing the Shwedagon in real life, which was also exactly as I remembered it from my dream. Why would I stay? I planned to be in Burma for three months, just a summer. Still, I felt unmoored from everything that had come before, overcome with inexplicable nostalgia, like I'd finally made it home. Later I'd have an explanation for feeling that way, even if it wasn't one I wanted to accept at first. In the beginning, I let myself forget that I was farther from home than I'd ever been.

With Thiha it was exactly the opposite: I saw him dozens of times before I dreamed of him. Or seeing him in a dream was the first time I really saw him at all. I do believe that what we said to each other in dreams was truer than what we were able to say when we were awake, which was always stilted and never in a language either of us could completely understand. Maybe I just like to think that way because we didn't get to say goodbye in real life.

Now, the image of the moon above the Shwedagon seems like a still from a movie poster: not a lie, but just one face of the story. I dreamed it before I'd heard the word *kala* spit from someone's mouth like a stone, before I'd heard of the people who call themselves the Rohingya, before I knew there were Muslims in Burma at all. I keep coming back to that one image of the Shwedagon, of Buddhism, of Burma, even though now I can only see it through the filter of other memories: me lying in my own shit, too sick to stand up; the newspaper photo of something that had been burned so badly I didn't realize at first it was a corpse; the fear on Thiha's face the first night he came to my room; Bhante waving to me as I sat in the army truck, his robes hanging on his body like a curtain of dried blood.

I come back to that image of the Shwedagon because I miss being an eighteen-year-old girl whose worst offense was dreaming of a place she'd never been.

Or maybe everyone around me now is right—I was the one who was hurt the most by my actions. Either way, what I did is done. I was sure I was right in the beginning, and I'm pretty sure I'm right now, too. But those two ways of being right feel farther apart than the span of one lifetime can hold.

KO OO

Burma began for Adela Frost with a man chanting under his breath as he rolled sushi in the Edgerton Fields Academy cafetorium: sabbe satta avera hontu, sabbe satta abyapajjha hontu.

His voice was low and guttural, and his lips barely moved; the words seemed to vibrate directly from his throat. The sound was so soft that Adela might not have noticed it, had she not been early for lunch, and the cafetorium so quiet.

The man had coppery skin and black hair, and he wore a neat white cap and apron. Adela had never seen him before. Sushi was a new addition to Edgerton Fields's menu. ("That's prep school for you," her Dad would say.)

She walked over to the sushi counter, pulled forward by the man's voice. The name on his badge, which did not seem like a name to Adela at all, read OO.

"Excuse me . . ."

He looked up from his work as if awakening from sleep. His black eyes held hers.

"What are you saying?"

"I chant the Buddha's words of goodwill. May all beings be free from danger."

"Oh."

Adela looked more closely at his face. It was hard to tell how old he was. His skin was smooth, but the whites of his eyes were tinged with yellow. A sparse mustache, too thin to shave, shadowed his upper lip.

"Are you a monk?"

He set down his knife.

"I was a monk for some weeks, when I was a child. But everyone in my country knows these words."

"Where are you from?"

"Burma."

He pointed to a yellow sticker on his badge, emblazoned with the silhouette of a burgundy-robed monk. Underneath the image, in a script that looked like circles and fish hooks, it said သတ္တိ ရှိပါ.

"What does it mean?"

"That-ti shi ba," he said. "Have courage. The monks make a revolution, to get democracy for our country."

It was eleven-thirty, and students started drifting into the cafetorium, looking down at their phones.

"Burma," she repeated.

He smiled to hear it said.

"What is your name?" he asked, enunciating each word as if he'd practiced the phrase many times.

"Adela." She had always liked her name; it sounded like a character from a turn-of-the-century novel, one who'd do something brave.

"Ah-deh-la," he repeated.

"And you're . . . ooh? Or oh?"

"Ko Oo," he said. The last syllable was long. It sounded to Adela like a birdcall.

"Hi, can I have a smoked salmon roll with brown rice?" asked a girl who had come up next to them.

Oo nodded quickly at Adela by way of a farewell, then turned back to his sushi station. Maybe they'd told him not to talk to the students. Just barely, underneath the clatter of cutlery, she could hear his chanting begin again. She stood there for a moment, then turned reluctantly toward the salad bar.

It was no wonder that Adela would seek distraction at this juncture in her life. It was the middle of a long, drizzly March in a small New England town. Only calculus, world lit, two study halls, and a dreaded phys ed class stood between her and adult life. Ms. Alvarez had told her that she needed to restructure her senior essay on unreliable narration in *Heart of Darkness*, and she didn't want to do it. Graduation was approaching. Everyone else would fill the summer before college with internships and road trips. But Adela's own plans to spend the summer in DC with Greg had evaporated when he unceremoniously dumped her while he was home from Johns Hopkins over winter break. Now it was back to Dad's dusty old house in Hartford or into Mom's suddenly much less appealing apartment in DC.

Adela still had some friends in Hartford, but she didn't want to go back. Winning a scholarship to Edgerton Fields four years ago had been her way out of the most boring city in the most boring state in the Union. And her father shared her tendency to start things without finishing them; living with him would be like rooming with a failed version of her future self. Yet her mother might have disturbingly high expectations of what she should accomplish in the three months before she headed off to her hard-won spot at Pomona College. Adela had spent the morning skipping phys ed, feeding quarters into the Ms. Pac-Man game outside the mailroom, losing and losing. Monks protesting for democracy in Burma sounded fascinating.

A few days later, Adela was taking a shortcut behind the art building when she saw Ko Oo sitting at a picnic table by the cafetorium's loading dock. It was the first clear afternoon in weeks. He nodded in her direction as she approached.

"Hey," she said.

"Ma Ah-deh-la nay kaung la?" he asked.

"Uh . . ."

"You say, 'Nay kaung deh.'"

"Nay . . ."

". . . kaung deh." He was smoking a grayish-green cigar, and its smell reminded Adela of campfires. His wavy hair was compressed into the shape of the sushi cap that sat beside him on the table.

"Nay kaung la?" he repeated.

"Naygongday!" she said.

"You want to learn Burmese?" he asked, looking up at her, flipping the hair out of his eyes.

Adela stared at his long brown fingers holding the cigar. They looked different from her own stubby fingers, different from any hands she had ever seen. They were, she reflected, almost like the hands of a different kind of human altogether. His fingernails were flat and rectangular. Small white scars crisscrossed the base of his thumb.

"Sure," she said.

❀

They started meeting at the picnic table several times a week, during Oo's lunch hour, which coincided with the second of Adela's study halls. Adela learned that his full name was Oo Htet Win, but he told her to call him Ko Oo. *Ko*, he explained, meant older brother, although when she heard his life story she realized he was old enough to be her father. Ko Oo had come to the United States on political asylum in 1996. He fell into the ranks of what he called the "Burmese sushi mafia," which operated on the principle that any Asian person could give a Japanese restaurant an air of authenticity. This network had secured him his first job in New York and eventually gotten him this one, in the middle of nowhere. He lived with several other Burmese men in an apartment a long bus ride away.

What Adela really wanted was to learn the chanting she'd heard that first day in the cafetorium, but Ko Oo said a real monk would have to instruct her. The words were from an ancient language called Pali, one he insisted he was not qualified to teach. And although he had offered Adela Burmese lessons, they didn't spend much time studying language. Instead, he told her about his country. Adela never knew why he chose her to tell. Perhaps no one else had asked him about it. His Burmese friends knew all about it already and had stories of their own; he didn't seem to know many other Americans.

Whatever the reason, Ko Oo spoke to Adela like he had just been ungagged. He started with the Saffron Revolution. Just a few years earlier, saffron-robed Buddhist monks, like the one on the yellow sticker on his badge, had faced down soldiers in the streets, demanding an end to fifty years of military rule, chanting prayers of goodwill like the one she'd heard him reciting. It had been more than twenty years since Ko Oo had taken part in the 1988 pro-democracy demonstrations, before fleeing to the jungle to enlist in an army of students and ethnic minorities fighting the Burmese military. For most of that time, his movement's leader, a woman named Aung San Suu Kyi, was under house arrest. She'd been free since 2010, just after the military finally held multiparty elections. But Ko Oo told Adela that the elections were rigged. The army still controlled everything, the civil war was worse than ever in the North, and the "new democratic Myanmar," as the government called the country, was a sham.

Adela memorized all of it. Not just what he told her, but how: as if it mattered. Adela had never paid particular attention to world events—she was a *literature* person, as Greg, now majoring in political science, used to remind her—but when she listened to Ko Oo speak, she felt transformed. Burma was a story Ko Oo unfolded for her page by page, and the more she heard, the more it captivated her. The only thing she could compare it to was *Heart of Darkness*, which she'd read until the pages turned greasy. Every time she returned to that novel, there was some rediscovered phrase, some new insight revealed: *the bitter truth of colonialism and the chimerical depths of the human spirit*, as she'd put it in her senior essay. But Kurtz and Marlow weren't even real. Ko Oo's Burma was.

They would sit by the loading dock and Ko Oo would talk. Adela had trouble believing his stories at first; they were as far-fetched as the Greek myths her father had read to her as a child, and just as dark. For instance, Ko Oo's family had lost their life savings when Burma's dictator, Ne Win, canceled all the currency notes in his own unlucky number, on the advice of an astrologer. Ne Win had also abruptly declared that cars should drive on the right instead of the left side of the road, leaving his citizens to smash into each other as he retreated to his private golf course. And he had ordered the army to open fire on student demonstrators, leaving some, like Ko Oo, bleeding in the streets.

Soon Adela suspended her disbelief. After all, what did she know about being a battalion commander for a rebel army in the jungle, hunting wild animals for meat and plotting how to wound the junta's soldiers? "Kill a soldier," Ko Oo explained, "and you get one man. Wound him, you get three; two must carry him out!" Sa Galay, the Sparrow, they called him, because he was so quick on his feet. He even told Adela that an amulet his mother had given him, a tiny bronze Buddha encased in plastic, protected him from being killed by a gun. It still hung around his neck. His wife was back in Burma; she hadn't been able to come to the United States. Once he told Adela she was dead. The details in his stories always changed, and everyone seemed to have more than one name, more than one past. Still, these borrowed stories became more vivid to Adela than her own life, and sometimes she'd lie awake at night repeating them to herself like incantations. She was too shy to ask him to chant for her again, but the sound stayed with her, underneath everything.

❀

It was Adela's roommate, Lena, who persuaded her to go to Burma. Lena had encouraged Adela's friendship with Ko Oo on the principle that it was a healthy distraction from Greg, and from Joseph Conrad. One night in April, Lena and Adela sat on the small, flat roof outside their dormer window, drinking mugs of chamomile tea and looking out across the forest at the highway beyond. As they did that whole spring, they were talking about the future.

"How much have you got so far?" asked Adela.

"Almost fifteen hundred." Lena was cycling to Oregon as a fund-raiser for the environmental organization she'd be interning with for the summer, and she'd already surpassed her goal just a week after announcing it on Facebook.

"Oh My Goth, that's great," said Adela, failing to disguise her melancholy beneath their silly private joke, the origins of which neither of them remembered but which had something to do with Lena's sophomore-year boyfriend's bad taste in music.

Adela looked over at Lena to gauge whether it might be acceptable to shift the conversation to her own woes, and then she plunged ahead.

"It's just like I'm living in this past version of what I was supposed to do, what I thought I wanted, but I'm afraid and I'll never do what I actually want to do . . ."

"What do you want to do?"

"I don't know, roll sushi? Be a writer?" Adela laughed, but Lena's face was serious.

"You know what I hear from you?" Lena cocked her head to one side, pausing for emphasis. She had a formidable stare, perfected while fighting for various causes as president of Edgerton Fields's Student Action Club.

"What?"

"Fear."

It was true, Adela realized. She'd said she was afraid. But what did she have to fear? She wasn't Ko Oo, running from the army or nightmares of jail and torture. She was just a girl obsessed with *Heart of Darkness*, trying to get over a boyfriend who wasn't that great in the first place.

"Oh, Dellies," said Lena. "You'll figure it out. Go to DC, I'm sure your mom can hook you up with something."

Adela felt her throat tightening. Other people seemed so sure of themselves. Greg, for instance. She thought back to their last conversation, which she had begun determined to prove she held no grudge against him and had ended unsure if she could bear to stay in touch.

"So, looking forward to your internship?" Adela had asked him. She couldn't figure out how to talk around their now defunct summer plans. He'd be interning at the New America Foundation, borrowing his uncle's apartment in Adams Morgan. Adela had hoped to split her time between his place and her mom's, maybe picking up some shifts in the gift shop at the Hirshhorn Museum, where her mother worked as a curator.

"I was just chatting with the guy who hired me today, the one who went to Yale? The people there are all really cool. We were talking about that ridiculous KONY2012 campaign."

Adela had seen the video—it had gone viral that spring. It was supposed to raise awareness about Joseph Kony, an African warlord, leading to his capture. Like everyone else, Adela had posted it on her Facebook page; she'd found it inspiring. Kony was from the Congo, the setting for *Heart of Darkness*, and so Adela felt a particular connection to it. The dismissive tone in Greg's voice annoyed her.

"Well, they must be doing something right, it's gotten millions of views. At least they're trying to do something."

"It's just so . . . simplistic!"

Adela could hear the excitement in Greg's voice, his determination to convince her. A year ago she'd found it sweet, his earnestness in making sure that she understood things the way he did.

"Well it sounds like a simple situation."

"Not really, but anwyay," Greg said quickly, moving on instead to a long anecdote about "office politics" at the New America Foundation—as if he needed to emphasize that he was going to work in an office while she still toiled away in the library.

"Hey," said Lena, nudging Adela. "Are you OK?"

Adela rested her head on Lena's shoulder. "Yeah. No. Sorry. I was just thinking about Greg. When you asked what I was afraid of—I'm afraid of becoming like him."

"Like how?"

Adela sighed. "Well, besides the fact that he was a total jerk to me. It's like nothing is real to him. He formulates all these opinions, but it's straight out of the books he just read in some class. He thinks he's too cool to actually do anything, or believe anything."

"Well, yeah," said Lena, as if this had always been obvious.

"I want to—do something."

It sounded vague, Adela knew. But she was tired of analyzing literature, interpreting what other people said about love and death, good and evil. She wanted to *be* good, she realized with embarrassment. She wanted to *feel* love.

"So do something," said Lena.

Adela took a sip of her tea and looked away. "Like what?"

"Go to Burma."

❀

That night Adela dreamed she was a planet circling the golden spire of a pagoda. When she told Ko Oo about it, he insisted it must be the Shwedagon, the most famous temple in Burma and a symbol of its ancient empire. The photo he showed her on his phone did look familiar—she couldn't think where she'd have seen the temple before. It was a sign, he said, and the voice that told her to stay was her own karma guiding her.

Adela imagined herself visiting the temple Ko Oo described. She would go in the early morning, when the attendants had just swept the grit from the marble steps and all the good housewives brought fresh flowers to adorn the Buddha statues. It would be like a pilgrimage, like completing a mission that had been given to her by the universe.

Once Adela made the decision, it was easy. The Myanmar Volunteers United application took her half an hour to complete. She emphasized her emergent skills in conversational Burmese, which Ko Oo had promised to start teaching her in earnest. Plenty of people went during their gap years before college, so why not just a summer? She didn't have to be at Pomona until late August.

There were some obstacles to overcome. MVU required a three-month minimum commitment, which meant she'd have to leave before Edgerton Fields's semester ended. Calculus was easy—she could take the final early. If she went to phys ed every day, she could complete her hours in time. That left world lit.

Ms. Alvarez was Adela's favorite teacher: skeptical and a tiny bit mean, with a great, slightly snorty laugh. But she was big on class participation. So Adela formulated a plan and then proposed it to Ms. Alvarez the next day after class: not only would she finish her senior essay on Conrad, she would also blog about her experiences in Burma on Edgerton Fields's International Studies webpage, which Ms. Alvarez moderated. "*And* read Orwell's *Burmese Days*," Ms. Alvarez added. "*And* connect it to *Heart of Darkness* and weave both of them into your blog posts."

Adela beamed with relief. "No problem!"

Then there were her parents. MVU's respectable-looking page, with its FAQs and links to travel agencies, helped. Her dad was on board right away—it seemed like a "good experience"—but her mother needed some convincing.

"Burma?? Isn't it called Mee-an-mar now? And who is this Ko Oo?" Adela had forgotten that Ko Oo had figured into her scrambled explanation of her plans.

"Yeah, it's also called Myanmar. And Ko Oo—well, he's like a visiting scholar at Edgerton Fields," Adela lied, cringing. "You know, the whole International Studies Program?"

"Oh," her mother said. "And the plane ticket?"

"Well . . ." Adela offered. "I know Grandpa Douglas was going to give me something for graduation. I was going to ask for a new laptop, but my old one is fine for now. What if he paid for my ticket instead?"

Adela's mother was hesitant at first. But fortunately Grandpa Douglas, who had served in the Pacific during World War II, was very eager for Adela to visit the Bridge on the River Kwai, which connected Thailand and Burma. Adela was ecstatic when her mother called her back with the news.

"Done! I'll take a bunch of pictures for him. I can blog about it for Ms. Alvarez! And Mom. You know if I come to DC I'm just going to be moping around the house all summer."

"True."

Silence.

"I just want to make sure this is the right thing for you, honey."

"It is, Mom, it is!" Adela practically shouted into the phone. She took a breath and then continued more soberly. "Just read the testimonials on MVU's website. Everyone says it's *life-changing.*"

"I just want you to be safe. There could be—"

"It's safe! They just had elections! The government is totally stable. No need to go all cray-cray."

"Adela, why do you have to speak that way?"

"I'm not writing a paper, Mom."

"You've never traveled on your own, and you've never left the United States."

"I went to Montreal with my French class! And, I won't be alone. MVU has a bunch of other volunteers there."

"Adela, you're eighteen!" her mother cried, a note of hysteria entering her voice.

"Exactly! I'm eighteen."

"Barely."

"And I'm practically on my own already. Technically, I could go whether you wanted me to or not. Not that I'd do that."

Her mother sighed, and it was a sigh Adela knew, a prequel to consent.

"Fine."

"Thank you!"

"Burma? Really?"

"Mom, everyone does this. Greg went to El Salvador, Lena went to Senegal . . ."

Again, the sigh. "You fly back through DC. *And* I'm coming to Edgerton Fields for Parents' Weekend before you go. *And* you're coming home for Thanksgiving."

"Fine, fine, fine."

A week later, Adela received an email welcoming her to MVU's 2012 roster of volunteers. She would be teaching English at a school in a Buddhist monastery. She rushed to the picnic table to tell Ko Oo the news.

He nodded approvingly. "Many poor children study in the monastery," he explained. "The fee at government school is very high."

He dug a roll of yellow Saffron Revolution stickers out of the tasseled shoulder bag he carried and presented one to Adela.

"You see, the monk are heroes for us."

Adela carefully affixed the sticker to her laptop.

Ko Oo settled back on the bench and lit a cigar. "Just some years ago, you cannot bring a sticker like this into the country. Now it is OK."

He paused to consider, exhaling a puff of smoke, and then went on.

"Not really OK," he said, tipping his hand back and forth in the air, "but a little bit OK. The government, they speak only with their mouths. Still, some foreigners can go to Burma. International-community"—a phrase he used often and with a solemn faith that Adela found touching—"can help our country."

On Adela's last night at Edgerton Fields, Ko Oo told her to meet him at the picnic table when his dinner shift ended at eight. Taking her familiar shortcut behind the art building, she glimpsed a bunch of freshmen practicing for the end-of-the-year talent show in the amphitheater. The talent show was an Edgerton Fields tradition, always held the night before graduation, and she and Lena had been planning to revive their two-person punk band for the occasion. The seniors always got to perform last, and there were tears and emotional speeches. Adela didn't care about the graduation ceremony itself, but she'd been looking forward to the bittersweet night before for years. But suddenly the talent show seemed silly to her. It felt right to leave everything behind for Burma.

Ko Oo had brought a thermos of smoky green tea—the best tea came from the hills of Burma, he said—to toast to her journey. He went over the simple phrases he'd taught her again, and she let him laugh at her terrible accent.

When their cups were empty, Ko Oo turned serious. He gave Adela his mother's address and reminded her to visit his family. He hadn't seen them since he'd fled to the jungle more than twenty years earlier. They were able to talk on the phone sometimes, but never for very long. Ko Oo worried that the army would punish them for contacting him.

"My mother has suffered enough for me," he said.

"I just wish you could see her yourself."

Ko Oo shook his head. "Cannot. They will know who I am. You are American. You can go where you like. You can visit her, no problem."

Then he unclasped the leather cord around his neck and handed Adela his amulet. It had kept him safe through the demonstrations, he said, through his years in the rebel army, after he crossed the border into Thailand, and all the way to the United States.

Adela held it up to the light. Up close, she could see that an eerie blue-green patina covered the tiny statue like phosphorescent dust. The Buddha sat cross-legged in his plastic case, hands draped over his knees.

"But you need it!" cried Adela, pushing it back toward him, coveting it nonetheless.

"Do not need," said Ko Oo. He gestured around at the quiet campus. "Lucky already."

The end of his cigar glowed red as he inhaled, and then the air grew smoky between them.

"You be careful, naw?" he said.

"Of what?"

"People have suffered a long time."

"I know."

Ko Oo had told her about forced labor, about soldiers raping ethnic minority girls and burning villages, about soldiers who were children themselves.

"Even in Rangoon," he continued. "You cannot know what can happen. The situation is delicate."

"I'll be OK," said Adela, laughing.

It would be a months before she'd realize that he was telling her to be careful for other people's sakes, not just her own.

Ko Oo shifted on the bench so they were facing each other.

"Yes, Ah-deh-la," he said, pronouncing her name in that funny way he had. "You are OK."

They were silent for a while.

"We keep in touch on Facebook, naw?" he said, gesturing to the sky, as if the digital world stretched above them.

"Definitely."

"Thadi ya ne meh," Ko Oo said. "I remember you."

"Thadi ya ne meh," repeated Adela.

They sat in silence for a while, and then Adela stood up. They shook hands with awkward formality, and she walked off into the darkness.

THE SLAP

"Peh byouk! Peh byouk!" A woman picked her way through piles of trash in the street, bracing a tray on her head with one hand and leading a child with the other. A breeze was blowing into the open-air lobby of the guest-house, and Adela smelled fried onions, and a sulfurous odor that she realized must be sewage. At seven-thirty in the morning, the air already felt like a warm bath.

"Peh byouk!" the woman called out again. Adela didn't know what the words meant, but she figured the woman must be selling whatever kind of food was piled on the tray she carried. Adela admired her balance as she navigated around sleeping dogs and broken pavement. She imagined the woman getting up early to prepare the little packets of food. A thrill went through her. This was Burma!

Adela went back over the trip in her mind. Lena skipped class to drive her to the airport, squeezed her tightly on the pavement outside, handed her the water bottle almost forgotten under the seat. Adela stood for a moment on the sidewalk after Lena drove away, suddenly panicking. How had anyone let her do this?

Then she remembered Ko Oo's words. Be brave. Hadn't he said that? She rolled her suitcase into the airport, went through security, found herself on the plane with *Burmese Days* open in her lap. But her eyes wouldn't stay on the page, and she spent most of the first flight staring out the window, imagining herself making this journey in reverse three months later, dreaming of what would happen in between. In Tokyo, Adela ate airport sushi, thinking of Ko Oo. Sometime this week, before MVU's volunteer orientation ended, she planned to visit his mother and give her the photo she'd taken of him in front of Edgerton Fields' impressive library, wearing a button-down shirt, his sushi cap nowhere in sight.

A child's wail broke the humid morning. Adela looked up to see the woman with the tray reach down and slap her boy on the side of his head, gracefully but very hard. He fell silent immediately, and they continued on their way down the street and out of sight. *Ouch*, thought Adela, touching her ear. She wavered between sympathy for the two of them and settled on the child.

On the table beside the remains of her breakfast was a thick book, *Burma: Insurgency and the Politics of Ethnicity*, which she paged through trying to learn the acronyms for the many armed struggle groups that had been fighting the government: the KIO, the KNU, the SSA. Greg had mailed Adela the book just before she left Edgerton Fields, and he'd inscribed the inside cover: *Adela, Burma is complicated. Have fun.* —*Greg.* The gift had taken Adela by surprise; Greg had recently changed his Facebook status to "in a relationship" with another poli sci major at Johns Hopkins, a cheerful-looking girl with glasses and glossy blond hair.

Adela had texted Greg about her Burma plans a week before she left, just so he'd know she wouldn't be lurking around DC all summer. He'd called her a few seconds later.

"Three months, eh?" he said, shouting above the noise of what sounded like a party. "Not sure what you can accomplish in three months."

"Better than your three-week Habitat trip to El Salvador that supposedly made you an expert," Adela replied.

"We'll see how long you last," he teased.

It was the kind of flirting that had brought them together, and it sent a pang of wistfulness, annoyance, and reluctant hope into the pit of Adela's stomach.

"No, seriously," Greg added. "*Everyone* wants to go to Burma right now."

Even now, recalling those words, Adela couldn't help smiling. Here she was, where everyone wanted to be. But the civil war and repression described in Greg's book didn't seem to have any relation to what Adela had seen when she'd gotten off the plane in Rangoon the previous night. She'd expected soldiers everywhere, oppressing the downtrodden. But the airport was quiet. A woman in a tight green uniform stamped her passport with hardly an upward glance. She rolled her suitcase out onto the pavement, found a taxi, and did her best to repeat the phrase Ko Oo had written down phonetically in Burmese, with the English underneath: "Will you go to Golden Land Guesthouse?"

The driver nodded, and they set off, with Adela in the passenger seat on what was, disconcertingly, the wrong side of the car but the right side of the road. It was from the open window of this taxi that she leaned as she glimpsed the moon above the Shwedagon Pagoda in real life. The driver removed his hands from the wheel, brought his palms together, and raised them to his forehead as they passed the temple. Adela copied his gesture. He said something she didn't understand. The voice that had visited her dream returned. *Stay here.*

Yet her mind always seemed to drift to the past or the future, to Greg or to Pomona or to the desk in the basement of the library where she had spent so many hours poring over *Heart of Darkness.* But what was the point of being in Burma, she berated herself, if she wasn't really *here?* Adela rededicated herself to noticing her surroundings. Her first blog post was due at the end of the week.

Outside the Golden Land Guesthouse, the street was filling up with people balancing packages on their heads and cyclists dangling bags from their handlebars. Yet no one seemed to spill anything, even though the road was so narrow that when cars came barreling through honking their horns, everyone had to squeeze up against the buildings on either side. **Men as well as women wear sarong-like garments called loungyis,** she planned to write in her blog. She'd read nearly that exact sentence in her *Lonely Planet,* so she'd have to add something to make it her own. **It's a tradition that is shared in India. But it's still kind of hard to get used to seeing men in skirts.**

A line of monks in burnt orange robes filed by with huge black bowls in their hands. Adela watched as the little boy who'd brought her breakfast ran out and gave each of them a packet of rice and a tangerine. She wished she'd brought her camera downstairs. It had been a birthday gift from her father the previous year, during her brief but intense period of interest in photography. Back at Edgerton Fields, she'd hardly used it, but now that she was here, she'd have plenty of opportunities.

"Adela?" A girl with a long brown braid stood in front of her table. "I'm Sarah, from MVU."

Adela had expected someone younger, or somehow younger-looking. As they chatted, Adela tried to place what made Sarah seem so confident. She carried one of those tasseled shoulder bags that Ko Oo had, like a badge of her right to be in Burma. She told Adela she had lived in Yangon (as she called it, not Rangoon, as Ko Oo had been saying) for the past four years. In addition to working at MVU, she had started an income generation project for women.

"Jayzu beh," Adela said to the boy who cleared away her breakfast dishes. She hoped Sarah would ask where she'd learned Burmese, and she could tell the story of Ko Oo.

But Sarah just cleared her throat. "Let's head over to the office."

Adela stood up. "I'll just go up and get my bag."

"OK," said Sarah, and then hesitated. "And you might want to change your shirt, too."

Adela looked down at herself, heat rising to her face. She had read MVU's packing list with great attention: *No tank tops. No tight clothing. Burmese people are very modest.*

"Why?" Her voice trailed up at the end, as if she were unsure of whether she wanted to sound sheepish or challenging.

"It's just kind of see-through."

Adela took in Sarah's outfit: a loungyi and a long-sleeved, button-down, collarless shirt.

"People in Myanmar are pretty conservative," Sarah said, without apology or spite.

"Yeah, of course," Adela muttered.

Back in her room, Adela examined herself in the mirror: brown cargo pants, practical sandals, and a lightweight cotton tunic with pretty embroidery on the sleeves. She'd gotten it at a fancy sporting goods store near Edgerton Fields, and it was holding up to its promise not to wrinkle. Yet with the sun shining through the window, she saw that despite the tank top she was wearing underneath, the outline of her body was indeed visible, down to the slight meatiness around her waist. She pulled off her tunic and put on a big black T-shirt she'd planned to wear as pajamas. For good measure, she wrapped her shoulders in a multicolored silk scarf her mother had given her.

Poking out of this eccentric outfit, Adela saw her same old face in the mirror, framed by dirty blond hair that had gone frizzy in the humidity: eyebrows she was too lazy to tweeze, lips that were a little too thin. The blue-gray eyes that Greg had told her were her best feature were still red from the plane's dryness. If she had been expecting Burma to transform her, it hadn't happened yet.

When Adela came downstairs, Sarah didn't comment on her new outfit. The MVU van was waiting in the street, and Sarah joked with the driver in Burmese as they made their way to another guesthouse to pick up two more volunteers. The boys—as Adela thought of them, although she wondered if she was supposed to call people "men" and "women" now that she was practically in college—were pre-med majors who'd be volunteering in a private clinic several hours from Yangon. Hearing them talk about malaria and dengue fever, Adela started to wish she had some more skills more useful than analyzing literature. And as they told Sarah how glad they were they'd been posted together, Adela began to ponder living in a monastery alone, or rather, surrounded by Burmese people. The prospect of her trip had been so exciting, and her relief so great at arriving at a plan for the summer, that she had not thought much about what her daily life would be like. Now, a film of queasiness began to settle over her enthusiasm.

As the van chugged through traffic, Adela peered out the window, trying to reinterest herself in her surroundings. She found the city beautiful in a rundown way. There were big old mildew-stained buildings, little muddy alleyways, and roadside shops where people sat on tiny stools sipping drinks. The van pulled up next to a truck with open sides that was shockingly full of people, their bodies pressed together, their faces vacant. Men were standing on the bumper and clinging to the railing in back. One of them spat a mouthful of blood onto the street.

When they reached the office, the other volunteers had already arrived. As Adela looked around, she was disappointed to see young people not so different from herself, wearing sporty sandals and loose clothing. They must each have their own story, she realized, their own reasons for coming here. Although she didn't consider herself extraordinary, she didn't like to think of herself as just one of a wave of volunteers who came for the MVU training each month, went off to different parts of the country, and flew home three months later. But there they were, the seven of them: two girls doing a gap year, the junior pre-med majors, a couple of recent college grads, and one odd retiree from England.

Kip, an MVU staff member with wire-rimmed glasses and a few days' stubble, asked the volunteers to introduce themselves, say where they were going, and explain their fears and hopes for their time in Myanmar.

Adela couldn't get used to hearing "Myanmar." Ko Oo always said Burma, and he'd told her that anyone who called the country Myanmar supported the current evil government. But Adela couldn't imagine that included Sarah or Kip. Out of loyalty to Ko Oo, Adela would keep saying Burma, even after she realized that plenty of people who opposed the government called the country Myanmar, too. Burma was the place she'd dreamt about; Myanmar was the place she actually ended up.

In the listing of fears, the volunteers ranked highly the prospect of getting sick, which hadn't even occurred to Adela. To "give back" and to "help people" were their main hopes. Adela was shocked to discover how clichéd her own ambitions sounded when they came from the mouths of others. Thus, when her turn came, she blurted out the only other thoughts that came to her mind: "I hope I can learn better Burmese, and I'm afraid I won't like living in a monastery." Everyone laughed, except Sarah, who raised her eyebrows.

Next, Kip showed a PowerPoint about Burma's history and politics. Most of the content was already familiar to Adela. She had to stifle a laugh when one of the pre-med students asked whether they would get to meet Aung San Suu Kyi, the famous leader of Burma's democracy movement. But some of the volunteers seemed better informed than Adela herself. One guy had made a documentary film about a political asylee, like Ko Oo, who worked as a janitor at his college. A girl wearing a long skirt over flesh-colored stockings explained that she had started a tutoring program for refugees at her church; she spoke an ethnic minority language called Karen as well as Burmese. Adela knew about the ethnic minorities, but Ko Oo had never mentioned any religion other than Buddhism. **There is a sizeable Christian minority in Burma, as well as Muslims and Hindus**, she blogged in her head, piecing together some bullet points from Kip's presentation.

Somewhat wearily, Sarah reviewed some common points of confusion for newcomers. The mouthful of blood Adela had seen the man spitting onto the street was actually betel nut juice. The yellow paste on people's faces was thanaka, a sunscreen made from tree bark. Sarah cautioned that it was offensive to touch people on the head or point one's feet at them. The volunteers should ask permission before taking people's photos. Monks couldn't touch women.

"But is Myanmar *safe*?" asked a girl with the exact same sandals as Adela. "I mean, for women?"

"Pretty safe," said Sarah. "You should take the same precautions you would at home—avoid walking by yourself after dark, don't count big piles of money in public..."

The girl looked uncertain, and it did seem to Adela that Sarah was dismissing the question.

"So, is it like India," the girl continued, "where women are second-class citizens?"

Sarah narrowed her eyes. "I don't know if that's a fair assessment of India, but in any case, here, no. Of course gender roles differ, but I don't think you'll find it uncomfortable. Women's role in Buddhism is different from men's, so you have to be careful about that. Just keep your eyes open, listen to what people are saying, and you'll be fine."

"Okaay," said the girl.

Adela wondered if anyone else would pursue the point. She was tempted to ask what was different about women's role in Buddhism, but while she tried to remember the name of the monastery where she'd be volunteering, Sarah moved on to a slide called "Myanmar since the 2010 Elections." The fellow who'd made the documentary film interrupted her.

"To call them elections is an exaggeration. There was no independent monitoring!"

"Well, they certainly weren't perfect," said Sarah.

"You can't deny there's been progress, though," said the girl who'd asked about India. "I mean, we wouldn't even have been allowed to come here three years ago."

A certain impatience to participate, to contribute, began to arise in Adela. She had never been one to stay silent in classes or discussions, even when she had trouble thinking of anything particular to say. It was a curious fear of being left out or underestimated, of being what Greg would call "a non-factor." Since she was a child, this fear had coexisted with her shyness, so that in large groups she vacillated between skeptical silence and blurting out whatever came to mind. Her four years at Edgerton Fields had pulled her toward the latter extreme. Everyone was sharing their opinions, why shouldn't she state hers? She tried to remember something specific that Ko Oo had told her about the elections, but instead a question came to mind that she'd always meant to ask him.

"If the elections were so bad, why didn't the UN do anything about it?"

Everyone in the room, even those who'd been disagreeing a moment before, even the elderly English man, united in rolling their eyes and chuckling softly. Adela felt herself blushing, and in order to have something to do, she cleared her throat. But beneath the embarrassment was another feeling, a thrilling feeling, of being somehow in over her head, out in the real world.

She tried to backpedal. "I mean, I know the UN doesn't have an army or anything, but they do monitor elections, so . . ."

"The generals would never let them see what really happens," said the filmmaker.

"Yeah, I know," said Adela, as if that had been her point all along.

Sarah looked around, slightly bemused, then went on with her presentation. Adela struggled to pay attention and then gave up and tried to memorize the details she'd just learned. There was something refreshing about feeling so utterly foolish: it was like being plunged into cold water, like being slapped. The feeling emboldened her. This was only the orientation, she reminded herself. By the time she got to the monastery and started meeting actual Burmese people, she'd know more. And by the time she made her way home at the end of the summer, she'd be an expert, at least compared to Greg.

At lunchtime Sarah's assistant, Ma Soe, brought in sodas and Styrofoam boxes of fried rice. Adela tried out the Burmese phrase for "Nice to meet you," which was puzzlingly long. Ma Soe smiled politely, as if she was used to volunteers and their need to please.

The afternoon was free, so Adela decided to walk back to her guesthouse. It was after one o'clock, and the pavement was hot as a griddle. She saw a shop selling the tasseled shoulder bags that Sarah and Ko Oo had, and she used some worn, colorful bills to buy one with a beautiful black-and-gray pattern. She put her daypack inside of it and continued on her way, feeling resourceful.

Up ahead Adela saw a huge, brick red, seemingly abandoned building that took up an entire city block. It was set in the middle of a yard overgrown with trees and vines; a high barbed-wire fence surrounded it. There was a sign on the gate, and Adela thought she'd take a photo so she could ask someone later what it meant. She snapped a few pictures, and they were coming out quite well, with sunlight streaming through the ramshackle towers.

The man who tapped her on the shoulder was extremely old. She could not remember ever having been touched by a person so old. His long white hair was tied in a topknot, and he wore gigantic black glasses that were taped together at the bridge of his nose. In perfect British-accented English, he said, "Do you know this building?"

He was standing just inches from her, and his breath smelled of onions. A lone tooth poked up from his lower jaw. Adela stepped away.

"No. What is it?"

He seemed to delight in her ignorance. "This is the Secretariat Building, where General Aung San was killed. Surely you know Aung San?"

As Adela hesitated, he continued talking. "The father of Mrs. Aung San Suu Kyi, and the father of our democracy, assassinated on the eve of our independence from the British! He was our last hope for uniting the peoples of Burma. You see, I make a habit of visiting this site. The cornerstone of our democracy. And you see its condition! Now I ask you, what would cause it to fall into disrepair?"

Adela didn't have an answer, but the man didn't wait for one, either.

"We must point the finger at ourselves," he said, stabbing the air near his heart. "We cannot blame every Tom, Dick, and Harry. After all, it was my countryman who shot Aung San, perhaps at the behest of the British, but under his own steam nonetheless! We must only compare our so-called golden land with that of our sister colony, India, in order to see our own failings," he finished, resettling his glasses on his nose.

It sounded like he had learned English from a nineteenth-century grammar book. He must have lived under British rule, thought Adela. She resolved to read the section of *Insurgency and the Politics of Ethnicity* on the colonial era, which she had skipped over in favor of more recent history; she considered herself relatively familiar with colonialism after reading *Heart of Darkness* so many times.

While Adela was marveling at the size of the old man's ears, which stretched nearly to his chin, he took out a handkerchief and mopped his brow.

"When did you arrive?" he asked.

"Actually, I just got here yesterday."

"I see. And what will you be doing for us?"

The "for us" sounded strange to Adela, as if, without providing some service, she'd have no right to be in Burma.

"I'm volunteering at a monastery school."

His head bobbed up and down, the loose flesh below his chin wobbling. "Oh, very good. So many foreigners come now."

"Really?" To Adela, the opposite seemed to be true—she had never been among so many people who looked so little like herself.

"It reminds me of colonial days. Oh, yes! What a top-notch idea!" He covered his mouth and tittered politely. Without another word, he turned and hobbled away.

Adela stood there for a moment, piecing together what he'd said. Which "idea" was he talking about: British rule, or foreigners coming to Burma now? Marlow's line about colonialism came back to her like an old friend: "What redeems it is the idea only." In the essay she'd cobbled together for Ms. Alvarez before she left, Adela used the quote as evidence of his unreliability as a narrator; Conrad, she argued, genuinely rejected colonialism, but he wanted to show how easy it was for people like Marlow to justify it despite all the brutality they'd seen. The strange thing about that line, she'd always thought, was that she couldn't help being inspired by Marlow's words, at the same time as she knew they weren't supposed to be true. Ideas *could* redeem things, couldn't they? And here was a man who had lived through the colonial era, and he seemed almost nostalgic for it. Adela watched his retreating form, bent double over his cane, silhouetted against an ancient tree. Quickly, almost secretively, she snapped a photo.

KALA

The next morning after breakfast, Adela set about posting on Facebook the photos she'd taken. Sarah had warned the volunteers not to count on Internet access; even in Yangon, it could be spotty. Indeed, the guesthouse's connection was extremely slow. The lovely picture of the old man she had encountered at the Secretariat Building failed to upload, but she managed to post one shot of the ruined compound. Adela waited, feeling a little prick of energy each time someone Liked the photo.

"OMG, jealous!" wrote a junior Adela didn't remember friending. "So nostalgic . . . sun setting on the British Empire, dude," said a boy from her art history class. "Very lovely seeing home!" commented Ko Oo. "Miss you so much I can. not. Function!!" wrote Lena.

Adela diligently Liked each of the comments, then looked out at the street.

Already Burma seemed less strange to her, more textured. The woman from yesterday, the one who'd slapped her child, was alone today. She stopped to spoon boiled beans into a plastic bag for a monk who was passing by with his alms bowl. While the previous day had seemed hot to Adela, she realized that it hadn't been, really—thick clouds had blocked the sun's full force. She opened the blog post she was working on. **The morning sky is bright blue. Light falls on the street like honey. A skeletal gray kitten nibbles at grains of rice on the margins of a trash heap. A man in** a sweat-stained undershirt and nylon track pants clears his throat and spits enthusiastically into the gutter. A teenage girl wearing tiny purple shorts and a tank top squats on the pavement, tending to some donuts that bob in a wok full of sizzling oil. The last bit made Sarah's criticism of her see-through shirt seem a bit unfair. Although most people do wear loungyis, she continued, young people belie the stereotype that all Burmese people wear traditional, modest clothing.

The MVU van pulled up with Sarah's assistant Ma Soe at the wheel, and Adela packed up her things and hopped in. That day the volunteers would visit a hospital where Ma Soe's sister worked, which Sarah had said would help them understand the "infrastructural challenges" the country faced.

When they arrived at a ramshackle building behind an open-air market, Adela assumed they were making a stop along the way. But Ma Soe parked in the courtyard and beckoned them out of the van.

"Is this the—" Adela wondered out loud.

"Hospital," Ma Soe finished.

The volunteers shuffled out of the van and followed Ma Soe up a staircase stained with splatters of red that Adela now recognized as betel juice. A dog lay on the landing, her belly heavy with pups. Adela hurried up the stairs and found herself in a wide hall with beds on either side.

The hospital was my first real shock in Burma, she'd later blog, next to a photo of the hospital's humble entrance, in a post she spent quite a bit of time composing, relying heavily on Word's thesaurus function. I expected to see poverty, in the abstract—people on the streets and such. I did not expect to see someone dying, alone, on a bare mattress set on a metal bedframe, in a room filled with such mattresses, each one hosting a person in some state of agony. I knew this person was dying because he or she did not look like anyone I'd ever seen before. Their feet were turned inward and seemed to be curling up like dried leaves. The person's mouth was open, and now and then the cheeks sucked gently inward. The person's head was wrapped in a scarf, and the eyes roved slowly back and forth, as if watching a film that only they could see. Now and then, the person would cry out as if struck with a cudgel.

"Why isn't anyone helping that person?" Adela asked, a little too loudly. They were being led through the patients' hall on the way to meet Ma Soe's sister.

A handful of men in white coats stood at the bedside of another patient, rifling through some papers. They glanced up at the troop of young men and women, and then quickly away. A few people in street clothes—relatives, Adela guessed—crouched by patients' bedsides, wiping brows and offering bottles of water. One person held a bedpan under a sheet as a patient noisily relieved himself into it.

The other volunteers were stone-faced. Despite the hospital's open-air design, the smell was oppressive—the odor of sewage with which Adela had recently become acquainted mingled with stale grease and sweaty mattresses. They kept walking, but they never seemed to get to the end of the hall. At every step, Adela encountered new and horrifying sights: two thumb-sized cockroaches explored a banana peel peeking out from under a bed; one patient inserted his long pinky nail into his nose and then examined his prize. Adela was light-headed, and her hair felt heavy as an animal pelt on her sweaty neck. When they arrived at the tiny office at the end of the hall, she snatched one of the few chairs right away.

The volunteers wedged themselves into the little room. Ma Soe's sister had to sit on a desk.

"There's someone out there who needs your help," said Adela, pointing down the row of beds to the dying person.

"Yes," replied Ma Soe's sister. Her thick white nurse's outfit looked terribly inappropriate for the weather.

"What is wrong with this place?" said the filmmaker. "Why don't the beds have any sheets on them?"

"Yes," the nurse said again, sounding tired. "At public hospital in Myanmar, you must bring your own sheet. Or family may bring some."

"What if you don't have any family?" asked the girl who thought India was sexist.

The nurse nodded. "Yes, this happen. Then—" she said, gesturing to the patients behind us.

"So when you have a heart attack," asked Adela, eager to join the fray, "you have to be like, 'Just a minute, gotta get my pillow?'"

There was a pause, and the nurse furrowed her brow, perhaps confused by Adela's attempt at irony.

"I think so."

There was a discontented rumble among the volunteers, who had worked themselves up into quite a state of indignation.

"The doctors seem to be sitting on their bums," noted the old English guy.

"If you want medicine or treatment, you must pay first," explained the nurse.

"And if you don't have the money?" demanded the filmmaker.

"You just lie there," said Adela flatly, answering for Ma Soe's sister. It felt good to be caught up in the volunteers' tide of collective outrage.

"How do you find the strength to do this everyday?" asked the girl who tutored refugees.

The poor nurse looked to Kip and Sarah; perhaps she was wishing that her sister hadn't convinced her to introduce this batch of new arrivals to Myanmar's health care system. "I try to make our patients comfortable," she said.

The guys who were headed for the clinic looked aghast. Adela did not envy them. Perhaps, she thought, teaching English wouldn't be so bad after all.

After the question-and-answer session reached its awkward conclusion, the volunteers filed out to the courtyard, where a stand was selling noodle soup. Adela wasn't hungry, but she bought a bottle of cold water, and then another.

"Can I give this to one of the patients?" she asked Kip.

"Um, I guess so," he said, looking around for Sarah, then shrugging.

Adela left everyone else to eat their soup, saved up a few breaths of fresh air, and re-entered the patients' hall with a growing sense of mission. She found the right bed and sat down beside it. The person did not register her presence. Up close, Adela could see it was a woman. She raised the straw so it was inside the woman's open mouth. The woman had no reaction. Adela didn't want to pour the water down her throat, but she looked so thirsty. Her skin was nearly black, and her lips were dry and purple. At a loss for what to do next, Adela retrieved a tissue from her new tasseled bag, poured some cold water on it, and placed it on the woman's forehead. The woman's eyes snapped open, and she started to groan: "Uhn, uhnnn, uhn." The bedside relatives had stopped what they were doing to stare at Adela.

"Kala," one of them hissed.

Adela realized they must be talking about her. She passed quickly from feeling angry to uncertain to downright foolhardy. What was she trying to accomplish? The woman on the bed was louder now, and Adela felt everyone's eyes on her. Although she knew it was ridiculous, her mind went to reruns of "Grey's Anatomy" and "House," seeking ideas for what to do next. Finding none, Adela picked the wet tissue off of the woman's forehead and balled it up in her hand. It was frightfully warm, and it dripped onto Adela's long skirt when she squeezed it in her fist. The woman closed her eyes, seemingly satisfied. Little bubbles of saliva foamed up at the corners of her mouth.

Adela stood up and backed away from the bed. Had she killed the patient? No, the woman's chest trembled with each shallow inhalation. Firmly, but not too fast, Adela turned and walked out of the room, leaving the bottle of water sweating by the bed. There were no trash cans, so Adela threw the tissue into a bush on her way out of the building, then reached for the little bottle of hand sanitizer in her bag.

Back in the courtyard, Adela found a bench in the shade and shakily sat down. Vaguely, she could hear the other volunteers talking in small groups nearby, slurping up the remainder of their noodles. Adela couldn't imagine eating. She couldn't remember feeling, physically, anything in her life like she did that afternoon. She felt like she was being buried alive in sweat made solid, like her clothes had been sweated onto her body so that they rubbed against her skin in a scummy mass. She ran her fingernail over her arm, and it came away brown, as if she were oozing mud from the center of her soul.

Kip sat down next to her. "Hey," he said.

Adela stared at the ground, unable to meet his eyes.

"Pretty intense, huh?" he offered.

She took a shivery breath. "I just—" she began, feeling her voice slip into that high register it did before she started to cry, "I just have a lot of questions, and—"

"I know," he said, like he was soothing a child. "I know, I know, I know."

Then she was crying, trying to make as little sound as possible. How did people live here? How could the world be like this, while back at Edgerton Fields, students were curled up on couches drinking lattes or doing yoga on the lawn? Kip set a hand on Adela's shoulder, keeping distance between them. She knew it wouldn't be appropriate to move any closer to him, but in fact there was nothing she wanted more than to bury her face in his neck and sob. She concentrated on the checkered pattern of Kip's shirt until her jaw relaxed and she stopped wheezing.

When Adela looked up, she was relieved to see that the other volunteers were absorbed in conversation. The noodle vendor busied himself collecting the bowls they'd left around. She took a deep breath.

"I'm OK."

"Good," said Kip.

"I'm sorry."

"Don't be."

They sat for a while.

"A bunch of us are going out for dinner tonight," he said. "Want to join?"

"That would be awesome," Adela said gratefully.

❀

When Adela reached the restaurant, in a recently renovated hotel downtown, Kip and his friends were already there. The walls were creamy white and the candlelight flattered the small groups of people gathered around dark wooden tables. The air conditioning felt good after the balmy night air, but tropical plants all around created a verdant backdrop. As she walked over to Kip's table, she was glad she'd worn her black dress with just a scarf over her shoulders. After a shower and a nap, she felt recovered from the day, ready to try to be charming.

Adela sat down next to Kip, and he introduced her around the table: someone who taught at the British Council, a beautiful girl who worked for the Alliance Française, and a guy from Seattle who was studying anthropology. They smiled at Adela, then went back to their conversation about a new gym that was opening up. A waiter in a white shirt brought a menu, and she was surprised to see its contents: wood-fired pizzas, rocket salad, calamari. She ordered a pizza and a mango smoothie.

"Oh my god, I'm starving," she said.

"Yeah, this country will do that to you," said Kip.

"Sarah's not here."

Kip chuckled. "She doesn't come to places like this."

"Why?"

"Sarah—how can I say it? She's kind of become Burmese."

"What do you mean?"

"This kind of thing makes her uncomfortable, or guilty or something."

Adela looked at the stylish foreigners dining around them, thinking of what the old man in front of the Secretariat Building had said; there *were* a lot of them. Several Burmese couples sat in the corner, but they seemed to be the only locals except for the wait staff, who hovered off to the sides with their hands clasped behind their backs.

"But it doesn't make you feel that way?"

"I can take it," said Kip, leaning against the banquette. "For some good wine," he said, gesturing to a carafe on the table, "I can stand a little guilt."

He filled Adela's glass, then raised his own. Apparently there was no drinking age in Burma.

"To the new Myanmar," he said, gesturing around the room.

Adela couldn't tell if he was being ironic. This restaurant was such a strange contrast to the hospital where they'd been only hours before.

"So, are you feeling a little better?"

In fact, she was struggling to get over the bitterness of the wine. Sometimes she and Lena snuck a bottle of Strawberry Hill into their dorm room, and she'd had sips of wine here and there, but finishing the whole glass seemed like an ordeal.

"Oh, yeah, thanks." Remembering the woman she'd tried to help, she asked, "Hey, what does *kala* mean?"

Kip sighed dramatically. "Don't tell me it's come up already."

"Yeah, I was giving water to a patient at the hospital, and someone called me kala."

"Probably wasn't directed at you," said Kip. "Technically, *kala* means 'foreigner,' but mostly it's used for Muslims, especially Indians or Bangladeshis, anyone with dark skin. It's not a nice word. Something like the n-word back home. It drives Sarah nuts."

"Oh," said Adela, surprised. "Yeah, the way they said it, it was like—" she began, searching for words. "It was creepy. I knew there were some Muslims in Burma, but . . ."

"Yeah, it's becoming kind of a problem. Buddhists are getting really nationalistic. There's this whole Burman supremacy thing."

"Burman, like—"

"The majority ethnic group. They're mostly Buddhists. They think the country is being overrun or something, even though Muslims have been here for centuries."

Adela felt a blog post in the making. Probably Greg didn't even know this stuff. "Wait, but is that why no one was helping that woman in the hospital? Because she was Muslim, or Indian?" She did have dark skin, Adela remembered. A hint of the outrage that she'd felt that morning returned, somehow out of place in the fancy restaurant.

"It's possible," said Kip. "But it might have been she just didn't have any relatives around. You probably noticed no one was getting much help. Suffering is pretty equal-opportunity in Myanmar," he finished with a chuckle.

Adela swirled the wine in her glass. Already, it was tasting better to her. She listened to Kip's ongoing monologue and reworked it in her mind:

Although most Westerners think of Buddhism as a peaceful religion, conflicts have recently broken out between the majority Burman, Buddhist population and Muslims. Some people say Muslims have lived in Burma for centuries, but others say that many have recently come over the border from Bangladesh. The international community has been struggling with how to intervene.

Just then, the waiter came up, holding their food on a tray. They paused as he set it down.

"But that's terrible, just hating all Muslims? It's, like, racism! It reminds me of home," said Adela, thinking of Greg's tirades about the rise of "patriotic xenophobia" after 9/11. She'd been just a kid in 2001, but she remembered her usually mild-mannered father getting into a shouting match with some people who were boycotting a Pakistani-owned gas station near their house.

"I know, totally," said Kip. "And the government doesn't do anything about it. If anything, they fan the flames. Keeps people's minds off other things."

He took a sip of wine. "It sounds bad, but they really aren't ready for democracy."

When Adela reached for her glass, she saw that the waiter was standing right next to her. For a split second she felt like she'd been overheard saying something rude, but it was Kip who'd said it, and he didn't seem troubled at all.

Still, the waiter had an odd look on his face. "How is everything?" he asked, as if he'd been trained to use that specific phrase. Yet his intonation was off; he emphasized "everything" instead of "is," which made the question sound more momentous than it usually did in restaurants.

"Great!" Kip smiled without looking up. The waiter stood there a moment, then he turned and walked away.

As Adela chewed her pizza, she tried to reconcile what Kip had said with everything Ko Oo had told her. It seemed patronizing to say Burmese people weren't ready for democracy. Ko Oo and his friends had risked their lives for it.

All the same, Adela had started to realize that Ko Oo had left some important details out of his stories about Burma. The hospital was awful, there was no doubt. But people seemed to be trying to make things better, even if the government was insincere in its efforts at reform. Why should Ko Oo be so cynical? Also, he had never mentioned any problem with Muslims. Buddhism was important to him, but Adela couldn't imagine he would hate people from other religions. She felt a pang of nostalgia for their talks. If only she could meet him at the picnic table and ask him about everything she'd seen, she would feel more confident.

Kip went on to tell Adela about a recent outbreak of fighting between government forces and the Kachin people in the North, and they didn't mention Muslims again. Adela was relieved that the people at the hospital hadn't been talking about her. In fact, she thought, she'd done the right thing by trying to help someone who might have been unfairly ignored otherwise.

Over the coming weeks, this incident would slip into the blur of that first week along with everything else she didn't understand. It was only later that the word *kala* would come back to her, like the shadow in every photo that you finally realize is a smudge on the lens.

When they'd finished their food, Kip pushed away his plate. "Looking forward to another fun-filled day of orientation tomorrow?"

"Dude, I can't take it," said Adela, shaking her head.

"No, tomorrow should be pretty mellow. We're just going over health stuff and visas at the office."

"I think Sarah hates me," sighed Adela, hoping to be corrected.

"No, that's just Sarah. She's a good person." Kip paused, considering. "She's a *really* good person. I think she's just had this job too long. Her heart isn't in it. It's just a way to pay the rent so she can keep working on her women's project."

"What is her project, anyway?"

"It's like a business co-op. She gets poor women from different backgrounds together and organizes trainings and helps them get loans. Actually she's started working on the whole religion thing, too. The idea is to create relationships, so people have a harder time hating each other. Pretty unlikely, if you ask me. But don't mind Sarah. She's just blunt. If you get in trouble, she's got your back."

"Good to know."

The others were gathering their things. The waiter, familiar with foreign ways, brought each person a separate check. Adela was surprised by how expensive her meal was. Kip threw down a handful of bills, and she wondered how much he and Sarah were paid.

They walked out to the curb. A fleet of taxis and bicycle carts stood outside the restaurant. Adela's head was muddled by the wine, and the night air felt good.

"Hey, have you ever taken one of those bicycle things?" she asked, gesturing to the carts.

"Sidecars. Yeah, they're fun," said Kip. "It's not far to Golden Land."

He waved as he hopped into a taxi. Adela walked over to the carts, less sure of herself now that she was alone. Most of the drivers appeared to be asleep.

"Golden Land?" she said to no one in particular, forgetting how to ask in Burmese.

One fellow nodded and motioned her up. She clambered onto the wooden seat and he stood on the pedals to get going.

As they slid along the street, Adela leaned back and looked up at the moon flying through the tree branches. It had waned since the day she arrived. Still, it was beautiful. She thought of asking the driver to take her past the Shwedagon, but she had no idea how far away it was. A look at the passing taxis showed her how slowly they were moving, and the driver's calves strained with each push, so she let it go. She'd have to visit in the early morning, as Ko Oo told her she should. And she had to visit his family. It felt important, having promises to keep. *I should keep them*, Adela thought, as they rolled through the night.

THE GATE

It was an ordinary gate, made of iron and painted red. Above it, an arch bore the monastery's name, in Burmese script and in English: YADANA YEIKTHA. One morning in early June, soon after the MVU orientation had ended, Adela rang the doorbell beside this gate, and she heard it chime somewhere far away. She stood there for a few moments, peering through the bars, then she turned back to the road. There was not much to see, just a noodle stand and an auto repair shop. It had taken nearly an hour to get there by taxi, and as they drove, the modest skyscrapers of Yangon diminished into two-story shop-houses and finally into scattered buildings. The place where they'd arrived seemed to be nothing more than a village. Leaving the city, Adela had felt panic rising in her body with the clouds of dust on the road. She did not want to be this far out; she felt Kip and Sarah and civilization slipping away. But waiting in front of the gate with her bags, she tried to compose herself. She had come to Burma for a reason.

Later, Thiha told her that he was the one who opened the gate, but in Adela's memory it was a monk she came to know as U Pyinnya. Whoever opened the gate, she rushed through it without a backward glance. The gate was never locked except at night, and she could have left anytime. But over the next few months it would come to seem like a boundary she could not easily cross, and the world inside the monastery became the only one that was real to her. Inside, life was simple, stripped down to its essential parts: sitting, walking, or lying down. Eating, bathing, or sleeping. Speaking, or not speaking. Each choice was simple, right up until the moment when she looked back and realized that somewhere along the way, she must have chosen wrong.

U Pyinnya was a solidly built man, a head shorter than Adela, with a round, friendly face. "Miss Ah-deh-la Fa-rost!" he said, giving her surname two syllables. "You have come."

"Tway ya da wun tha ba deh," said Adela, using the phrase for "nice to meet you," which she had finally mastered.

"Oh!" he gasped. "You can speak Burmese! You must have some Burmese friend in the past?"

"Yeah," said Adela, recalling as she did so that she had not visited Ko Oo's mother. The day she'd intended to go was unbearably hot, and the lure of an air-conditioned cinema outing with the other volunteers had been too much to overcome. She told herself she'd visit later, when her Burmese was better.

U Pyinnya led her to a tree-shaded building. There was a blue-tiled patio strewn with leaves, and a sliding door led into a room with a whiteboard, two long tables, and a dozen plastic chairs.

"Your classroom," he said.

"How many kids are there?" she asked, a little confused. From Sarah's PowerPoint, she'd been led to expect a palm-leaf shack with low benches where children wrote on slates.

U Pyinnya looked surprised. "Oh, no, no. You will not teach the children," he said. "You will teach to the monks."

"Okaay."

U Pyinnya did not seem to notice Adela's trepidation. "Yes, our monks want to learn English. Some foreigners come to meditate. The monks are difficult to talk with them. Now, Myanmar can be easily visited. We can share our Buddha's teachings. Our abbot instruct us to invite the foreigners here. But we feel very shy to speak."

"Oh, I see." It was just as Sarah had warned the volunteers: they might not end up doing what they thought they'd be doing. They were supposed to go with the flow.

Once Adela considered this new information, she was relieved. She didn't have any younger siblings or cousins; she hadn't known any child well since she'd been one herself. Adults seemed easier. She could do what her teachers had done: make them read things and ask them what they thought.

When she looked around the room again, her attention was piqued. In the corner an ancient desktop computer and printer sat on a wooden table.

"Do those work?" Adela asked, pointing to them.

"Oh yes," said U Pyinnya. "We must read the email from our foreigner guests."

"Are there any foreigners here now?"

"There is one lady meditator from Taiwan. You live in the dormitory with her. I will show you now."

He gestured to a water cooler. "Would you like some drink?"

"No, I'm good."

"No, I'm good," he repeated, puzzled.

"I mean I'm fine, I'm not thirsty. 'I'm good,' means I don't need anything now."

"Ah, I see!" he said, brightening. "Ma Ah-deh-la, I think you will teach us a lot!"

"I hope so."

"And, excuse me, what state do you come from?"

"Well … I'm moving to California," she said, trying to focus on the future, and finding it too complicated to explain that she lived in one place while each of her parents lived in another.

"Ah, yes, like the 'Hotel California,'" he pronounced soberly.

"Yeah," she said, surprised by his familiarity with classic rock.

U Pyinnya gestured across the compound, and Adela pulled her suit-case behind her to a cluster of huts set amidst a grove of banana trees. A woman in pink robes emerged from one of them.

"Daw Pancavati," the monk said by way of explanation.

"Daw Pan-cha-wa-ti," Adela repeated carefully, reminding herself to add a note to her blog: **The Burmese language features honorific kinship terms that may be unfamiliar to English speakers. "Ma" is used to refer to women around one's own age; "Daw," for older women, like Burmese democracy hero Daw Aung San Suu Kyi**.

U Pyinnya spoke to Daw Pancavati in Burmese, then turned to Adela.

"You are … good?" he asked.

"Yes, I'm good!"

"Good! I am good too!" he repeated. "Lunch is at eleven o'clock, in this one here," he said, pointing to a large white building across the courtyard. "You can meet Bhante Pandita-blah-blah-sa after lunch."

That was not what he said, but that was what Adela heard. It would be a long time before she saw Bhante's name written out, or anyone's—the syllables melted together so that she only got a general sense of people's names the first several times she heard them. At that point Adela's Burmese was still elementary, but the few words she knew let her coast along. She just kept nodding and smiling, probably leading people to believe she understood much more than she actually did.

"Then you can take rest," continued U Pyinnya. "The monks are busy in the afternoon. We begin our class tomorrow morning."

"OK."

He left. Adela turned to the woman in pink, Daw Pancavati. Her face was soft and unlined, and her head was shaved. A delicate smell of camphor wafted up from her robes. Although she was a few heads shorter than Adela, she pulled the suitcase away and dragged it behind her toward a two-story building across from the dining hall. Inside was a hallway with a dozen identical doors and a row of toilets at the end.

Daw Pancavati opened one of the doors and gestured Adela inside. There was a metal bunk bed with a thin mattress on the bottom. A string with several hangers on it stretched between the bed frame and the one tiny window. There was a woven mat on the floor. In the corner was a jug of water with a cup turned upside down over the lid. The stub of a candle was melted onto a bedside table.

Adela remembered to leave her shoes at the door, just as Sarah had instructed them. Daw Pancavati set the suitcase in one corner.

"I apologize for our room. Very narrow," she said, moving her hands close together to illustrate its size.

It looked to Adela like a prison cell. She couldn't bring herself to say what she knew she should, that it was fine, no problem. Instead, she stood there chewing her lip.

"You need something?" Daw Pancavati asked, searching Adela's face.

"No, thanks. See you at lunch."

Adela heard Daw Pancavati close the door gently behind her. She sat down on the mat, staring at each object in turn as if waiting for its transformation. The panic that had arisen first at the airport when Lena had left her—and again during the taxi ride to the monastery—returned. There was no desk, not even a chair! Sulkily, Adela hung up her clothes and left everything else in her suitcase, since there was no place to put it.

She went to the water jug and examined the plastic cup on top, which was gray around the edges from many mouths. It was in need of washing, she decided. She slipped back into her sandals and walked down the hall to the bathrooms. There were two stalls with squat toilets set into cement, and buckets of water beside them to flush with. Kip had given the volunteers squat toilet instructions, so Adela felt prepared; she'd even remembered to bring her own toilet paper.

Next to the toilets were two rooms with sinks and water tanks. As she pushed open the door to one, a rat, its fur wet and spiky, darted from the water tank out the drainpipe beside the sink. Adela squealed in disgust, then tiptoed in. By the sink she found a peach-colored lump of soap veined with dirt, and she rubbed the rim of the cup with it. Fearful after Kip's talk on water-borne illness—giardia, dysentery, and cholera—she rinsed and dried the cup with her towel before returning to her room to fill it from the jug.

The water was warm and tasted like soap. Adela lay down on the bed, which smelled of mildew and mothballs, and recalled what Sarah had said: "The first twenty-four hours is the hardest. Please, don't call us before then. Try to give it a week." Without those instructions, Adela knew, she'd already be searching for a phone. She hadn't had a clear picture of the monastery in her mind before arriving, but she had imagined she'd feel the same sense of peace she had in her dream of the Shwedagon. Instead, she heard a whiny voice arising inside of her, complete with the asterisks she would have used in a message to Lena: *I *cannot* live here.* Adela scolded this voice into submission, channeling Greg: *Come on, Adela. You're the one who wanted to see the real Burma.*

Perhaps, she encouraged herself, she just needed to explore the monastery. She rallied for a pre-lunch walk.

Outside, it felt as if the air were actually being heated, as if someone had left open the door to a vast oven. Slowly, she paced the monastery's perimeter, thinking of how she'd describe the place. **The monastery is laid out in a square, with a golden structure that looks like a soft-serve ice cream cone at the center: the stupa. At the top of the stupa is a spire** similar to the one at the Shwedagon but smaller; the little bells that hang around it tinkle in the breeze (she'd need to insert two photographs here). The base is decorated with mysterious altars, stone water-tanks, and half-melted orange candles.

Near the stupa was a hall with a massive golden Buddha statue at the back. From the top floor of this building, Adela heard a cloud of sound drifting down. Voices, she couldn't tell how many, were chanting as Ko Oo had chanted in the cafetorium the day she met him: Buddho yo sabbapaninam saranam khemamuttamam. It comforted her; she had come to the right place.

From a building at the far end of the compound, she heard children shouting in unison, their voices rising and falling in a droning melody. When she passed by, she saw that it fit Sarah's description of a school: crowded and loud. She was glad not to be involved.

In the corner opposite the school, there was a building with monks' robes drying in the sun out front. Adela veered away from it. There are some places in the monastery where women aren't allowed. Men's and women's roles in Buddhism are different, she added, quoting Sarah, knowing she'd have to add some specifics later.

On her way back to the dining hall, Adela saw the collection of huts where Daw Pancavati lived, set amidst leafy banana trees. Outside of one, a man in a soaking wet loungyi was standing by a water tank, the upper half of his body covered thickly in lather. As she watched from a distance, he used a bowl to splash water over his chest. So that was how the "shower" worked, Adela thought. The man didn't have a shaved head, so she knew he couldn't be a monk. Who were all these people? One man was sweeping leaves into a little basket. A woman was squatting in front of a hut washing clothes in a bucket. The monastery was like a village unto itself.

In the other corner lay the main gate and the office, which Adela had already seen, so she headed back toward her room. On the way she passed a dormitory identical to hers, from which several women in brown loungyis and white shirts were making their way toward the dining hall. They didn't talk amongst themselves or look up, but instead proceeded slowly, their hands folded in front of them.

Adela concluded that it was lunchtime, so she followed them. In a manner that showed she'd been observing Adela from afar, Daw Pancavati fell into step beside her. She led Adela to a low table in the corner of the dining hall, where many dishes were arrayed under a dome-shaped plastic fly-shield. Other people started to file in and group themselves around similar tables—men and women in brown loungyis and white tops, ladies in pink robes like Daw Pancavati's, and other people in regular clothing who walked around filling water glasses. Daw Pancavati motioned for Adela to sit down, and then held up a hand to show her she should wait.

The monks came in. Adela saw U Pyinnya and a dozen others, led by one elderly monk who leaned on a cane, take seats on a platform. There was a long wait as various people approached to spoon food onto the monks' plates. Everyone else put their palms together and held them in front of their chests, so Adela did the same. Finally, the elderly monk began to eat, and everyone bowed down, touching their foreheads to the floor three times before turning to their meals.

The food was the only thing that kept Adela at the monastery that first day. It was exceptionally delicious. She hadn't yet eaten much Burmese food. Golden Land offered a Western breakfast, and with the exception of that first night with Kip she'd eaten alone at cheap Indian restaurants or with other volunteers anywhere they could get french fries and ice cream. The monastery food was a revelation: a pumpkin curry with tofu and lemongrass; grilled eggplant in a smoky salad dressed with lime juice; fresh ginger sliced thin and mixed with cabbage and crunchy seeds; and some kind of sour, savory soup that Adela couldn't get enough of. There was a salad that Daw Pancavati whispered was made of pickled tea leaves, studded with peanuts and fried garlic.

Adela was embarrassed at how much she was eating, but Daw Pancavati seemed pleased. She kept spooning more food onto Adela's plate. Adela wondered if she should reciprocate, or whether it was something only nuns did. She was fairly sure Daw Pancavati was a nun, but what did the brown-and-white uniform that the other women wore mean? Adela wanted to ask, but the room was nearly silent.

Eventually, Adela looked around and saw that she was the only person still eating. She wiped her mouth.

"Eat slowly," said Daw Pancavati.

"It's OK, I'm finished."

"Laphet yay thauk ma la?" she asked, offering Adela a steaming cup of something.

Adela took a sip. She expected instant coffee or strong green tea, like the kind Ko Oo had served her, but it was as creamy and fragrant as the lattes Adela loved but not so bitter. She slurped it up.

"What is this?"

"Laphet yay. Our special Burmese tea."

"It's really good."

Daw Pancavati smiled. "Do you need some rest?"

Adela thought of her dismal chamber. "No, I'm fine."

"Then I take you to our abbot, Bhante Panditabhivamsa."

As they walked away from the dining hall, Adela saw an old woman squatting behind the building, holding a small child in her arms. A man in a plaid loungyi was scraping the leftovers from lunch onto a plate for her. She started eating it right there on the ground, pushing food into the child's mouth with her fingers. It was the image of poverty Adela had expected when she had pictured Burma, and she found it oddly reassuring.

They entered the hall with the golden Buddha at the back. In front of the statue, the elderly monk was seated on a platform. Daw Pancavati walked ahead of Adela across the polished wooden floor, knelt down with her knees tucked under her, raised her palms to her forehead, and bowed three times. Adela, watching out of the corner of her eye, tried to imitate these movements.

The monk observed them, blinking sagely. When they were finished, Adela looked up at him with undisguised curiosity.

"Ah-deh-la Fa-rost, from Cali-for-nee-ya," he pronounced. Adela was startled that U Pyinnya had already told him where she came from. She could not decide if it was unsettling or reassuring that so much communication was going on behind her back.

"Yes," said Adela, trying to be as polite as she could.

"Very good you come to our monastery."

"Yes."

"You teach our monks English."

"Yes."

There was a long pause, and Adela wondered if their conversation had ended. The monk sat there regarding her impassively. From time to time he burped gently. It was hard for Adela to guess how old he might be. His eyebrows were white and wiry, extending a good inch from his face, like tufts of feather on an owl. Yet his face was plump and his body looked sturdy, as if his cane were a prop he could toss aside at any moment.

"You call me Bhante," he finally said.

"OK."

Daw Pancavati whispered to her: "Hman ba, Bhan-tay."

Adela repeated this phrase. Bhante smiled. There was another long pause, during which Adela could not help looking around at the objects in the room: the golden Buddha statue with a tray in front of it holding a glass of water and some miniature bananas; a radio in the corner; an orange washcloth on a small table next to Bhante's hand. She tried to fit the objects into some kind of sequence. What did Bhante do all day?

When she looked back at him, his eyes were closed and his lips were moving. Her legs were falling asleep and her knees hurt where they pressed into the floor. Sweat pooled inside her bra. Daw Pancavati, seeing Adela's discomfort, gave her a signal to bow once more. Adela wondered if she'd have to do the same routine with the monks in class every day. How many times a day could you bow?

Adela stood up to go. Suddenly she wanted to be alone, even if it meant going back to her depressing little room. As she reached the door, she turned and saw Daw Pancavati shuffling backward on her knees and then carefully lifting herself into a standing position, without ever turning her back to Bhante, and somehow without disturbing any of the mysterious folds of her pink robes.

"I think I'd like to rest," Adela said when they were outside.

"Yes, rest."

"What does it mean, 'hmabba, Bhante'?"

"'Hman ba, Bhante,' 'Correct, Venerable Sir.' You say this when he speaks to you."

"Like, no matter what he says, that's what I say?" asked Adela, unable to conceal her incredulity.

"Yes," replied Daw Pancavati cheerfully.

"And to the monks also?"

"'Hman-ba, Hpaya.' 'Correct, my Buddha.'"

"Why do I call them differently?"

"Bhante Panditabhivamsa is very important monk."

"And you? You're a nun, right?"

"Yes, kind of nun. But no need to say something special for me. You just say, 'OK.'"

"OK." Adela planned to write it all down when she got back to her room.

"And when's dinner?" she added, imagining another tasty spread.

Daw Pancavati looked at her blankly for a moment. "Oh," she said. "No dinner. Monks do not eat after noon."

Seeing the look of disbelief on Adela's face, Daw Pancavati added, "At teatime you may take fruit juice."

Sarah must have known about the absence of dinner, and yet she hadn't told Adela, perhaps sensing she'd have asked for a different posting. No dinner? For three months? Adela mentally sorted through the contents of her suitcase. There might be a package of almonds from the airplane.

"Or," said Daw Pancavati, brightening, "there is noodle cart just outside our gate."

"Um, OK. When's teatime?" asked Adela, trying not to sound hostile.

"Five o'clock," she said.

"Thanks," Adela replied, afraid that if she looked into Daw Pancavati's kind, attentive eyes, she would start crying.

❀

When Adela woke from her nap, it was nearly five, and she leapt out of bed terrified that she might miss teatime. As she was rushing out of her room, she stopped. A woman in a long brown skirt and white blouse was coming out of the room across from hers. There was nothing remarkable about the woman's short black hair or stocky figure, yet she appeared to be moving in slow motion, like a mime. She pulled the door shut so slowly that her progress was almost undetectable. Without pausing, but at the same speed, she turned and began walking—if one could call it that—toward the exit, staring at the floor in front of her and placing her feet so softly that she seemed to be avoiding invisible landmines. Adela deduced that it must be the "lady meditator from Taiwan" that U Pyinnya had mentioned. She didn't look like she was meditating; she looked like a zombie. Nonetheless, Adela decided to introduce herself.

"Hi, I'm—" she began, and then she stared in amazement as the woman's head turned mechanically toward her, and then her eyes turned within her head, millimeter by millimeter, to regard Adela. The lady meditator met Adela's eyes for a moment, nodded almost imperceptibly, then began inching her head back in the opposite direction. As Adela stood there stunned, the woman continued toward the door.

"Okaay," she couldn't help saying out loud.

Daw Pancavati was already at their table when Adela arrived. There was a pitcher of juice, another cup of tea, and a small bowl of chalky candies that tasted pleasantly of maple syrup.

At her elbow, someone placed a tray of papaya and pineapple chunks. That was the first time she saw Thiha, although she was so focused on food that she only registered him as the helper who was taller and perhaps better-looking than the others. No, maybe she remembered his wrists: she could picture the way the veins snaked through his brown forearms, the way he set down the tray without making a sound.

No other tables got fruit, and Daw Pancavati didn't take any. Adela ate every morsel and then walked back out into the broiling evening, her stomach overfull and aching.

Still, knowing there would be nothing more until breakfast, she couldn't stop herself from investigating the noodle cart. She thought longingly of how she and Lena used to drive themselves out to the Pancake House before curfew, even after a full dinner, just to gorge themselves on starch and talk about the day.

As Adela let herself out through the gate, the noodle seller was already packing up, but she gestured to a plastic stool when she saw Adela coming. The woman worked with speed, dicing up cabbage leaves and something Adela guessed was dried meat. Adela was awed by the amount of oil the lady poured into the pan and concerned to see the meat sitting out in the sun. The odor of frying garlic was enticing, but when the plate of noodles arrived, Adela could only take a few bites. She nibbled on the cabbage leaves and pushed the rest aside, feeling bad for leaving so much food on her plate. Then she held out a few crumpled bills.

"Manahpyan!" said the lady, pointing to her watch. Tomorrow, same time.

Adela nodded and smiled, internally resolving never to return. Then she turned away quickly, not wanting to see what would happen to the remainder of her food.

Afterward she strolled up the street. The auto repair shop was closing up, and a few young men squatted in front of it, smoking cigarettes and staring at her. Inside the open-fronted shop-houses, kids looked up from their plates to gape as Adela passed. Their parents ignored her, stuffing rice into the children's mouths by hand. As dusk fell, scabby dogs crawled out from under the cars and trotted around in a pack, nipping the air near her ankles. Adela hurried back to the monastery. It was a relief to slide Yadana Yeiktha's red gate closed behind her.

SABEH

The next morning Adela stood in front of the whiteboard in her class-room, facing five monks: U Nyanika, U Suriya, U Agga Dhamma, U Silak-khanda, and U Pyinnyathami. The first thing she asked them to do was make name tags. The longer names did not fit on the tags, and thus she came to call them U Pyinnya, U Sila, and so on.

All of them had shaved heads and wore red robes, so at first it was dif-ficult for Adela to remember who was who. U Pyinnya was easiest; she met him first, and he had a round face and wire-rimmed glasses. U Agga was the youngest, the smallest, and a compulsive smiler. U Nyanika had dark skin and bushy eyebrows that nearly joined in the center; he had a tendency toward querulous interruptions. U Sila was pale and had an unexpected smattering of freckles across his cheeks; he was from Shan State, Adela learned, and some of his relatives lived across the border in Thailand. U Suriya, the oldest and most serious monk, had eyes so deep-set and cheekbones so prominent that it seemed his skull was trying to press its way out of his face. He rarely spoke.

Adela asked the monks to introduce themselves and tell a little about their lives. Each of them began with an elaborate apology for his weak-nesses in the English language, requested her forgiveness for any mistakes he might make, and asked that she have patience as she corrected his errors. Adela nodded obligingly each time. From the monks' speeches, she learned that they ranged in age from twenty to thirty-seven, and that some of them, like U Pyinnya, had been monks since they were ten or twelve years old, whereas others had been ordained more recently. Only a few of them were from Yangon; the rest were from far-flung places and considered it a great opportunity to study in this monastery.

Finally, Adela introduced herself. "I'm Adela. I can speak a little Burmese. I'm from America. I'm eighteen years old—" and then she stopped, because the monks seemed somehow shocked. "OK, I'm eighteen years old, and I just finished high school, so—"

"What subject do you study?" asked U Nyanika.

"I'm going to study literature."

He looked crestfallen. "I studied engineering," he said.

"Great. Well, let's get started. First, I'd like to, um—." She paused. She had planned for the introductions to take much longer, and she was at a loss for what to do next.

She was glad when U Pyinnya piped up. "Excuse me, Teacher. Sayama Ah-deh-la, not easy to say," he noted.

Apparently, 'sayama' was teacher. Ko Oo had called her Ma Adela—Sister Adela—and in truth it was hard to pronounce, tending to merge into one word.

"Feel free to just call me Adela."

"No! We must call you 'Sayama' first, for you are our teacher, and you call us 'U,' for mister."

"I think Phyu Phyu is good name for you," offered U Agga.

"What does it mean?" she asked.

"Miss Very White."

She wrinkled her nose. "Very white?"

U Agga gestured to his arm. "See? Black. Very ugly. Not like you."

"I don't want to be called—" she protested, but U Suriya interrupted.

"What day of the week she is born."

Adela looked it up on the computer. Saturday.

"Ooh! Unlucky," said U Sila.

"Ta, Hta, Da, Dha, Na," said U Nyanika. "It must start with one of these letters."

U Agga frowned. "Those letters are not good. What about Sabeh? Means 'jasmine flower.'"

"I like that," said Adela. "Sabeh."

"It is not correct day of the week," said U Suriya.

"She is American, who will know?" asked U Agga.

U Suriya nodded, and it was decided.

The name later came to seem like her first mistake, as if her Burmese self were wrong from the beginning. At the time she liked it because it sounded pretty, but later she loved the words that came after it. *Sayama Sabeh, have you eaten rice yet? Ma Sabeh, will you drink tea? Ma Sabeh is clever! Ma Sabeh is not like other Americans. Ma Sabeh, Ma Sabeh.* Thiha would say it while he stroked her hair. There was a nursery rhyme about Ma Sabeh that he sang to her. Adela could never remember the words, but the tune still ran through her mind. He never asked her what day of the week she was born, and she didn't learn the day of his birth, either. Maybe he avoided the topic because he didn't want to tell her that Thiha wasn't his real name.

Once the question of Adela's Burmese name had been settled, an hour of class time remained. Luckily, U Pyinnya had a suggestion. "Four kinds we need to study," he said, counting them off on his fingers. "Speaking, reading, writing, and listening."

"Oh, good idea," said Adela. "Let's start with speaking. You want to talk to the foreigners who come to the monastery, right? Why don't you pair up and one can pretend to be the foreigner, one can be the monk. The foreigner has a problem, and—"

"The foreigner is sick!" suggested U Agga.

"Yes, the foreigner is sick, and you need to ask what is wrong." The others looked uncertain. They consulted amongst themselves in low voices.

"OK, U Agga and U Sila, you guys work together!" said Adela, hoping that her enthusiasm would spur them to action. "U Nyanika and U Pyinnya! U Suriya, I'll work with you! Practice together first, and then you will perform for your classmates!"

It was the kind of activity Adela had done in her French classes. She busied herself writing some health-related vocabulary on the board.

As it turned out, the monks were very good at making up dialogues. The "foreigners" suffered from fever, headaches, and diarrhea; the monks advised that they see doctors and seek out medicines. By lunchtime, Adela felt that she had won them over.

"OK," she said. "Tomorrow, writing! We will write our life stories!"

"Sayama Sabeh also," said U Pyinnya. "Also write the life story, naw?"
"OK," she agreed happily. They seemed to like her. The monks stood up, chanted "Thank you, Sayama Sabeh!" in unison, and walked over to the dining hall, with Adela following at a respectful distance behind them.

❀

Adela had hoped that the monks' stories would be full of drama and intrigue, like Ko Oo's. However, the next day when they read their assignments aloud, they followed a formula that made them nearly indistinguishable. U Sila had the best handwriting, so his was the one Adela saved:

> My name is Sai Sai. I was born in Hsipaw, in Shan State. My mother is Nang Rak and my father is Sai Leng. My father and mother plants rice paddy. I have three older sisters and one younger brother. We are Buddhist and we are from the Shan ethnic. We live happily on our farm. But my parents have no money to send me to school. When I am ten years old I go to the monastery for "Shin Pyu ceremony." I become the novice monk. There I can learn to write Shan language and Burmese language. I learn the Buddha teachings and my mind become calm. When I am twenty years old I become the fully ordained monk. I get my name "U Silakkhanda." I can come to Yangon for study.

Adela asked the monks to fill in the parts she thought were missing from their stories: what they had wanted to be when they were little (this question confused them, except for U Agga, who had wanted to be a rock 'n' roll singer), which of their siblings they liked best (they all had a favorite, and it made Adela feel lonely), and where in the world they would go if they could go anywhere (America was a popular choice, although U Pyinnya insisted that it was excellent karma to be born right here in Burma, where one could easily study the Buddha's teachings).

Then Adela read them her story, which she had labored over, tearing up several more elaborate versions before settling on this one:

> My name is Adela Frost. I like to read and do yoga. I haven't decided yet what kind of job I want, but I'm planning to major in English. Sometimes I think I want to be a writer, but I also want to help people. I was born in Hartford, Connecticut. My dad still lives there, but my mom lives in DC. I'm moving to

California for college. This trip to Burma is my first time leaving the United States, except one trip to Canada. I like it here because the people are very kind and the food is delicious.

After she read it aloud, the monks had many questions: her parents' names (Joseph Frost and Barbara Cooper), what they did for a living (librarian and curator), and how many sisters and brothers she had (none). The last part was hard for them to believe. They asked Adela if she'd had any siblings who had died. She explained that her parents had divorced when she was small, and the monks nodded knowingly. Some had seen similar situations in American movies.

"And what religion you worship?" asked U Sila.

"Um . . . my parents were both raised Christian, but they didn't take me to church or anything when I was growing up. So I guess I'm not religious?"

The monks looked perplexed, and consulted amongst themselves for several minutes.

"I mean, I haven't found any religion that really makes sense to me yet," she added during a lull in their conversation. "But I definitely respect all religions. And Buddhism seems really . . . great."

"The Buddha had grown up in a palace, like a prince," pronounced U Nyanika, in what struck Adela as a non sequitur, "and when he come out he sees three man: the old man, the dead man, the sick man. And then he can realize, the world is not as he had known before! There is sickness, aging, and death also."

"Yes, and he goes out from the palace, and begins his meditations!" continued U Sila, as if the Buddha's life story had some connection to Adela's.

"In past life, Sayama Sabeh lives in Burma," said U Pyinnya with conviction. All the monks nodded.

"Really? How do you know?" she asked.

"If not, how can Sayama Sabeh learn Burmese language easily?" he asked, laying out his case. "Many places in the world to go, but Sayama only come here. Sayama can eat Burmese food, also," he noted approvingly.

"Ma Sabeh is not like other Americans," added U Agga. "Not like ones from the movie." It was difficult to tell if he was disappointed or trying to give her a compliment.

"So if I lived in Burma in a past life, why did I get reborn in America this time?" she asked, skeptical yet intrigued.

"Maybe some bad luck!" said U Pyinnya.

Adela wasn't sure how it could be bad luck if all the other monks wanted to go to America most, but she liked to entertain the past life idea. Just to see their reaction, she told them the dream she'd had about the Shwedagon before she came. They became serious. It was certain, they said, that she had lived in Burma before.

๛

Sarah was right. The first twenty-four hours were the hardest. After that I fell into a rhythm: I drag myself out of bed each morning for breakfast at six, then go back to my room to study _Insurgency and the Politics of Ethnicity_, which is really helping me understand the history of this country. The ethnic groups are easier to remember now that I can connect them with people I know: U Sila is Shan, U Agga is half-Mon and half-Burman, and so on. After doing my reading, I wash my clothes in a bucket, just like Daw Pancavati showed me, and hang them in the sun behind my dormitory. I go to teach the monks at nine, then gorge myself at lunch; the food is amazing. There's no dinner in the monastery, but I've gotten used to it more quickly than I thought I would.

Everyone rests after lunch, even the people who wear regular clothes and help out at the monastery in order to earn good karma (it's called doing waya wutsa in Burmese). I usually take a nap as well—it's too hot for anything else. Then I take a shower, stamping twice outside the bathroom door to scare off the rats and the giant cockroaches.

Adela looked up from her computer and smiled. Her hair, fresh from the shower, fell cool and wet on the back of her neck. Maybe she'd send this post to Greg. He'd have to be impressed—he knew how much she hated bugs. The blog was turning out to be, she felt, quite a good outlet. At first, she'd written Lena elaborate emails relating each experience she'd had, but then she'd have to write separately to her mom and dad in addition to doing the blog, and with limited time on the Internet, it made more sense to do it all in one go.

Then she could take her time preparing for class the following day, printing out news articles she could read with the monks or inventing scenarios to act out. Adela had the office to herself; U Agga chatted with his brother online, but he usually did so in the early morning. In fact, she had most of the day to herself. She saw the Taiwanese meditator often, yet the woman never gave any sign of acknowledgment. Adela's sightings of Bhante were rare, but when she glimpsed him from afar, he always gave her a Miss America wave, putting his hand up in the air and then rotating it on his wrist, as if he'd read somewhere that it was the proper way to greet foreigners. Somehow, he made this gesture, like all of his other movements, seem dignified and formal.

The only person she talked to regularly, aside from the monks, was Daw Pancavati. Every evening before teatime, the nun would help Adela with her Burmese. In the meditation hall above the dormitory or at a table in the courtyard if the weather was fine, Daw Pancavati would lay out a set of kindergarten textbooks, flimsy little pamphlets with cartoon drawings and nursery rhymes. She read them out loud to Adela and had her chant them back line by line, just as the children in school did. Adela had filled a notebook with phrases from these lessons and from her conversations with the monks, who seemed as eager to teach her Burmese as they were to learn English. She'd started learning to write the alphabet, laboring to make her handwriting as smooth and round as Daw Pancavati's. Adela was impatient with her progress, but Daw Pancavati showered her with extravagant praise at the end of each lesson: "Ma Sabeh is clever! Learn very well!"

The evenings were quiet. Adela walked around the compound until darkness fell. Sometimes she sat outside the main temple, looking up at its golden spire and listening to the monks performing their evening chanting with the Burmese meditators. It was at those times that she approached the sense of peace and awe she'd experienced in her dream of Burma, the feeling of arriving home she'd had when she'd first heard Ko Oo chanting prayers of goodwill for all beings.

As Adela recalled these pleasant feelings, a message from Ms. Alvarez popped up, its little ping jarring her out of her thoughts. *Nice observations, Adela. But what about* Burmese Days? *And more on the Buddhist-Muslim conflict? Try to keep your tone consistent. It's fine to write on different topics, but this should be more of a literary/political analysis, and less of your diary.*

Adela chuckled. Did Ms. Alvarez ever sleep? And what did she know about blogging? Blogs were supposed to be personal. She scrolled back through her first, tentative post on loungyis and thanaka.

Already, she looked back scornfully on the girl who had worn the wrong shirt, the girl who'd been disgusted by the hospital. Occasionally, when she caught a glimpse of herself in the mirror at the back of the dining hall, it took her a moment to recognize the person she saw. Her hair had curled softly in the humidity and her skin had an unfamiliar sheen. Skipping dinner had left her looking slightly gaunt, her body a little more like the Burmese bodies around her. She was Sabeh now, and Sabeh belonged in Burma.

SAVAGE CUSTOMS

It was several weeks after Adela arrived that she saw the photo. She was doing research for her post about the Buddhist-Muslim conflict, which had been slow going:

Over the past few weeks there have been clashes between Buddhists and Muslims in Rakhine State, near the border with Bangladesh. The conflict centers on a group of people called the Rohingya, Muslims whom the government does not recognize as citizens. Some Buddhists use the derogatory term "kala" to reference this group, or others of South Asian descent.

Kala: she heard again the hiss of that word as she remembered crouching by the dying woman's bedside in the hospital. She wished she had a picture; she could hardly remember the woman's face, just the sound of that word, the smell of rot, and the heat that had blanketed everything.

But she needed some photos to accompany her post. The *New York Times* had a slideshow next to the article she'd just read. It was preceded by a warning: *Some images are graphic and may be disturbing to readers.*

Adela clicked through the images of burning houses and angry crowds until she came upon one that stopped her. It showed the charred remains of a palm-leaf hut against a background of lush green foliage, almost as if a black-and-white photo had been superimposed on one in vibrant color. The effect was actually quite beautiful. In front of the hut was a fallen log, charred and smoking, with a pink plastic sandal melted over it. She looked back at the log, and it was not a log. She zoomed in on a blackened, claw-like hand. She looked away for a moment to be sure, and then back.

Adela felt her breath coming in and out of her body, and she looked at her own pale hand resting on the table. For a moment she thought of what was beneath the skin: bones, blood, little pink stringy bits like the ones she'd sliced through with a scalpel when they'd dissected cats in anatomy class her sophomore year. The boys in her class had joked about how the cats had been killed—with electric shocks, or with poison—and then they'd moved on to how they'd choose to die themselves: in their sleep, from a gunshot wound, or leaping from a building. No one chose being burned alive.

In the article's sidebar, a new comment popped up: "As I am a Burmese Buddhist, these KALAS are Terrorist to me. Just kill them."

Adela shuddered. The last sentence reminded her of the famous phrase from *Heart of Darkness*, the one Kurtz scrawled at the bottom of his "Report on the Suppression of Savage Customs": "Exterminate all the brutes!" She understood why a mentally disturbed colonial official from the 1800s would want to exterminate the natives. But for a Buddhist to talk that way about someone from their own country? This whole post she was writing just didn't fit into what she'd experienced in Burma. Buddhists were doing this? She couldn't imagine U Pyinnya or Daw Pancavati mildly irritated, much less wanting to kill an entire religious group.

She heard Greg's voice in her mind: *Adela, you're so naïve.* She looked around the empty office and imagined the monks in their identical saffron robes, shaved heads bowed over their papers. What did she really know about them and what they believed? What did she really know about this country at all?

Adela was staring at the rain clouds gathering over the pagoda's spire, with the photo still blown up on the screen, when U Pyinnya came in.

"Sayama Sabeh," he greeted her. "What do you do now?"

Adela slapped her laptop shut.

"Nothing much," she said. Then, wanting to fill the silence, she added, "You can say 'Nothing much' when you are not doing anything special."

He nodded. "Ah! We have this in Burmese also."

Adela didn't remember the rest of the conversation, but as soon as U Pyinnya left, she got back online and read a few more articles, then plunged back into her blog.

The violence was sparked when some Muslim men were accused of raping a Buddhist girl. Ten Muslim men were lynched

She paused. That was the word the *New York Times* had used, but wasn't it only something that had happened to black people in the American South? She backspaced.

Ten Muslim men were killed. Houses were burned.

She could hear Ms. Alvarez's voice in her mind. People usually use the passive voice when they're trying to make you forget who's doing what.

Adela deleted the lines and started again.

Buddhists killed ten Muslim men and burned some houses. The UN recalled some of its workers, and authorities called for calm.

It was crazy. Buddhists burning a village? She'd ask the monks about it. They would condemn the violence; they would reassure her that real Buddhists weren't involved. She printed several copies of the *Times* article, folded them up, and took them back to her room.

❀

That night Adela dreamed she was drowning, yet she woke up parched, as if she'd drunk a gallon of seawater. Rain hammered on the roof. The monsoon was coming, the monks had told her, and the heat would subside.

After breakfast, Adela borrowed Daw Pancavati's umbrella and ran over to the office, copies of the article tucked into her shoulder bag. Some of the print was smudged, but the type was still legible. She set the papers out on the tables to dry while she waited for the monks to arrive.

U Sila came first. He picked up the article and read the headline.

"Very terrible," he said.

"Yes, very bad," Adela agreed.

"You know these things from your own country," he said.

"Yeah," she said, a little surprised that he'd made the same connection she had. "Since 9/11 it's gotten a lot worse."

He shook his head sadly. The others came in as a group, neat and dry under their special orange monk umbrellas.

U Pyinnya nodded vigorously when he saw the article. "Yes, we must discuss this one," he said. "Sayama Sabeh must understand our country."

"Yeah, I have to say, I don't really understand." Adela was relieved. "But maybe we can do something about it, something to help."

"Yes, we can do," said U Agga, smiling. "Why not?"

"Yeah, like maybe some kind of fund-raiser, or public statement, just to let people know that this is not OK."

All the monks nodded, and Adela felt herself getting excited. She could actually *do* something.

"I should speak about one matter," said U Nyanika. "I am Rakhine people, from Rakhine State. Our Rakhine people are Buddhist for thousands of years. Our kingdom, Mrauk-U . . ." He went on for some time about an ancient kingdom with a famous Buddha statue that had been stolen by a Burman king. Adela didn't see what it had to do with Muslims, but she had learned that U Nyanika didn't like to be interrupted, so she waited for the other monks to intervene.

"Like I say," U Sila finally jumped in. "You have the same problem in America. Muslims come and bomb your towers."

"Well, that was different," Adela said slowly. "Wait a minute, so you're saying . . . so you're saying this conflict, it's the Muslims' fault?"

Maybe when she and U Sila had agreed that the situation was "very terrible," they hadn't agreed on why.

"Yes, of course their fault. They do this this riot and raping."

Adela looked around the room in utter disbelief. The other monks nodded, confirming U Sila's charge. U Pyinnya, seeing his teacher frowning, piped up. "Sayama, of course you know about our national races?"

He and Adela had discussed the civil war previously, when he'd seen her reading *Insurgency and the Politics of Ethnicity*; he said he felt sympathy for all the ethnic peoples, and he wanted peace. He supported Aung San Suu Kyi, and his older brother had participated in the same 1988 demonstrations that Ko Oo had.

"In my opinion," U Pyinnya began gently, "these people are not Myanmar people, not our national races. They come from Bangladesh, only recently."

"These people? But there are Muslims all over Burma, right?" Adela asked. Her heart was beating fast. She had that feeling again, of being in over her head, of being dropped into cold water. "They can't all have come from Bangladesh."

"Maybe some," U Pyinnya admitted.

The other monks looked down at the article with knitted brows. Perhaps they didn't understand the English, Adela told herself. Maybe she wasn't communicating clearly enough.

She tried again. "Say they did come from Bangladesh, don't they have human rights just like everyone else?"

"I think we must protect our culture," said U Nyanika haughtily.

"But what does it have to do with culture?" she asked. "People can be from different religions and still have the same culture. Like, in American culture, there are people from many religions, from many races. I mean, there are African Americans, and—"

"Your country is very different to ours," interrupted U Nyanika. "Then, you cannot understand our Myanmar people."

"I have read about this problem in your country also," said U Sila. "Some people come in by secret from Mexico, with no passport, make many babies."

"But they're not Muslim. And anyway, there's nothing wrong with Mexicans. I love Mexicans!" Adela insisted desperately, glad that no Americans were there to hear how silly she sounded.

U Sila shook his head in bewilderment.

"Not all Muslim are bad, only about 99 percent," said U Nyanika with great seriousness, as if he were quoting a well-known statistic. "Did you know 100 percent of the rapes in Myanmar are done by kalas?"

Adela couldn't believe what she was hearing. Kip had said that *kala* was like the n-word. How could a monk use it?

"In Myanmar we are Buddhist for long time," said U Nyanika. "But now some are changing. Some Muslim marry Myanmar women, so their children will be Muslim. The mosque give them money for taking Myanmar wife. I know this one from my own experience in my hometown."

Adela found U Nyanika's theory so bizarre that she didn't know how to respond. She tried a different tactic. "But the whole country *isn't* Buddhist. There are Christians here, too, right?"

"OK, fine, Christian is no problem in Rakhine State," said U Nyanika. "Very small number. And," he said, stabbing at the article, "this is not correct. So-called Rohingya are not 'minority.' They grow and grow! It is we Rakhine who are minority now, minority in our own state. Many years ago these Muslim people have an army. They try to separate and take over!"

His voice was louder now, and he leaned across the table toward Adela.

U Pyinnya patted the air between them. "Sayama, I know it sound strange for you. You come here just some weeks ago. But we face this problem a long time, naw?"

"They're not a problem, they're ... people," she gasped.

"Sabeh has any Muslim friends?" U Nyanika demanded.

"Well ..." she searched her memory. There was that freshman in her phys ed class. "Yes! Yes, I do! And all of my Muslims friends are very nice, very kind."

U Nyanika practically shuddered with disgust. Then U Agga jumped in, smiling as he explained that Muslims only went to stores owned by other Muslims.

Adela was shocked. She had never encountered such blatantly prejudiced statements. Edgerton Fields had a strict code of conduct related to hate speech, and even the most subtle comments could leave one open to accusations of racism or sexism. By comparison, she found the monks' views of Muslims almost laughably straightforward. She felt like she had entered another place and time, like she was Atticus Finch in *To Kill a Mockingbird*, standing up against injustice. But it was so confusing; she didn't want to argue with the monks, she wanted to go back to the place in the conversation where she thought they agreed about how to fix the situation in Rakhine State.

Only U Suriya, the oldest monk, had stayed quiet. Adela had thought of him as the least friendly, but now she appealed to him for help.

"U Suriya, what do you think?"

His deep-set eyes were so dark Adela couldn't see his pupils. "Monks should not involve in politics," he said.

That silenced the others.

They didn't read the article that day. The rain-spattered copies still lay on the table at the end of class. Adela threw them in the garbage.

❀

The electricity was patchy for a few days, so Adela couldn't get on the Internet. She wondered what was happening in Rakhine State, but in a way she was relieved not to know. Inside the monastery, everything was fine: breakfast and lunch came on schedule, there were torrential rains every afternoon, the monks chanted in the evenings.

But at breakfast and lunch, Adela looked at the people around her in a new way. What did Bhante think of Muslims? Was he the one filling the monks' heads with these ideas? What about all the meditators? Daw Pancavati? As the lady from Taiwan moved around in slow motion every day, did she harbor hatred toward people who didn't share her beliefs?

Adela's conversation with the monks had disturbed her, but all the same she longed for the harmonious relations they'd had before. So she tried to see things from their perspective, as Sarah had recommended the volunteers do whenever they encountered something that confused them. People say all kinds of things they don't mean, Adela told herself.

Although she wasn't sure what to write anymore, she tried to wrap up her blog post: **Surprisingly, some monks actually support the Buddhists who have been attacking Muslim people. They'd never participate in the violence, but they at least pay lip-service to some racist ideas. Of course, they are just exercising their freedom of speech and stating their views, which people couldn't do in Burma for many years because of the repressive government. Some Buddhists might have had negative experiences with Muslims that caused them to form a stereotype. It's not so different from the kind of "us vs. them" thinking and dehumanization of "the other" that we see in *Heart of Darkness*. But ... there's still a lot I don't understand.**

Adela thought it was a crappy ending for a blog post, but she got a lot of good feedback. *This is messed up!* Lena commented. *I thought Buddhists were supposed to be peaceful.*

Even Ms. Alvarez was pleased. *I appreciate your on-the-ground reporting, Adela. But it's good that you realize you have more to learn.*

Somehow, getting the story out made Adela feel better. She felt able to face the monks again. Over the next few days, they seemed to warm to her as well. U Pyinnya said that they had enough reading knowledge and they should work more on speaking, which was his way of telling Adela not to bring any more news articles to class.

Thus the monks voted on a new topic to discuss: favorite foods. With the aid of a dictionary, they described fruits Adela had never tasted: durian, rambutan, jackfruit, and mangosteen. U Nyanika held forth on the superiority of Rakhine mohinga, the fish soup in his home state, while U Agga insisted that Yangon mohinga was best. Adela told them about bagels, pizza, and the sushi stand where Ko Oo worked. No one mentioned Muslims again.

Adela did not forget what was happening in Rakhine State, but she let her mind stray from the photograph of the burned body, from the vein pulsing in U Nyanika's neck when he said the word *kala*. The monsoon had come, and instead of taking walks in the evening she sat under her dormitory's awning, listening to rain pounding on the roof and watching everything turn muddy and green. She was making progress with the Burmese alphabet, too. The first phrase she learned to write was the one from Ko Oo's sticker: သတ္တိ ရှိပါ. Have courage.

SICKNESS, AGING, AND DEATH

Whatever else happened to Adela while she was in Burma, one personal landmark would remain: it was there that she lost control of her bowels in public.

It happened at breakfast time in late June. She'd felt queasy all morning, and she hoped that some rice would settle her stomach. But midway through the meal her heart started pounding, and she realized she had to get to a toilet right away. Walking back to her room or even making it to the door seemed unlikely. Shakily, she stood up and half-stumbled, half-ran for the exit. Just over the threshold, in morning sun, she knew: it was happening. She crouched down, shitting and throwing up at the same time, feeling for a moment a sense of total release that was almost pleasurable. Then everything went dark.

When she opened her eyes, Daw Pancavati was squatting on the ground beside her. From the smelly wetness all around, Adela could tell that the situation was even worse than she had feared. She wanted to stand up, but when she tried to lift her head, the trees above her started to spin. Daw Pancavati consulted with the waya wutsa guys, who loomed over Adela, talking in hushed voices. The strongest men of the group returned with a clean white sheet, which, to Adela's horror, they rolled her onto in order to bear her aloft toward the outdoor water tank. She looked up at the sky, feeling like a wounded elephant or a humbled queen, as they swayed across the compound. She was so weak that it was difficult for her to hold in her mind the sense of mortification she knew she should have. The men positioned themselves under her shoulders, their heads politely averted, while Daw Pancavati poured water over her clothed body, cleaning her as best she could.

As soon as Daw Pancavati finished, Adela passed out again. When she woke up, she was lying on a mattress covered with a plastic tarp, wearing a T-shirt and a loosely-tied loungyi. She had never been in this room before. Pink curtains hung in the windows. An array of little medicine bottles and jars of camphor ointment were arranged on a low table. Daw Pancavati sat on the floor nearby.

"Where am I?"

"My room," said Daw Pancavati.

Adela started to cry. Daw Pancavati had taken her, shitting and stinking, into her own room. Adela wanted her own mother very much, but she was so far away. Daw Pancavati laid her dry, cool hand on Adela's forehead.

"Hpya nay deh." Adela knew the phrase from the monks' dialogues. Fever.

Daw Pancavati brought a cup with a straw in it, and Adela sipped some mild orange liquid. She felt it trickle down into her stomach with an ominous gurgle. She lay back for a moment, then bolted upright. Daw Pancavati held a bowl for her as she vomited, soiling the loungyi in the process. Then Adela sobbed with abandon. How much shit did her body contain?

Daw Pancavati made comforting noises and wiped Adela like a baby. Then she held Adela upright just long enough to deftly change the tarp and loungyi. Adela's body felt light and empty, as it were filled with helium.

"Now sleep," said Daw Pancavati.

"Don't leave me," Adela begged.

Daw Pancavati shook her head, laughing a little.

❀

The next day Adela kept some liquid down, but she couldn't eat. Daw Pancavati cut up a banana into little bits and tried to feed them to Adela like she was a baby bird, but they tasted like chalk and Adela spat them out. Her whole body seemed to vibrate with illness; her lower back, her inner ears, even her nostrils throbbed with discomfort. She slept most of the time, waking for odd intervals in the day or night. The nun slept on the ground by Adela's side, changing her loungyi countless times. Adela half-remembered crouching on a squat toilet, with Daw Pancavati holding her up.

She had all kinds of dreams. Terrible ones that she'd killed someone and she was running from the police through a green field with a rainy sky above, tripping over logs that were corpses, their hands grasping her ankles and holding her fast. She had ordinary dreams that she was going about her daily life back at Edgerton Fields, that she'd never come to Burma. The most vivid dreams were a return to infancy. She was carried, her diaper was changed, she suckled milk from a warm breast. Everything was blurry, but the feeling of safety was profound.

Adela worried, in her semi-lucid moments, that she had been acting like a baby, too. Every time she woke up she was terrified that Daw Pancavati had left her. But the pink-robed nun was always there, sometimes sleeping, sometimes eating rice and fruit in the corner, nothing with a strong smell that would turn Adela's stomach.

Other people came in, too. The tall man who had brought fruit to their table on the first day held Adela's wrist between his fingers and watched as Daw Pancavati stuck a thermometer in her mouth. Bhante came too, or maybe Adela only imagined him, sitting on the floor in the corner, chanting: sabbe Buddha assmasama, sabbe Buddha mahiddhika, sabbe dasabalupeta vesarajjehupagata. The rhythm of this chant entered Adela's dreams, irritating and compelling at the same time.

During this time two questions obsessed Adela's fevered mind: whether she should leave Burma, and why she had come in the first place. What had she wanted, and had she gotten what she wanted? She had been in Burma a month. Had it been long enough? Should she go back to DC and spend her last summer before college relaxing and putting together photo albums? She worried about getting sick again, or about never getting well at all. Ko Oo had been right, she decided; Burma was dangerous. She could die here, lying on Daw Pancavati's floor.

Weighing against those fears was a motivating sense of shame, and her determination not to admit that she'd been naïve when she'd imagined what Burma would be like. Adela remembered the discussion in the MVU training, in which she'd suggested the UN monitor the elections, and every-one had laughed at her. She was not the same person anymore, and she wanted to prove it. She was not scared of giant cockroaches. She had seen firsthand things that people back home only read about in newspapers, the underbelly of the "New Myanmar": the appalling hospitals, the discrimination against Muslims.

Perhaps that was why when Daw Pancavati suggested calling MVU, Adela made her promise she wouldn't. Adela didn't want Sarah to see her in this condition. She worried that Sarah would blame her for getting sick, and that indeed it was her own fault. Maybe she'd eaten the wrong things or hadn't washed her hands enough. The only way to overcome her shame was to come through the ordeal stronger than she'd started it. Greg's teasing words came back to her: *We'll see how long you last.* If she left Burma after a month, she would have to admit that he'd been right. Her mother would think she was flighty and reckless. Her father wouldn't judge her, but that would only reveal his low expectations.

A memory came to Adela from when she was nine or ten years old. Her father had taken her to a soup kitchen where he sometimes volunteered. She could see now that it was something he did irregularly and self-consciously, primarily so that he could think of himself as the kind of person who volunteered at soup kitchens, as the kind of person who took his daughter to soup kitchens in order to educate her about the world. At Edgerton Fields, Adela would learn to see her middle-class identity as shamefully boring, without the romance of poverty or the power of wealth. But at the time, going to the soup kitchen comforted her. She knew she was different from the men who shuffled into line for overcooked spaghetti. As she and her father walked to the parking lot, she'd asked him smugly, already knowing the answer, "Daddy, are we poor?"

Was her trip to Burma any different? Was it just a glimpse of what Greg would call "the Global South," with a dash of exoticism and the self-satisfaction of having "helped people"? Adela didn't formulate those questions so clearly when she was sick, but they played underneath her thoughts, unsettling her. Looking back, she would see clearly the presumptions that brought her to Burma: that the world was there to be seen by her, that she had every right to see it, that it was hers to dream.

※

One morning Adela awoke ravenous. Daw Pancavati was dozing against the wall, her head listing to one side. When she heard Adela stir, she startled awake.

"What time is it?" Adela asked.

"Morning."

"How long have I been sick?"

"Six days, thamee."

This news alarmed Adela. She had counted two days and two nights.

"But my visa is going to expire!"

MVU could only arrange tourist visas for volunteers, which had to be renewed every thirty days. She'd been planning a trip to Bangkok, but by now it would be too late.

"Don't worry, thamee, Bhante will take care of this."

"But how can he? I'm not—"

Daw Pancavati patted Adela's hand. "Bhante has a way."

Adela absorbed this information. His "way" sounded slightly illegal, but intuition told her not to question it.

"What is 'thamee'?" she asked.

Daw Pancavati smiled. "Thamee is 'my daughter.'"

Adela looked at the nun's dear face, her dark brown eyes, and the fine wrinkles that were visible in the morning light streaming through the pink curtains.

"What can I call you?"

"Amay is OK."

"Amay, Amay," said Adela, grasping her hand. Adela knew it meant mother without asking.

Adela looked down at her arms resting on the sheet, which seemed paler and thinner than before.

"Should I go to the doctor?"

"Oh. You say you do not want to go to doctor."

"Really?"

"Yes, you say, 'Stay here, stay here.' We want to take you but you really fight us. So we try to help you here. You do not want us to call your organization, but they call to us on the phone about the visa and we explain the situation to them."

Adela had no memory of refusing to go to the doctor, only of the conversation about MVU. She thought perhaps she should be checked, just to be safe, but she didn't want to end up anywhere like the hospital they'd visited. Kip had mentioned one private clinic in Yangon, but it was expensive. He recommended going to Bangkok for anything major, and he was careful to warn the volunteers away from village doctors.

"What kind of sickness do I have?"

"Maybe thway wun. I do not know English word."

"Do I need to take medicine?"

"Ko Thiha give you some medicines. He says if they make you better, then no more problem."

"Who's Ko Thiha?"

"The young man who come here. Like this," said Daw Pancavati, holding her hand high in the air to show that he was tall.

"Is he a doctor?" Adela knew she must be getting better, because she was starting to feel a sense of skepticism that had been impossible before.

"Kind of doctor," the nun agreed.

All sorts of questions occurred to Adela. What did that mean, "kind of doctor," and how much could she trust his medical knowledge? What had made her sick in the first place?

Yet she could not deny that she felt better. She could feel the vigor returning to her limbs, and when she checked for nausea, which had become so constant that she had stopped noticing it, it was gone. Her fear of dying seemed ridiculous now, and she hoped she hadn't mentioned it in her delirium.

"I'm hungry."

Daw Pancavati fetched a banana from the corner and got Adela a pillow so she could lean against the wall.

"Slowly, thamee."

Adela took tiny bites. It tasted like the sun. She sipped her way through a glass of the orange drink, and then Daw Pancavati brought out a bottle of Pepto Bismol, which she dispensed as if it were a sacred substance. "Left behind by one foreign meditator," she explained.

Finally, Adela was able to get to the toilet on her own. She didn't want to think about how many times she must have shat all over her bedding in the past six days. She called to Daw Pancavati for a clean loungyi and soap, and she bathed, feeling shaky but stronger. Daw Pancavati stood right outside the door, and helped Adela back to bed for a nap afterward.

Several hours later, Adela woke with a pounding headache. Daw Pancavati was sitting beside her, softly chanting. When she saw Adela was awake, she fetched a cup.

"Drink."

Adela closed her eyes and sipped from the straw, enjoying the trappings of infancy that she knew she'd have to give up soon.

"Tell me a story," Adela said.

"I do not know any story."

"Tell me about your life. How you came to the monastery."

Daw Pancavati was silent for a moment. Her mouth creased into a smile, but her eyes were dull.

"Thamee, that is a long story."

"I have time."

Daw Pancavati did not respond. Instead, she stood up and began tidying the room, sweeping nonexistent dust out the door and carrying away bits of garbage. Adela gave up on the idea of a story and closed her eyes as she listened to Daw Pancavati puttering around. But after Daw Pancavati had cleaned the room to her satisfaction, the nun poured herself a glass of water, leaned against the wall, and began to speak.

THE MUSTARD SEED

"I was born in Ngayabo, in Irrawaddy Delta. My father is rice farmer. My mother had pass away when I am a baby and my older sister cares for me, who is ten when I am born. We are six brothers and sisters."

"How did your mom die?"

Daw Pancavati looked at Adela as if she'd never thought of it before.

"I do not know. She is sick. No doctor in our village."

Adela contemplated a world in which one's mother died and no one knew why, or no one thought it important.

"We are six of us and we love our eldest sister very much. She cook our meals and she shows us how to take care each other, oldest to youngest. I am the baby and so everyone love me most. My older brothers help to my father in the rice paddy. Sometime we do not have enough rice. It is the time of MaSaLa—"

Daw Pancavati reached for Adela's copy of *Insurgency and the Politics of Ethnicity*, which she'd fetched in case Adela was well enough to read. She pointed to an entry in the index: Burma Socialist Programme Party.

"It is time of MaSaLa, and we have rice quota to send to our government. Sometime there is not enough and we have to borrow from the next season profit. Slowly we get the debt, and there is not enough money to send my two sisters and me to school. So they send only me. I want to be the English teacher. So I study also by listening to radio."

"What about your brothers?"

"They must work in rice paddy. So it is very special for me that I can go to school. I promise I will get the good job and support to my father when he is old. I still remember when we get the red scarf in school for Myanma Lanzin youth. I feel so proud of my red scarf! I feel so proud to see our flag! The government say we peasants are the best of the nation. I believe our government is the good one. Later I doubt, but when I am young I believe."

"So the government wasn't good then?"

"Hard to explain, thamee. U Ne Win, he take power for himself. In MaSaLa government maybe some are good. But for farmers, we need to send the rice quota, there is not enough for us to eat."

Adela tried to start a blog post in her mind, but her brain was too fuzzy. She closed her eyes, listening to Daw Pancavati's voice.

"Ne Win, he say he will keep our country together, keep all ethnic nationalities with peace. But he cannot. In this time, our ethnic groups fight a lot."

"Why were they fighting?"

"I don't know, thamee. Maybe they want their own place. Once a fight start, it will keep going, naw?"

"And didn't Ne Win cancel all the currency notes in his unlucky number, because his astrologer told him to?" asked Adela, remembering the story of Ko Oo's story of losing his family's savings. "He sounds like a crazy man."

"Yes, you can say he is crazy man. But sometime astrologer are right."

The monks had mentioned astrologers as well, when they were explaining to Adela why people born on Saturdays, like her, were supposedly unlucky. **Surprisingly**, she managed in her head, **many Buddhists find no contradiction between their faith and new age practices like astrology.**

Daw Pancavati nodded gravely. "It was astrologer who advise me to come to this monastery. But this will come later. First, I study very hard at school. When I am in Fourth Standard, my eldest sister has to get married. When she is pregnant, we are very happy. But when she give birth, there is some problem. My sister pass away along with her baby. After this my father start to drink a lot. He is so sad to lose his eldest daughter."

First her mother, and now her favorite sister, lost. Yet Daw Pancavati spoke in such a matter-of-fact way, as if it had never occurred to her to feel sorry for herself. Daw Pancavati wasn't trying to entertain Adela, the way

Ko Oo had, but there was a similar intensity to the way that they spoke about their lives. Adela found herself settling into her familiar mode of listening, memorizing, making the details her own.

"When I finish Tenth Standard, I want to become schoolteacher. But my father choose one man for me to marry. He is not from our village. The first day I meet him, this is the day we get engaged. I do not love him, but I must say yes.

"Why?"

"We are poor. Hard to find someone to marry the poor girl, naw?"

"Why did you have to get married at all?"

"Thamee, what can I do if I do not get married? Then I am a spinster!" she exclaimed with horror.

"But couldn't you just become a teacher and live on your own?"

Adela had resolved not to get married. She didn't know any married people who were happy. Even her parents' brief marriage, which had produced her, seemed like a mistake, at least in terms of their lives.

"I want children. And my father pick this man for me."

"Is that always the way it works here?"

"Sometime now young people can choose. But most want to marry the person their mother and father pick for them."

"Why?"

Daw Pancavati paused. She took a drink of water, and she made Adela drink, too.

"How can I explain? This is not the way in America, I know. Myanmar girl can be afraid to get in the bad situation. The parents know the family, they choose someone who is suitable."

"But was your husband suitable?"

"For me . . . for me, I do not know. I marry this man, and he take me to his village. He is not a bad man. He work hard in the paddy field. He does not drink alcohol. But he does not want me to be a teacher. He want me to have babies and take care of the house. After some years, no baby. So he divorce me and take a new wife."

"Maybe it was his problem. Did his new wife have any babies?"

"I do not know, I leave the village. Maybe no."

"Where did you go?"

"I go to Chin State, and I get the job as a schoolteacher. Not many people want to go to Chin State. It is very far. Still, I have to borrow money from my brother to pay bribe to someone so I can get this job easily. In Chin State, this is the happy time for me. I love my student very much. They try to help me too; their families cook rice and food for me, because I am teaching I cannot grow my own rice. They are like my family, my children. Really I want my own child. But I think no one will marry me again. I am small and very black, naw?" she said gesturing to her skin. "Not like Ma Sabeh."

Adela thought Daw Pancavati's delicate frame was lovely, and her skin was coppery brown. Adela certainly was large and pale by comparison; these qualities didn't necessarily seem like assets.

"No, I'm nothing special," Adela said awkwardly. "But what's Chin State like?"

"My village is near border with Rakhine State. Very small. People are poor there. They are, how do you say . . . not Buddhist, not Christian?"

Adela bolted upright. "Muslim?" The conflict in Rakhine State, and her conversation with the monks, came back to her like a half-remembered dream.

"No, no, not Muslim. They worship nat. Like a spirit. It is some traditional religion, before Christian, before Buddha."

"But are there any Muslims there?" Adela had never asked Daw Pancavati what she thought about the violence; learning that her closest Burmese friend shared U Nyanika's views would have been too much for her.

Daw Pancavati shook her head. "For me, I do not meet any Muslim."

"Because I was reading about these riots in Rakhine State—" Adela began, the visceral horror of the photo returning to her.

"This one is very sad," Daw Pancavati said soberly. "No one should do like this. Not Muslim, not Buddhist. I do not want to see people suffer this way. Buddha does not want this."

Adela felt her belly relax. "You're so right. I knew you'd think so." Adela decided to bring up this point with the monks when classes started again. They couldn't claim that the Buddha himself would have supported violence.

"But anyway, the Chin people were, like, pagan?"

"I do not know the pagan. Chin people have many rules about when and how to go, how to build the house, when to marry and when to plant the rice. I do not believe like this. But for my students I try to do it, because I love them very much."

"And when was it that you lived there?"

"I go there in 1992."

Adela hadn't even been born. She pictured her favorite photo from her childhood: her first Halloween, when her mother and father were still together, and had dressed her in a bunny suit to take her trick or treating. It seemed unbelievable that while her parents were coddling her through her childhood, across the world Daw Pancavati was struggling to follow obscure pagan rituals.

"I stay there happily in this Chin village for four years. But in 1996, I get a health problem. I have problem here," she said, pointing to her belly, "like you. I cannot get the medicine. They have only some herb."

Adela thought of being alone, in a place where people believed in spirits and herbs, and being as sick as she was.

"I am so lucky to be here!" she said, marveling at this fact for the first time.

"Yes, lucky," Daw Pancavati agreed. "I have to come back to Mandalay, three days travel, to go to hospital there. The doctor tell me not to go back to my village, the water is not clean. I need to go somewhere else. At that time, I hear from my brother that my father is sick. They need money for his treatment. My salary as teacher is very low. I go to the astrologer, ask him how I should do. He tell me I should come to a monastery in Yangon and study meditation. He give me this one," she said, pulling an amulet on a red cord out from under her robes.

"Like this one you wear," she said, gesturing to Ko Oo's amulet, which still hung around Adela's neck. Adela had almost forgotten about it. It hadn't done a very good job of protecting her from getting sick, in any case.

"But I do not listen to astrologer. I think this advice is wrong for me. I see now he was trying to spare me some suffering. At that time I think, if I go to monastery, how can I help my father? I hear about one job as housekeeper for the Burmese family in Malaysia. I think, if I can do this job two years, send money to my father, then I will come back to find work as a schoolteacher again."

"But you couldn't?"

Daw Pancavati sighed. "It is seven years before I can come back to Myanmar. When I arrive in Malaysia, it is the big city, Kuala Lumpur. There are high towers. I have never seen like this. My employer is the rich man. He have a wife, but she stay in a different part of the house. I am cooking and cleaning for them and their children. Soon I learn, this man ... he want housekeeper for another reason."

The nun stared straight ahead for a minute. Adela's mind closed around her friend's words. Daw Pancavati was so dignified, so brave, she had survived so much already. It was so unfair! Adela felt tears behind her eyes, but she held them back. If Daw Pancavati wasn't crying, what right did Adela have?

"So, he ..." Adela said, as gently as she could.

"Why he want me, I do not know. There are many other ladies he bring back at night. But sometime he take me. Because of this, his wife hate me, too. Even though I care for her children, she hate me."

Adela thought of reaching out to touch her friend, but she couldn't find the right place—her arm, her cheek, her hand—it all seemed too intimate. Instead she spoke.

"I'm so sorry."

Daw Pancavati nodded, but her eyes were glassy and fixed on places far away.

"Yes. Even he makes me bow down to him every day."

"But I thought you were only supposed to bow down to monks or the Buddha."

"No, sometime we can do for other people if they are really our jayzushin, our benefactor. Like mother and father, or teacher who support to us. We can ask forgiveness and show respect this way also."

"But there was no reason for you to bow down to him!" Adela said.

The nun looked down. Adela felt ashamed. There were plenty of reasons, just not ones she herself had ever had to take into account.

"I do not want to bow down for him. But I must do. After two years, I am pregnant—"

"So it was your husband's problem!" Adela couldn't help pointing out.

"—At this time I am already thirty years old. The wife hates me more, and when I am pregnant she gives me the hard work to do. But inside I am happy because I will have a child. How can I say how I feel at this time my son is born? I love him. I do not want him to grow up in this house. I do not want him to be a servant like me. But I have no choice. My employer does not pay me money. Many years, he pays me only the small amount. So I cannot send much money to my family. No one can help me. I do not know Malaysia language. Where can I go?"

Adela tried to think her way out of Daw Pancavati's situation. What would she have done? Tried to kill the employer? Run away? All of it could have backfired, leaving her worse off, in prison or dead, her son left alone.

The nun began to speak faster, as if the words tasted bitter in her mouth. "At this time I learn my father pass away. My employer does not even let me go home for funeral. For Buddhists, this is—" She shook her head, shuddering. "This is very bad. At this time, I think it can be the worst time of my life. But later . . ."

"Later it got worse?" Adela asked with disbelief.

"Yes, it get worse."

Daw Pancavati paused and looked thoughtfully at the blank wall. Adela wondered if the nun might end the story there, and she felt bad that she'd asked about the past at all. At the same time, she wanted to hear the end of the story. She didn't want to leave Daw Pancavati there, in Malaysia with her infant, lonely and abused.

After several minutes, Daw Pancavati let out a long breath. Then she began to speak again, as if she had only been pausing to find a way to continue.

"In 2004, my employer pass away from heart attack. It is not right, but I thank the Buddha for this. Finally I am free! The wife send me back to my home. I stay with my second sister and her husband. At that time my son is about four year old. My son, Than Naing, he has never seen the village. He like the fresh air very much and he plays all the time. I find some work in the school nearby so I can give a small money to my sister. I dream someday me and my son will have our own house. Slowly I save. When my son is five, I can send him to school. I am so happy he does not remember his father, and I also try to forget."

A smile came to Daw Pancavati's face, and then she winced. She furrowed her brow, whispered a few lines of a prayer, then took a deep breath.

"In 2008 Cyclone Nargis comes. The date is second May, on Friday."

Sarah had told the volunteers about the storm. More than a hundred thousand people died, millions were displaced, and the government turned away international aid. Local organizations and ordinary people had driven down to the Irrawaddy Delta with fresh water and packets of noodles to donate. That was when Sarah first came to Burma; she started out volunteering, then she worked for a relief agency before helping to found MVU.

"During the week sometime I stay in the village where I teach. So I am not at home. It is too early for rainy season, still very hot. Then we see some storm is coming but we do not know it will be the big one. I stay at the school with some other teachers. The next day, third May, is very bad storm. Our school is made of cement, and it is built on one small hill. It cannot blow away. We stay two days in the school. We have some water but no foods. All this time I think of Than Naing. I do not know is he with my sister, is he alright."

Daw Pancavati's voice became hoarse, as if her throat was closing around her words. Her face was calm, but she sniffed repeatedly. Finally her eyes watered, spotting her robe dark pink. Adela tried to let herself cry the same way, without making a sound.

"When I get back to my village, I cannot find Than Naing. My sister has died. Her husband say Than Naing does not come home from school on Friday. No one can find him. Every house is broken. My two brother also gone. It is four days before someone bring food for us. I do not care. I want to die. Only I do not have courage to die."

Have courage, Adela thought, remembering Ko Oo's sticker. What does courage mean, in a case like this?

"Some aid groups bring the large tent for us. We stay with many other people. It is raining all the time and dead bodies are rotten all around, of people, of buffalo. My one sister try to take care of me, but I feel I am already dead. Finally some ladies come to me. They come from Yangon to bring food and some blanket for our village. But they need some help with their record keeping. They say I know very well about this village, also I am schoolteacher. Can I help them with their work? I think my sister send them to me. At first I do not want to do anything but they keep asking me and I feel I should do this. I can help them easily. Also I tell about my situation to one lady. She explains to me about this Yadana monastery, where she had study the meditation with Bhante. Come to Yangon, she say to me. You can help in the monastery and you can know the Bhante Panditabhivamsa."

Daw Pancavati spoke the name reverently. Her eyes were dry now, and Adela's throat unclenched from the effort of keeping back tears. The worst of the story was over.

"At that time I remember what the astrologer tell to me. So I come to this monastery. First I only help by doing waya wutsa. Then I do one ten-day retreat with Bhante. He understand what I suffer. He tell me the story of the mustard seed. The Buddha find one lady with her baby who has died. She has become crazy woman, she carries her dead baby with her everywhere. Buddha says to her, 'I can bring your baby back to life, if you go and find one house where no one has died. You bring back one mustard seed from this house.' The woman is happy. She think she get her baby back. She go to every house she can find, but someone has died in every house. Now she can see! She can see everyone suffer the same. Everyone will die. And she become enlightened!"

Daw Pancavati's eyes shone with their familiar tranquility once again. But the story left Adela confused. How could death be comforting? Especially when it was unfair in some way? She thought of the dying woman in the hospital, and the charred corpse in the newspaper photo from Rakhine State. In Burma, death seemed somehow closer. It had never scared her before, because she'd had so little experience with the pain and sickness that came along with it. Now, life and death seemed to be knitted together in the same fragile fabric.

"I do my meditation every day," Daw Pancavati continued. "I chant with monks. My anger go away. I see clearly how this life is. Than Naing, he will die like everyone. I will miss him also and this cause me to suffer. Everyone suffer, everyone want things, and there is the end to wanting the things. This is the dhamma, the teachings of Buddha—my refuge! After one year I decide to become thila shin, like a nun for the Buddhist. Now I am here. I can stay very easily. I will live here and I can die here. I can help others to find the dhamma also."

Daw Pancavati closed her eyes and smiled. As they sat in silence, Adela searched for a way to respond. No one had ever told her a story like that, not even Ko Oo. What could Adela say besides that she was sorry, which seemed worse than saying nothing at all?

On one hand, hearing Daw Pancavati's story made Adela feel closer to her. On the other, it divided them. Adela lined her life up against her friend's. By the age of eighteen, Daw Pancavati had lost her mother and her sister and been married off. She was on her way to Chin State, where she'd get sicker and sicker. In order to accumulate such a measure of misfortune, Adela would have had to start when she was a baby.

And yet Daw Pancavati didn't seem to feel the unfairness of it all. Buddhism had solved everything for her, made all people equal in their suffering. But for Adela, Daw Pancavati's story proved the opposite. Sickness, aging, and death might be common to everyone, but some people got to experience them in much more comfortable surroundings than others. And Burma was the hardest place Adela could imagine.

She thought about it for so long that when she looked up, Daw Pancavati had nodded off, leaning against the wall. For the first time, Adela watched over her friend, as she had been watched over for the past week. Finally, Adela curled up closer to the nun and let her eyes close as their breathing fell into a common rhythm.

THIHA

The next day, Adela was able to sit up and eat rice. Daw Pancavati fed Adela with her fingers, the way Burmese people fed little children. Adela could not help feeling like a baby bird as she opened her mouth for the clumps of rice and bits of boiled egg that her friend had prepared.

Fortified by her meal, Adela started to feel guilty about being so slothful. She knew she'd been keeping Daw Pancavati from her other duties.

"You don't have to stay with me," Adela said, piling her dishes onto a tray. "I'll be fine."

Daw Pancavati hesitated, but Adela insisted, pointing to the copy of *Burmese Days* she'd been meaning to start.

As soon as Daw Pancavati left, Adela started missing her. But she couldn't very well call her back, so she picked up *Burmese Days* and began to read. She'd been saving this book for when she was done with *Insurgency and the Politics of Ethnicity*, trying to read something serious instead of her default novels, but she had finally accepted that finishing five hundred pages of dense nonfiction was beyond her. She was eager to lose herself in a story again.

Just as Joseph Conrad was posted in the Congo, she would start her next post, **George Orwell served in colonial Burma. It is interesting to compare their perspectives because—**

Yet the first few chapters disappointed her. She reached for her laptop.

Although reviewers describe *Burmese Days* as a "scathing critique of the British Raj," Orwell seems to dislike the Burmese just as much as he does the British. The main character, Flory, who is obviously based on Orwell himself, is spineless and self-obsessed. Then there's the corrupt Burmese magistrate, U Po Kyin; Dr. Veraswami, the pathetic apologist for colonialism; and Ma Hla May, Flory's vain and selfish Burmese mistress. The other British people in the book are even worse than Flory, but I'd expect them to be. It's telling that Orwell couldn't come up with even one sympathetic Burmese character.

But the book does reinforce one thing we—

Was it pretentious to use "we"? On the other hand, hadn't Ms. Alvarez told her to make it less like a diary?

—learned from *Insurgency and the Politics of Ethnicity*: the British really did make a mess of Burma. It was like they analyzed the central weakness in Burma's social fabric and created policies designed to exploit it. They separated the Burman-majority areas from Karen, Kachin, and Shan States for their own convenience, then treated each group differently, which sparked rivalries. It was a "divide and rule" policy, just like the one the Belgians had pursued in the Congo. Then the British imported workers from India, including Muslims and Hindus, whom the Burmans resented. It's no surprise that different ethnic and religious groups are in conflict today, because the British tried on purpose to keep them apart. The carefully orchestrated social hierarchies described in *Burmese Days* are even more insidious than the naked brutality and greed in *Heart of Darkness*, she concluded, feeling especially proud of her last sentence.

Yet one memory unsettled her: the old man outside the Secretariat Building had told her that all the foreign volunteers coming reminded him of colonial days. Did she have anything in common with Flory and the boorish officials at the club, who complained about the heat while the natives fanned them? Adela thought of the restaurant she'd visited with Kip, where the Burmese waiters had stood silently in the corners. "They're not ready for democracy," Kip had said, as if they couldn't understand English.

Adela had planned to meet Kip at the same place for her one-month check-in, which she'd missed because of her illness. MVU liked to conduct monthly debriefs with volunteers who were close enough to Yangon, in order to troubleshoot and assess progress. Earlier in the month, Adela had found herself looking forward to the meeting. She was proud of what she'd accomplished in her teaching, and she looked forward to describing it to Kip over a glass of wine.

Now the idea of going back to that restaurant seemed a little distasteful. Adela had seen the real Burma, or at least heard about it from Daw Pancavati. She'd become more like Sarah, she decided: content to wear a loungyi every day, happy eating Burmese food, even a little wary of other foreigners. And unlike Orwell, she loved the Burmese people she'd gotten to know. Maybe not the Muslim-hating U Nyanika, but most of them.

Adela was still immersed in these reflections when she heard Daw Pancavati's quiet footsteps on the porch. The nun entered, holding a piece of paper reverently.

"You are OK?" she asked, laying the paper on the table and pressing her hand to Adela's forehead.

"Yes, fine."

"Good." She presented Adela with the paper. "Bhante wants you to read this one, thamee. It is the sutta—words of the Buddha," she said, holding it out with both hands. It was titled REFLECTION ON THE THIRTY-TWO PARTS. Adela read it aloud.

This, which is my body, from the soles of the feet up, and down from the crown of the head, is a sealed bag of skin filled with unattractive things.

Adela laughed out loud. She thought of shit and vomit and tears that had flowed from her body over the past week.

"Unattractive is right," she said, and then kept reading.

In this body there are:
hair of the head
hair of the body
nails
teeth
skin
flesh
sinews
bones
entrails

undigested food
"Eew!" she exclaimed.
excrement
bile
Adela skimmed this rest of this impressive catalog with fascination.
fat
tears
grease
spittle
It concluded unceremoniously:
urine
brain.
The list was absorbing and exhaustive. At any other juncture in her life, Adela might have found it simply disgusting. It certainly didn't accord with her preconceptions of what the Buddha would say. Yet given her recent experiences, she had to admit it was true.

"Is this what Bhante was chanting when I was sick?"

"Bhante chanting? No, no. I chant for you when you are sick. I ask him for advice and he tell me to chant the Twenty-Eight Buddhas' Protection for you."

Adela was sure she remembered him, sitting in the corner of Daw Pancavati's room. And yet it now seemed outlandish that he would come into the nun's private room and sit four feet away from a violently ill American girl.

"Anyway, I need to thank him for arranging my visa."

"Yes. Two months you can stay here."

"But wait, how did he extend my visa without my passport?"

"I get it for him," said Daw Pancavati sheepishly. Adela had given the passport to her for safekeeping in the monastery's lockbox. "You are sick, and ..."

"Two months? How did he do that?" Kip and Sarah had three-month business visas, but they'd gone through masses of red tape to procure them.

"Meditation visa. We often make this for the foreigners who come here."

"Oh, that's clever. I hope no one finds out that I'm not really meditating."

"Well ... you will do. Yes. Bhante wants for you to do meditation here."

Adela considered her friend's earnest countenance. "Yeah, sure, I'd like to learn to meditate. Why not?"

"When you are better you can start with ten-day retreat."

"Oh—I mean, I don't know if I need to do a *retreat.*" Adela thought of the lady meditator from Taiwan, who'd left two weeks earlier. She could not imagine herself taking twenty minutes to walk to breakfast. In fact, she was eager to be back in her routine now that she was healthy again.

"I can just learn in the afternoons, or—"

Daw Pancavati was firm. "Bhante has arranged this."

Adela felt a small prick of resentment. She was ready to be back in her own room, teaching the monks and doing what she liked. She wanted to check Facebook and see what had been happening with the Buddhist-Muslim conflict.

"To study meditation with Bhante Panditabhivamsa is special chance for you, thamee," Daw Pancavati said quietly. "At this time, no other foreign meditators. You can have your own interview with Bhante every day!"

How could Adela disappoint her friend? It would only be ten days. She should adapt to the circumstances, as Sarah had advised them. It would make her a better person. And it would make a great blog post.

"OK, I'll do it!"

The nun grasped her hand. "I know you will do. I will help and support to you."

Just then, there was a knock on the door. It was Thiha, the tall one, the "kind of doctor." When he saw Adela sitting up, he seemed hesitant to enter. She wasn't a patient anymore, she was an American girl whose body he had seen and touched. Adela was embarrassed that this man had observed the unsightliest of the "Thirty-Two Parts" of her body that the sutta described.

Just as she was ready to look down, to look away, he smiled.

She smiled back.

Thiha spoke to Daw Pancavati in Burmese. The nun gestured toward Adela to indicate that the patient could answer for herself. He crouched down beside her.

How would she have described his face the way she saw it that day? He looked determined and calm, as if he needed nothing from her. She saw his lips, his neck, and the fine shape of his skull. He was wearing jeans and a T-shirt, unlike the other helpers who wore loungyis and button-down shirts.

"Hi," he said. The word sounded strangely informal, almost flirtatious.

"Hi."

"How do you feel?" His English accent was good.

"Better. I can eat today."

"Good. You need some more days' rest. And drink the rehydration salt," he said, nodding toward the orange liquid Daw Pancavati had been giving her.

Adela found herself looking into his deep brown eyes. She couldn't help but smile; she was worried she might laugh out loud.

"What did I have?" she asked.

"Dysentery. But not the bad kind."

Adela chuckled. "Hope I never get the bad kind."

He smiled again, showing a row of straight white teeth. Adela wanted to smile back, but she realized she was already grinning like a fool.

"Are you a doctor?" she asked, not suspicious anymore, only curious.

"I studied medicine."

She gazed at him, wondering why she didn't look into people's eyes more often. Were everyone's eyes like that, so quiet and alert?

He glanced at the books by her bedside.

"You interest in Burmese politics," he said, gesturing to *Insurgency and the Politics of Ethnicity*.

"Yeah. It seems pretty complicated." *You idiot!* she thought.

"Yes, complicated."

Did the room smell bad? Daw Pancavati had opened the curtains and burned incense at the altar, good. But what was she wearing? She looked down at her T-shirt and Daw Pancavati's loungyi. She was trying to think of another question to ask him, but he had already stood up and turned toward the door.

"I will go," he said.

Stay here! Adela pressed her lips together so she wouldn't say it. *No, leave! I'm disgusting right now!* He left the room. She waited for a few moments to pass.

"What's his name?" she asked Daw Pancavati, wanting to hear it again.

"Ko Thiha."

Thee-ha, she repeated in her mind. It was a quiet name, to match the way he moved. Adela didn't want to ask anything more, for fear her interest would seem too obvious.

"So, I think I can move back to my room today," she said instead.

Daw Pancavati helped Adela pack up her things, and they carried them over to the dormitory.

In the cool of the early evening, Adela walked slowly around the compound, waving to everyone she saw. She was in the office, emailing her parents and MVU to let them know that she was OK, when U Pyinnya found her.

"Sayama Sabeh thet tha thwa bi la?"

"Yeah, I'm feeling a lot better." She was pleased that she understood so many Burmese phrases, although she usually responded in English.

U Pyinnya nodded. "Good. You need to be strong for meditation."

"I guess so," said Adela, bemused that he had been in on the plot. "Then we can start classes again, right?"

"Maybe, when you finish."

The "maybe" unsettled her, but Adela put it out of her mind. Were the monks trying to get rid of her? Had they decided her questions about the Buddhist-Muslim conflict were unforgivable? Without her classes, she'd have no reason to stay at the monastery. But with her illness behind her and Thiha now in her mind, she had decided that she was definitely not ready to leave Burma.

That night, back in her own bed, she dreamed of Thiha. She was walking around the monastery at night. She knew she was doing something wrong, that she was somewhere she shouldn't be. Thiha was there too, in the shadows under the mango tree, then behind the dining hall. He seemed to be looking for something. Adela followed him. When they found each other, they embraced in a way that is only possible in dreams: so complete, so inevitable, but somehow unspecific. Thiha was himself and he was Greg and he was someone she had never seen; Adela was herself and she was Thiha seeing her. The same voice came to her from her Shwedagon dream, more intense and desperate: *Stay here. Don't let this end.* At the same time, she knew that it would not end, that it was already happening and that it would continue.

DUKKHA

One afternoon in early July, Adela walked as gracefully as she could across the compound in the brown loungyi, white blouse, and brown scarf that Daw Pancavati had prepared for her. She entered the hall with the golden Buddha statue, taking care not to move too quickly, and she knelt down in front of Bhante's platform. She didn't know if she should look him in the eye, so she alternated between staring at her hands folded in her lap and looking surreptitiously around the room. It was a long time before Bhante acknowledged her.

"I speak, you repeat," he finally said.

"OK." And then, remembering Daw Pancavati's instructions, "Hman ba, Bhante," Correct, Venerable Sir.

Bhante began to speak in Pali. Adela knew a few phrases, which they were supposed to recite inwardly whenever they bowed down before meals, but Bhante stopped her and told her to speak more slowly. Then he started intoning the Eight Precepts, which Adela was to keep during the next ten days.

I was ready for this part because Daw Pancavati explained it all to me in advance. I was promising to abide by the rules of the meditation retreat, which are only eight of the two hundred and twenty-seven rules that monks have to follow every day. I was supposed to avoid harming any living beings; not steal; "refrain from any sexual conduct"; not lie

(which would be easier since I actually wasn't supposed to talk at all, except to Bhante during our interviews); not take drugs; eat only before noon; "refrain from entertainment, beautification, and adornment" (and books do count as entertainment, so no more *Burmese Days* for the time being); and eschew luxurious beds and chairs (which I don't have access to anyway). And check out the schedule I had to follow:

4:00am	Wake Up
4:30–5:00	Metta Chanting (this means sending goodwill to all

beings)

5:00–5:30	Walking Meditation
5:30–6:30	Sitting Meditation
6:30–7:30	Breakfast
7:30–8:00	Walking Meditation
8:00–9:00	Sitting Meditation
9:00–10:00	Walking Meditation
10:00–11:00	Sitting Meditation

Sitting and walking meditation was literally all I did all day, except eat lunch, sleep, and go to my interview with Bhante, where I was supposed to report how my meditation was going and listen to him explain the dhamma, or the Buddha's teachings.

When I first saw the schedule, I thought it was a joke. When I realized it wasn't a joke, I thought it was just a suggestion of how to structure my time. But Daw Pancavati was pretty clear: I was supposed to follow it exactly. Still, I thought I might sneak back to my room and sleep if I got tired.

As Adela repeated the precepts, trying to keep her eyes away from Bhante's severe countenance, she decided it was probably better not to cut corners. He would definitely know. As Daw Pancavati had promised, there were no other foreign guests. There were plenty of Burmese meditators, but they stayed in a different dormitory and listened to Bhante's talks in Burmese earlier in the afternoon. Their activities seemed to involve much more chanting, although they were doing the same kind of meditation: vipassana.

So the point of vipassana meditation is to get insight, and there are actually specific things you're supposed to realize: dukkha, the suffering that characterizes human existence, anicca, the impermanent character of all things, and anatta, the illusory nature of the self. Anyone who realizes these points completely will reach enlightenment, or nirvana (neibbana, as it's called in Burmese). Daw Pancavati explained all this to me in advance, and at first, it seemed to spoil the surprise. Why meditate if I already knew what I was supposed to realize? And what if I had different insights, thoughts of my own?

But that first day, Bhante didn't mention any insights. Instead, he gave me instructions for sitting and walking meditation.

"Follow breath coming in and out," Bhante explained, placing a hand on his belly. "In, out. Observe. Long or short? Deep or shallow? Your mind go away from breath, no problem. Come back, start again."

He called U Sila to demonstrate walking slowly up and down the hall. Bhante described the movements of the monk's feet: *Lifting, moving, placing. Lifting, moving, placing.* Adela recognized the ponderous gait of the Taiwanese woman.

"You must be mindful of daily activities," Bhante continued when U Sila had noiselessly exited the hall. "You taste the food, you taste mindfully. Slowly slowly," he said, paddling the air with his hand. "You take shower, you shower mindfully. Whatever you do, thadi shi ya meh."

That-ti. Adela knew that word. It was the first Burmese word she'd learned from Ko Oo, as he told her about Aung San Suu Kyi and the Saffron Revolution.

"I must have courage," Adela said proudly.

Bhante's brow furrowed.

"No. Courage, that-ti. Mindfulness, thadi."

It happened all the time in Burma. She'd mistake one word for another. But later she couldn't stop thinking about this. Bhante was trying to tell her the same thing Ko Oo had tried to tell her, the one thing that could have saved her, and saved Thiha. She didn't need to be brave. She needed to pay attention. She needed to be careful for other people's sakes, not just her own.

Bhante continued. Adela noticed his tendency to use several more examples than were necessary to convey a point.

"You use toilet, you use mindfully. You drink the water, you drink mindfully. Even you fall asleep, you fall asleep mindfully."

Falling asleep mindfully seemed like a contradiction in terms, but sitting and walking did not seem difficult. In fact, Adela was eager to begin. She still had four hours to practice after teatime and before bed.

After Bhante's explanation was over, Adela walked as slowly as she could to the dining hall. Out of habit, she smiled at Daw Pancavati as she sat down. The nun glanced downward. Adela wasn't supposed to communicate; even smiling counted. There was no fruit for her that day, only juice and tea. Adela didn't miss dinner anymore, but she did like her teatime fruit. Mangos had come into season, and on the temple compound there were two different kinds of trees: one that produced sweeter fruit, and another a tangy and addictive variety that she adored. Adela wondered if there'd be any mango at breakfast. As she sipped her tea, craving mangoes, she noticed for the first time how gently Daw Pancavati raised her teacup to her lips. Not in slow motion, as the lady meditator had, but carefully, as if she were noticing every movement. Indeed, the spirit of mindfulness pervaded all of the nun's gestures, even when she deftly put out her hand to catch a spoon Adela had knocked off the table.

Drinking slowly made teatime last longer, so the sky was getting dark by the time Adela made her way up to the meditation hall on the second floor of her dormitory. It was empty all day, except when Daw Pancavati swept it in the morning and freshened up the offerings in front of the Buddha statue. Sometimes they held their Burmese lessons there when it was rainy. Adela liked the smooth wooden floors and the view over the rice fields. On this evening, Daw Pancavati had lit the candles in front of the altar, and the sitting Buddha, with his long fingers draped over his knee, looked inspiring and serene.

Adela began with walking meditation. The hall was long, and she wondered how many times she'd have to cross it to fill an hour. For the first few steps, she noted each movement of her feet, remembering how U Sila had done it. It was relaxing, and soon Adela found herself gazing out onto the darkening rice fields. By the time she reached the windows, she was lost in thought. She nearly bumped into the wall before catching herself. She stopped, turned carefully, and rededicated herself to *lifting, moving, placing*.

Before long, Adela had crossed the room several times without noticing. When she consulted her watch, twenty minutes had passed. Spending another forty minutes in this manner seemed pointless, so Adela decided to switch to sitting meditation.

She found a mat and some cushions in the corner of the hall, arranged them underneath herself, and sat down. Then she remembered she was supposed to bow three times at the beginning and end of each session, so she roused herself to complete the ritual. Bowing before meals had always been a task she rushed through, but now there was no reason to hurry. She said the words Daw Pancavati had taught her: Buddham saranam gacchami, Dhammam saranam gacchami, Sangham saranam gacchami. I take refuge in the Buddha, I take refuge in the Buddha's teachings, I take refuge in the sangha, the monks and nuns who carry on the Buddha's ways. The words didn't mean much to her, but she liked the feel of the cool floor against her forehead.

Finally, Adela settled herself onto the cushions and tried to feel her breath coming in and out of her lungs. But her breaths weren't long and calm, as she thought they should be. In fact, she felt like she could hardly breathe at all, as if there were some obstruction that prevented her from inhaling. She shifted a little on her cushion, stretched her back, and tried to breathe deeply. In, out. In, out.

The first thing Adela realized was that she was obsessed with Thiha. While half-paying attention to her breath, she scraped back over her memory for any interaction she'd had with him. Her first day at the monastery, he'd put fruit on her table with his lovely arms. Once she'd seen him giving leftover food to the old lady with the child behind the dining hall. He had knelt down to scrape the rice onto the woman's plate so kindly, and he'd given the child a fresh banana. Then there were times she'd seen him when she was sick, which she could hardly remember, and which made her body tense with shame and disgust.

But how could she not have noticed him, how could she have avoided really seeing him until after she'd gotten well? Had he been one of the guys who'd lifted her on the sheet when she first got sick? She prayed he had not, and she hoped that Daw Pancavati had somehow shielded him from the worst of her illness. She preferred to rehash the vivid, electric minutes when he'd visited her in Daw Pancavati's room. She remembered his smooth brown skin and the quietness in his eyes. There must be ways to orchestrate casual meetings between them—maybe she could start helping out in the dining hall, or she could invite him to her English classes. Most of all, Adela dwelled on her dream, which she relived in hopes that she would dream it again that night.

Half an hour later, Adela's legs had fallen asleep. Itchy pins and needles made it impossible to concentrate on the breath, or even on Thiha. Her hips ached, like chicken bones that someone was slowly pulling apart before eating. When she abruptly stretched her legs in front of her, the sensation of

blood rushing back into them made her cry out in pain. Surely it wasn't supposed to be this way. She'd watched the monks sitting cross-legged for hours
while they did their nightly chanting. Nor did the Burmese meditators seem
to have any problem. They didn't even use cushions, and their legs lay peacefully on the floor. Adela's knees stuck up in the air and her back slumped. She
must be sitting the wrong way, and she resolved to ask Bhante about it the
following day.

Although the hour wasn't nearly up, Adela stood and practiced walking
again. At first it felt good to move, but before long she wished she could
sit down. She tried continuing her blog post in her mind, but she couldn't
summon the detachment necessary for what Ms. Alvarez would consider
an appropriate tone. Instead, she chatted to Lena in her mind: *I was a total
failure at meditating. It was like staring at a wall. And it was *incredibly* pain-
ful.* Lena! She had so much to tell Lena! *I got dysentery. I crapped my pants
about fifty times. I have a crush on the guy who cured me. Oh My Goth,* she
typed in her mind, falling back into their familiar personal language, *you
would not beeleeve how cute he is . . .* Indulging in these thoughts, walking
back and forth, an hour passed quickly. Adela decided to skip the next sitting
meditation and go to sleep. If she was to wake up at four, when the bells rang,
she would need the rest.

Back in her room, though, she couldn't fall asleep. It was only eight o'clock.
Suddenly *Insurgency and the Politics of Ethnicity,* which was sitting on the
table by her bed, seemed irresistible. What was the difference between those
two rebel armies in Shan State, the SSA and the SSA-S? She could look it up,
or ask U Sila later; he was from Shan State. She could run to the office right
now and look it up on her computer. She promised herself she would only
check the comments on her blog, read the subject lines of her emails, and
scan Facebook without liking anything, leaving no trace of her presence. But
Adela didn't want to break her vow to renounce "entertainment" on the very
first night of her retreat, so she lay there favorably comparing Thiha to Greg
until she fell asleep, wondering if that counted as breaking the Third Precept.

❀

It still felt like the middle of the night when the morning bell clanged.
Adela had gotten used to ignoring it, but on this morning Daw Pancavati

knocked on her door to make sure she was up. It was pitch black outside, and the electricity had failed, so Adela had to hold her flashlight with one hand while she brushed her teeth with the other, stamping her feet to keep the cockroaches from running over her toes. *For the record*, she thought of writing to Lena, *it is difficult to brush one's teeth "slowly, slowly."*

The schedule instructed her to proceed to the main hall for metta chanting. The prospect of saying prayers of goodwill for all beings, as Ko Oo had in the cafetorium so long ago, had appealed to Adela. However, at five in the morning, Adela found it a struggle to stay awake, much less to summon up any goodwill. It would be the only time all day that she was surrounded by all the Burmese meditators and the monks, so Adela tried to feel at least a sleepy solidarity with the others. Yet their alert and beatific faces were a reprimand. Adela gave up her effort to focus on the words, closed her eyes, and worked on her next blog post: **It is paradoxical that Buddhists are supposed to send goodwill to all beings, yet some apparently don't see a contradiction with killing or attacking Muslims. It really seems strange. I wonder if Thiha or other people like him . . .**

Adela realized she'd dozed off. She bit the inside of her cheek to stay awake, but it only worked for a moment, and then she fell back into a daze, waking up to find her head slumped into her chest or tipped onto her shoulder. Breakfast, breakfast. Breakfast was coming next.

It was hard to eat mindfully. Adela seized her fork right away when she saw the food, forgetting to bow. Daw Pancavati gently touched her hand, and Adela dropped her fork and squeezed her friend's fingers, desperate for some interaction. Daw Pancavati disentangled herself without looking at Adela.

Why did they have to make yellow bean curry? Adela hated yellow bean curry, or she realized that she hated it while she was "mindfully tasting" it. Its chalky sulfurousness coated her tongue. Even the sweetness of the tea stung her throat. Everything was unsatisfactory and not at all how she remembered it.

The morning of sitting and walking was a blur. An ache developed right between her shoulder blades, and it wouldn't go away no matter how much she shifted around. She longed to take a yoga class and have a long soak in a hot bath, but only hours of meditation and a cold bucket shower awaited her.

Lunchtime came: stir-fried spinach that was too salty and rice that tasted faintly burnt. Adela kept careful watch for Thiha as she walked back from the dining hall, but he was nowhere to be seen. Was he gone for a few days, or permanently? If he'd left, how would she find him? If he'd left, what hope would propel her through the remaining days of this retreat? How could she have lost him before she found him? She wanted to look for him during the rest period after lunch, but instead she fell heavily into sleep, her body exhausted by less than a day of meditation.

❀

By the time Adela reached her interview with Bhante, she was bursting with things to say. What a relief it would be to speak to someone! But as she bowed down before him, she wished that her interviews were with someone she felt more comfortable with, such as Daw Pancavati or U Pyinnya.

Bhante waited silently for Adela to begin. She knew she was supposed to start with, "Bhante, I have done eight hours of sitting meditation and seven hours of walking meditation," but instead she said, "I keep falling asleep."

He nodded. "When this happens, you must note, 'sleepy, sleepy.' Note position of your body at this time."

"Hman ba, Bhante."

He nodded to show she should continue.

"And I was thinking that it might be better for me to start with shorter meditation periods, like maybe half an hour? Because—"

"When you think this way," he interrupted her, "you must note: 'thinking, thinking.' Then return to the breath."

Adela's faith in Bhante's wisdom was fast diminishing.

"Hman ba, Bhante."

"And daily activities?"

Adela hesitated. It seemed petty. "Um, the food tastes bad? When I taste mindfully."

"Good!" he said, smiling at her for the first time. "Sensation can be pleasant, unpleasant, or neutral. When it is pleasant, note 'pleasant, pleasant.' When it is unpleasant . . ."

Adela didn't listen to the rest, because she knew what he was going to say.

"Anything else?" he asked, raising his tufted eyebrows.

"When I sit, my legs hurt."

This also seemed to strike him as good news. "Notice this pain. How is the pain? Where is the pain? Pain is like this or like that? Pain is your good friend. When pain go away, you miss your good friend," he said, smiling widely.

Adela was becoming increasingly impatient. She could permanently injure herself by seeking out pain. And Bhante, who had at first struck her as sensible and benign, was starting to sound downright sinister.

"Anything else?" he asked.

"No, Bhante."

He nodded, closed his eyes, and then began to speak.

"Dukkha, suffering. Anicca, impermanence. Anatta, not-self. Three kinds. First, dukkha. You born, you have dukkha. You get old, you have Dukkha. You get sick—" here he paused, snapped open his eyes, and looked at Adela. "Ma Sabeh get sick last week. Dukkha, naw?"

"Dukkha," she admitted.

"Ma Sabeh sit, get pain in her leg. Dukkha, naw?

"Dukkha."

"Ma Sabeh taste food, it taste bad. Dukkha, naw?"

"Dukkha," she said, although she wanted to add that it wouldn't be dukkha if they'd stop making yellow bean curry.

"Ma Sabeh cannot have the thing she want. Dukkha, naw?"

She thought of Thiha. "Dukkha."

Bhante nodded, considering his point to be proven. "Buddha teach this way. In life, dukkha." He sighed with satisfaction. Then he took a deep breath, resettled himself, closed his eyes, and continued.

"Anicca. Everything arise and pass away. Breath arise and pass away. Pain arise and pass away." At this moment, he burped gently, as if to make his point. "Wind in the body, arise and pass away."

He opened his eyes. "Ma Sabeh also, arise and pass away," he said, chuckling in a manner that struck Adela as somewhat mean-spirited.

Adela had no specific beliefs about heaven, hell, or an afterlife. Both of her parents had rebelled against their strict Catholic upbringings and

advised her to choose a religion (or not, no pressure!) when she was ready.
Her mother still went to church on Easter, while her father was suspicious
of all organized religion. Although Adela hadn't arrived at any particular
convictions, she found her mind rebelling against the idea that she was no
different from a breath, or one of Bhante's burps.

Sensing that she wasn't quite convinced, Bhante went on.

"Ma Sabeh body, stay here forever?"

"No."

"Ma Sabeh feel angry. Stay angry forever?"

Did she seem angry? She managed a smile. "No."

"Ma Sabeh now awake. Stay awake forever?"

"No," she said, thinking of her cozy bed.

"One hundred year from now, any Ma Sabeh here?" he asked, raising
his hand to his forehead and scanning the horizon for an imaginary Ma
Sabeh.

"No . . ." Adela replied, her attempt to conceal her sullenness wearing
thin.

Her legs had fallen asleep and she wanted to stretch them out, but she
knew she wasn't supposed to point her feet at Bhante. She shifted her knees
to one side.

"Now, anatta," he continued. Adela was intrigued to hear what
he had to say. Suffering seemed fairly straightforward, but the claim
that there wasn't a self made even less sense to her than the idea of
impermanence.

"Body is not-self. So, Ma Sabeh can make body be sick or not sick?"

"No."

"Ma Sabeh can make legs be long or short?"

"No."

"Ma Sabeh have many body part," he said, gesturing to his own portly
physique. "Leg, foot, hair, hand. These body parts are self?"

Adela looked down at her hands. Her nails could have been cleaner. She
thought of what she'd learned in biology class: human skin cells are dying
and sloughing off all the time, and they become the dust that we vacuum
up.

Then she turned over her hand to look at the scar on her wrist.
She and Lena, under the influence of Lena's depressive sophomore
year boyfriend, had gone through a brief phase in which they'd cut

themselves with safety razors. Adela had done it only half-heartedly, in solidarity with Lena, but one time she'd cut too deeply, glimpsing some fatty yellow goo under her skin before blood gushed forth. This brief vista into her own body had alarmed her, and she'd never cut herself again.

Now Adela could see violet-colored veins roping their way over the small bones of her wrist. Not her. Not another person. Just stuff—tissue, elements, some of the Thirty-Two Parts from the Buddha's list. Suddenly there was a kind of flowering in Adela's mind. At that moment, she knew something that she'd never be able to un-know. She knew from her own experience, the way she knew that objects fell to earth. What Bhante had said was right. It was—it must have been—insight.

Adela smiled, this time sincerely. "No, Bhante, body parts are not self."

He paused, as if he sensed he needed to let her realization crystalize before moving on.

"Ma Sabeh feel sad. Ma Sabeh can decide, be sad or not be sad?"

Adela felt her skepticism returning. She could certainly do things to make herself sad or not. Sometimes she did choose to feel a certain way. The morning after the first time she'd slept with Greg, he'd left her room without waking her up. By noon, when he rushed back to explain he'd had an exam to make up, she had practically excised him from her heart in order to save her dignity. She'd decided not to be sad. Still, she knew what Bhante wanted her to say.

"No."

"Ma Sabeh have consciousness. Ma Sabeh now awake. Ma Sabeh can decide, pay attention to this or that?"

Adela didn't want him to think she wasn't paying attention to what he was saying.

"Yes."

He chuckled. "Ma Sabeh can pay attention to breath one hour?"

"Maybe not a whole hour . . ." she conceded.

Bhante sprang to life. "Ma Sabeh cannot pay attention! Ma Sabeh attention is like the monkey, jump to here, jump to there. Ma Sabeh say, 'Stop!' Ma Sabeh consciousness do not listen."

His judgment seemed rather harsh. And something else occurred to Adela.

"Well, who's saying stop?" she asked, feeling clever.

Bhante paused. "Sometime," he said. "You look up at moon in the sky. Moon is there, no problem." She thought of her dream of the moon above the Shwedagon Pagoda.

"Small pond is there. You see moon in pond. Moon is in pond, or no?"

Adela considered his question. "Well, the reflection—"

"Wind blow, moon in water fall apart," he interrupted. The image came to her clearly, ripples breaking up the silvery light.

"OK, done," he said, closing his eyes and preparing to receive her bow.

PARADISE

The next day came and went, and the third day arrived, and it was no easier to get up in the morning. The constant chatter in Adela's mind didn't seem interesting anymore; it was downright insipid. How could she think of the same things, day in and day out? It was like a merry-go-round: *I'm hungry Where's Thiha My back hurts Are there going to be mangoes at breakfast My back hurts Is Thiha ever coming back.* She wondered how she could be so boring.

Bhante's dhamma talk that day was about the Five Hindrances that could interfere with meditation: sense desire, aversion, restlessness, sloth and torpor, and doubt. By this point, they all sounded familiar. Adela's meditation periods were marred by each one—the desire for a bowl of chocolate ice cream, an aversion to the mosquitoes that buzzed near her ears, a restlessness so strong that sometimes she stood up and whacked her meditation cushion several times just to expel some energy. Sloth and torpor made her eyelids droop. She wrestled with doubt over whether this retreat was beneficial and character-building or masochistic and pointless. Still, Adela was comforted by the idea that everyone in meditation retreats struggled the way she was struggling.

As if he were reading her mind, Bhante added a caveat. "Some people have only small problem with these Hindrances. Some people," he noted, gesturing to Adela, "many problem."

"Why?"

"Depend on past karma."

She'd heard the word karma before, of course. Mostly, she'd seen it on tip jars back in the United States.

"So karma is like . . . what goes around comes around?"

Bhante had already been talking for quite some time, and Adela only wanted to confirm that she had the right idea. However, he lifted his eyebrows, reinvigorated, as if he were preparing to begin an entirely new topic.

"Karma, we Burmese call *kan*." He moistened his lips with his tongue and then continued.

"Why some person rich, some person poor?"

Adela had an answer to that question, which she'd gleaned from Greg's diatribes on economic policy. But she guessed that Bhante didn't want to hear it. Sure enough, he proceeded with a series of rhetorical inquiries.

"Why some person very clever, some person not clever?"

Genetics, thought Adela.

"Why some person born with two arm, some person only one?"

Exposure to toxins in the womb?

"Because of kan," he pronounced with delight.

"Um—" she interrupted, thinking of the Muslims whose huts had been burned, and of Daw Pancavati, whose child had died in a cyclone, "do you mean it's their fault that they're born with only one arm? Like they're being punished?"

Bhante shook with quiet mirth. "No one need to punish you! Your own actions punish to you! This is the result of some actions in your previous life. But, your kan is only one of twenty-four conditions, five processes. Also the kan of your mother and father are involve. Each result, many causes. But this is sure: the seed make the fruit. Good action make good result! Bad action make bad result!"

Adela knew she shouldn't interrupt again, but a question that she had never quite formulated before, but which she realized had been bothering her for quite some time, burst forth: "But what if you're trying to do a good action, and there's a bad result anyway?"

"Good intention and skillful action, wise mind, then good result. Maybe you cannot see, maybe in one thousand years good result come. Good intention, unskillful action, unwise mind . . . bad result!" He grimaced.

It seemed unfair. Wouldn't one want to see the good results of one's good deeds? And what if one hadn't had the chance yet to accumulate skill and wisdom?

"And there's nothing you can do? If you have bad karma from your previous life, you're just—" She hesitated, refraining from saying, "screwed."

Bhante shook his head. "No, no. You do good action, make merit in your lifetime. Help people, get good kan for next life."

"But . . . what happens if you do a lot of good things, but you had really, really bad karma from your past life, so you can't make it up?"

"Next life, not so good. Maybe you become the dog or the mos-quee-to." Bhante made a buzzing sound to make sure she'd understood. "Then you cannot be a Buddhist!"

She realized that this was the closest Bhante had come to addressing the Buddhist-Muslim conflict. She wanted to ask him if Muslims had bad karma. Was that why some Buddhists thought it was OK to burn their houses? Was that how he justified what was happening, that people deserved what they got? But Adela couldn't ask, because she was afraid to hear how he'd answer.

"So if there's no self . . . how do I have a next life?"

"Not you. Your kan."

"So, my karma has a next life?" she asked incredulously.

"No, no," said Bhante with a hint of impatience. "Ma Sabeh kan go into another body."

"But, I don't understand—"

He silenced her with a raised hand.

"Ma Sabeh have the computer," he said, pronouncing it kun-pyu-taa.

"Yes."

"Ma Sabeh send the message, read the news, go here, go there." He pointed to and fro.

"Yes."

"Ma Sabeh understand how the *kun-pyu-taa* work?"

"Um . . . no."

"But still, Ma Sabeh can use this *kun-pyu-taa.*"

"Yes."

"Ma Sabeh does not understand. Still, *kun-pyu-taa* work. Ma Sabeh do not understand kan. Still, kan work." He settled back, making little grunts of satisfaction.

This analogy didn't make much sense to Adela, but she liked talking about herself more than she liked listening to Bhante's disquisitions.

"So what do you think, do I have good karma?"

He nodded. "Chances of birth in human realm can be very small. Very precious. Also Ma Sabeh has big body," he said, pulling at the air around his waist as if to indicate rolls of fat. "Ma Sabeh is healthy. Ma Sabeh father is the rich man. Ma Sabeh is born very far away, but Ma Sabeh find the Buddha dhamma! Good kan."

However positive it was to be considered fat in Burmese culture, Adela resented the implication. Her mother always said the women in their family were "big-boned," not fat. And Adela's father wasn't exactly rich.

Yet she saw Bhante's point. She did sometimes feel that she had more than she deserved. But that was exactly what confused her about karma. Daw Pancavati was so much nicer than Adela; why had her life been so hard? If karma was real, why did dictators like Ne Win accumulate money and power while good people were abused?

Yet Adela could hardly focus on these thoughts, because during the past twenty minutes she had been ignoring the growing fullness of her bladder, and now she had a vicious urge to pee. The interview had run longer than usual, and she knew she would have to walk extremely slowly back to the dormitory to relieve herself. So she nodded as if karma had been explained to her satisfaction, thanked Bhante, and began the process of extricating herself from the hall.

Adela was still thinking of Daw Pancavati's karma as she walked to the dining hall for teatime an hour later. She added up the bad things that had happened to her friend: being born poor, her family members dying, being raped, losing her son. How could the nun be so tranquil despite everything? What had she found during her meditation retreats that Adela hadn't?

Adela was late arriving, and Daw Pancavati was already finished taking her evening refreshment. She had set the teapot where Adela could reach it and placed a few lumps of the chalky sugar-candy, which was the only exception to the no-eating-after-noon rule, on Adela's plate. Her bare feet hardly made a sound as she glided over the wooden floor toward the door.

The nun's example had already influenced Adela, who was used to stomping around, rattling the cutlery as she plopped herself down to eat. Now that she was on retreat, she at least pretended to move carefully. All she had to do now was make the reality match the appearance. She resolved to try harder. If Buddhism could bring Daw Pancavati peace after all that she'd suffered, Adela really had no excuse.

The inspiration was fleeting. By the end of the fifth day of her retreat, Adela was once again near giving up. She didn't understand how moving slowly could be so exhausting. Her knees ached whether she was sitting or walking. True, she had become better at concentrating on the breath. Just as Bhante had promised, the chatter of her mind quieted. But it left blankness in its wake. In, out, in, out. What was the point? Except for her one moment of insight during Bhante's first dhamma talk, when she realized that her body was not her self, she didn't think she'd experienced anything she was supposed to.

Five days were enough, she told herself. She did want to continue to meditate, just not during all of her waking hours. Thus, as she fell into bed that night, she decided that the next day at her interview, she would tell Bhante that she was cutting short her retreat. She knew it would be disrespectful to stop without telling him; she had to un-take the Eight Precepts, or else she'd never be allowed to sleep in a comfortable bed again. And she couldn't very well barge in on him outside of their scheduled interview. She would have to wait until the following afternoon.

❀

The sitting meditation before breakfast was always the hardest for me. I was sleepiest and hungriest then, and I had come to dread it. But that morning, the morning of the sixth day, something happened to me. It was like sitting in the darkness of the eye doctor's office, straining to read the blurry letters, when suddenly the correct prescription was flipped into place. Except my eyes were still closed. My whole body relaxed, but the sensation of my breath coming in and out became crisp and distinct, occurring at the exact moment that I noted "in, out." It was like tumbling through a trapdoor into the present moment, like falling into step with reality instead of always being a few seconds ahead or behind.

I brought my attention to the place between my shoulder blades that always hurt. It didn't hurt. I practiced pausing my breath. My attention paused with it. It was as if the sun was directly above me, so that my attention, which had always shadowed my body at a distance, was

suddenly aligned with my physical self. It was like closing out all the extra programs running on a computer so that one—the important one—could work the way it was supposed to. It felt amazing.

The only time she'd had a similar experience was when she and Lena had taken mushrooms their junior year—although she decided not to include this detail in her blog. They'd walked out into the forest behind campus, and the forest was so forestlike, so sublime, that Adela lay on the ground and smelled the earth, unresistant to the dampness seeping into her clothing. The feeling of nonresistance that Adela felt that morning in the meditation hall was so powerful, so familiar, that for a moment she feared that someone had slipped her some drugs.

She sat there breathing in and out until she heard the bell for breakfast, and then she opened her eyes. The Buddha statue sat in front of her, eyes downcast, deathless and beautiful. *Stay here*, she thought.

She could not stop feeling the in and out of her breath. It was there as she bent her body for the bows, and it was there as she walked to the door, her feet pressing into the ground. She realized, with terror and elation, that she could not stop meditating. As this thought arose, she noted, "thinking, thinking," just as Bhante instructed her. She tried to let her mind wander, and it would not go. She tried thinking of Thiha. "Thinking, thinking," responded her mind.

She descended the stairs one by one, each footfall a revelation. So this was what it was like to walk! This was what is was like to breathe! All that had been a drab background to her inner dramas moments earlier was rendered in technicolor. The sweeper's rattan basket, abandoned at the dormitory's entrance, cast such exquisite shadows on the dust! The morning air was impossibly cool, and she took little sips of it, as if it were life-giving ambrosia. And it was! She was alive, she was breathing. She spent several minutes watching the sun break through a purple cloud on the horizon, its rays like a light show that only she could appreciate.

It took Adela a long time to get to breakfast. Daw Pancavati was waiting for her, and she spooned food onto Adela's plate reverently, aware that something had changed. Yellow bean curry. Adela raised the spoon to her lips, felt it entering her mouth, noted the expectation of how the food would taste and the actual taste. There was the same sulfurous undertone, with a little more lemongrass that morning. Unpleasant, but not extremely so. The difference was, the unpleasantness didn't disturb her. It came, and it went. It didn't belong to her. She noticed it as indifferently as she noticed the color of the beans, the slant of the light.

Then Adela had her second real insight: being in the present moment, paying attention without resistance, was paradise. How could a simple thing like grasping a water glass be paradise? How could she never have realized it before? Her father's attempt to expunge all Judeo-Christian lore from her mind must have failed, because the image that arose was of the Garden of Eden. Adela felt like she had been forgiven. She realized why Daw Pancavati called Buddhism her "refuge." Adela saw clearly how afraid she'd been, how much energy she'd wasted trying to avoid discomfort instead of simply letting it come and go.

After breakfast, Adela spent forty minutes walking to the meditation hall. It didn't matter what she was doing, because every action was equally interesting and worthwhile. Sitting, walking, taking a shower, she had no preference. She watched pleasant and unpleasant sensations arise and pass away without clinging to them. She remembered the Taiwanese meditator, how even her eyeballs had moved slowly. How long had that woman stayed in this state? No wonder she hadn't been interested in making small talk with Adela, when she could enjoy the bliss of turning a doorknob or lifting, moving, and placing her feet.

Suddenly Adela felt a rush of tenderness for the lady. How hard she must have worked on her meditation! How wonderful it was that she had found such serenity! Adela waited a moment for the familiar stab of jealousy, the feeling of inadequacy that usually followed her recognition of other people's accomplishments. It did not come. Instead, she felt overwhelming love. It was a kind of love she'd never felt before, certainly not for a stranger. Dear, stocky Taiwanese lady! Adela wished that wherever the woman was she was well fed and well rested, and that she was continuing her meditation practice.

This, Adela realized, was metta, goodwill. Every morning they chanted, sending metta to all beings. Bhante had given Adela a lecture about metta on the second day of her retreat, explaining how different it was from the love she felt for her parents or her "boy friends," as he put it. "Lust," he'd said—and Adela had been shocked to hear him pronounce the word—"is opposite of metta." But metta had remained abstract to her. She'd thought that love for all beings sounded like a contradiction in terms, that real love required special preference. But next to this new feeling of metta, Adela had to agree that the attachments she had felt in her life previously were small and sullied with self-interest.

To test the limits of this metta, Adela tried to direct it at other people. Her mother, who was probably worrying about her at this very moment. Her father, whom she'd often found herself being mean to because she didn't like to consider how similar they were. Ko Oo, who'd led her to this amazing country and given her his own amulet for protection. Greg, with his endearing and futile need to be right. Lena, who searched so hard for intensity. The man who worked in the mailroom at Edgerton Fields, to whom Adela had never spoken. Daw Pancavati, her Burmese mother. Sarah, her nemesis, her role model. U Nyanika, whose views were so distorted by his fear of Muslims. Adela felt the same rush of tenderness for each person, whether she liked them or not, whether she knew them or not. She stood under the eaves of the meditation hall, directing metta at everyone. President Obama: what pressure he must be under! Mitt Romney: how hard it would be to face his huge family if he lost the election! Thiha. Ne Win. The mangy dog who ate the old rice that even the beggars left behind. The cockroaches who busily scuttled over her feet in the bathroom. How they struggled and strived and suffered, every one of them! The beings in the universe occurred to her, one by one, and she loved them with a love so pure that it could not settle on an object but flowed smoothly from one being to the next.

Adela arrived at her interview with Bhante still in the grasp of this strange paradise, unsure how to explain it.

"Something—happened—to—me," she managed, looking down at her hands folded in her lap.

Bhante squinted at her. "Yes. You have a little concentration."

Concentration wasn't the word Adela would have used. She felt a small chink open up in the blissful sameness of everything.

"Concentration come and go, arise and pass away. Nothing special."

Adela felt sure that he hadn't understood.

"No, no, I mean everything is paradise!"

"There is joy, and there is suffering. We must not cling to either one."

"I feel metta for everyone. Everyone!" she cried out, striving to feel it all over again and noting its absence.

"Metta is good. But Ma Sabeh must have uppekha also: equanimity. Mental formation, body sensation, these arise and pass away. Uppekha let Ma Sabeh stay stable," he said, flattening the air with his palms.

Then he closed his eyes, as if preparing for a long speech.

Adela burst out: "But I think I'm—"

Bhante's eyes snapped open. "Yes, you always thinking, thinking!" he announced with obvious disapproval. Little vertical lines creased the sides of his mouth, and he blinked rapidly.

If he hadn't interrupted her, what would she have said? As ridiculous as it would have sounded, she could not rule out that she would have claimed enlightenment. Later, she was glad Bhante stopped her. But at the time, Adela felt desperate for recognition, desperate to be told that she'd finally done something right.

Tears of frustration came to her eyes, blurring the image of Bhante sitting on his platform, as she heard him beginning a story.

"One time, a giant name Asurindarahu come to the Buddha. This Asurindarahu believe Buddha is nothing special and he plan in his mind, 'I will not bow down to this Buddha.' Asurindarahu think he himself is more large and beautiful to look at. He come to Buddha very proud. At that time, Buddha see what is in Asurindarahu's mind. So Buddha make himself appear very large, like a mountain. Asurindarahu is amaze! He is the size not even of the Buddha's little toe. 'Ah! I am so small!' say Asurindarahu. Buddha say to him, 'It is true you are bigger than other ones in your kingdom. But outside your kingdom, this is not true.' Then Asurindarahu bow down and worship Buddha."

Adela's peace of mind was fast evaporating. She could see that, in the story, she was supposed to be the arrogant giant. But she was only telling Bhante what she had experienced! True, Bhante hadn't used the word "arrogant," but Adela was sensitive to the accusation, which had been leveled at her by her mother during their arguments and once, indirectly, by Ms. Alvarez during a class discussion. And why was her size constantly thematized in Burma? She was of average height and weight in the United States. It wasn't her fault that the people around her were so short and malnourished.

Bhante continued, indifferent to the tears now sliding down Adela's cheeks.

"Not only sensation arise and pass away. Also mental state arise and pass away. Sometime mind is concentrate, sometime mind is confuse. Ma Sabeh must keep to practice, let mental state come and go. You must not meditate to get the blissful state," he scolded. "You must meditate for complete liberation—for neibbana." He pronounced this last word reverently, closing his eyes.

Adela gulped for breath, reaching for the calm it had brought her before. But it was as if she were waking up from a dream, willing it to continue by remembering scraps of it.

"Now I tell about the dependent origination, paticcasamuppada. All thing arise from causes and conditions . . ."

The talk was long and difficult to follow. Adela wanted to leave and meditate, to try to recapture the feeling that was slipping away from her. If she could just sit and watch the breath, she thought she could do it. So she put on her most attentive expression and tuned out Bhante's words. *In, out. In, out.*

Her efforts were fruitless. She left the hall an hour later, walking as slowly as she could. But her eyes wandered, her mind flitted here and there. And then something happened that thrust her back into the ordinary world: for the first time in a week, she saw Thiha.

He was standing by the water tank, his soaked loungyi clinging to his hips. Adela watched with something approaching alarm as he splashed water over his bare chest. Droplets tumbled off his body, glistening like diamonds in the sunlight, running down his brown back in rivulets. Adela felt slightly dizzy, as if she were at the top of a Ferris wheel, the ground far away. Thiha reached for a bar of soap, rubbed the lather casually over his lean, muscular chest and dark purple nipples, then scrubbed his armpits, where Adela could see smudges of hair.

Bhante's voice intruded on her reverie, his squat body superimposing itself over Thiha's in her mind. "Lust is the opposite of metta," he scolded, waggling a finger in the air. *No*, she protested weakly at the specter of her guru. *I'm just seeing, seeing, noting pleasant sensations.* Thiha pulled a dry loungyi over his body, deftly shimmied out of the wet one beneath, and reached for a T-shirt. Adela closed her mouth, which had fallen open.

Thiha's face was half turned away from her, and he did not look up. Yet Adela sensed that he knew she was watching him. She continued to walk deliberately, not looking up again, until she reached her dormitory. But instead of climbing the stairs to the meditation hall, she went back to her room, slumped in a corner, stared up at the ceiling, and thought.

How luscious thinking was! To let her mind run quickly over everything, like a tongue over delicious food, to digest the events of the past days!

Thiha was back. She longed to sneak out of her room and find him again, even if she could only stare at him from afar. Impatience flooded her body, washing away the last remains of her metta for all beings. But before she could fully devote herself to enjoying her crush, she had to sort out what had happened to her over the past few days. She struggled to bring her thoughts back to the spiritual matters that had concerned her until only a few minutes before.

She'd had, it seemed, some kind of fake enlightenment. It was embarrassing to admit it, but she had wanted to believe that the way she'd felt would continue forever. Bhante was right; she'd been puffed up with pride, like the giant in the story, unable to grasp her place in this new landscape. She had failed, but the process of failing had changed her. Burma had changed her. As she had at various junctures of her trip, she tallied up her achievements. Ma Sabeh: semi-expert on the Buddhist-Muslim conflict in Burma, dysentery survivor, knower of (albeit elementary) Buddhist truths.

She was determined to sort out the real insights from what Bhante would call "thinking." She pulled out her laptop and opened a new document.

What I Learned on My Meditation Retreat
1. My body is not my self.
2. Everything is paradise.
3. I can feel metta for everyone.

She knew these things were true, and she also knew that they sounded like the clichéd ramblings of a person on drugs. Furthermore, these insights were difficult to apply in daily life. She couldn't walk around in a stupor all the time, emoting metta at everyone. Already, she could feel the vividness of her realizations fading. If only she could talk to someone, explain what she meant in detail, her ideas might become concrete. But she still had four more days of the retreat.

It occurred to Adela then that she was lonely. Compared to her life back home, in which she and Lena dissected every experience and she spoke

with her mother several times a week, Burma had isolated her. She had
Daw Pancavati, but the nun was so virtuous that Adela couldn't really confide in her. It was a little sad, she thought, to have so many new experiences
and no one to tell.

Some time later, Adela found that she had an empty cup in her hand,
and that her lips were wet. Without noticing, she had gotten up and drunk
a cup of water. She had also missed teatime. No matter, she thought. Suddenly, she was full of energy. She would finish the retreat. She would use
her new understanding of Buddhism to help Buddhists realize that perse-
cuting Muslims was wrong. And she would make Thiha fall in love with
her.

BURMESE DAYS

Adela needn't have worried about the remainder of her retreat. The day after she unofficially gave up was Bhante's birthday, and the monastery was flooded with people for an extended celebration. Adela was surprised to see his birthday so elaborately commemorated; it seemed counter to the doctrine of not-self. At every meal, visitors flocked to serve him or touch the plate he would eat from. The monastery helpers were busier than ever, and Adela could hardly keep track of Thiha despite the fact that she had dedicated the whole of her concentration, sharpened by meditation, to monitoring his comings and goings.

In the commotion, everyone seemed to forget about Adela's retreat. Even Daw Pancavati was preoccupied with the arrival of some of her friends from the Irrawaddy Delta. Adela stopped waking up so early, and although she did spend a fair amount of time sitting and walking to keep up appearances, the object of her meditation shifted to her crush. She hadn't felt so overwrought since the beginnings of her infatuation with Greg. Whatever she was doing, she pictured Thiha watching her. Yet she could not be sure he was even aware of her presence. She had the urge to march up to him and demand, "Is this happening?" If he didn't know what she meant, it would be over. If he did, they were already halfway there.

On the day before Adela was scheduled to end her retreat, Daw Pancavati came to her room after lunch to tell her she should go to the main hall right away. All of the visitors would take the Five Precepts, with Bhante presiding, and Adela could end her retreat that way. Adela wasn't sure if it was merely for convenience, or whether Bhante could tell by casual observation that she wasn't really meditating anymore, but she was relieved.

Later Adela would remember walking with Daw Pancavati to the hall, waiting for her to break the silence. She was poised to humbly brag about her insights. But the nun didn't ask Adela about her meditation experience, then or ever. Adela would have liked to think it was because Daw Pancavati understood everything, forgave everything. But she could never be sure.

They sat at the back of the large crowd that had gathered in the hall. Old ladies in lace blouses fanned themselves. Young men in dress pants knelt up front. Mothers tried to coax their toddlers to sit still with their hands in prayer position. Bhante's long speech was in Burmese, so Adela didn't understand much of it, although she caught the words *kan* and *dukkha* repeated often. At the end, to her shock, Bhante peered over everyone's heads to locate her in the crowd, then called out, "Ma Sabeh nah lay la?"

Everyone turned toward Adela. If there was anything she understood in Burmese by now, it was the question, "Do you understand?" Although she had only the most general sense of his talk's meaning, she was too embarrassed to say anything but "Hman ba, Bhante." It wasn't even the proper way to say "I understand," but a ripple of approval went through the crowd. The foreigner had passed the test, without knowing much at all.

Then Bhante recited the Five Precepts, and everyone repeated them back. These guidelines were the same as the Eight Precepts Adela had been following, minus the ones about luxurious beds, entertainment, and eating after noon. And the Third Precept, the one about sex, was slightly different, although she didn't understand how. Adela gathered that it must leave room for reproduction, because there were plenty of children in the room.

Afterward, people wormed their way to the front. Some had envelopes in their hands, others held orange buckets filled with special monk supplies: orange towels, orange flip-flops, orange candles, and incense.

"What are they doing?" Adela whispered to Daw Pancavati, enjoying her newfound freedom to speak.

"They give dana, some offering for Bhante."

"But he can't possibly use all that stuff."

"He give to other monk." She gestured around the hall. "All our food, all our things, donated or bought with the donation. It make merit for our donor, good kan."

Adela thought of all the meals she'd consumed, all the laundry powder she'd used. It seemed wrong for her to be living off donations. They weren't intended for her, and she probably had more money than the donors did. She resolved to give whatever leftover cash she had at the end of her stay to the monastery.

With so many people in the room, the air was heavy with the tang of sweat. When Adela saw the line of people waiting to give offerings, she realized that the festivities were far from over. Bhante was conversing with each donor, then intoning blessings over their entourage.

Suddenly Adela was overcome with the urge to escape from the hall. Now that she was free from the strictures of the retreat, she wanted to change out of her brown loungyi and sweat-stained white blouse. She pointed at the door, waved goodbye to Daw Pancavati, then threaded her way through the crowd that had gathered behind them. Once she was outside, she took a deep breath of fresh air.

As she walked—at a normal pace, for the first time in over a week—toward her dormitory, she heard someone behind her say, "Hi."

It was not a greeting she had heard lately. She knew before she turned around who had said it, so she was able to compose a nonchalant expression.

"Hi."

They stood about six feet apart in the midday heat, which necessitated speaking louder than Adela would have liked.

"How do you feel?"

"Fine. Good!" Adela wasn't sure if he was referring to her illness or to the retreat, which he must have known about because of her clothing.

"Where were you?" she asked, realizing the moment the words left her mouth how much they revealed: that she had noticed his absence, even while she was supposed to be meditating, and that she considered them intimate enough that she deserved some account of his whereabouts. But something stopped her from back-pedaling. She let the words hang there, and she even started to wickedly enjoy the surprise on his face.

"I was visiting to my mother." He gestured back toward the hall. "She is here now."

Is she going to stay? Are you going to leave? Where does she live? Why are you staying at the monastery? Why do I want to take your hips in my hands and pull you toward me? Adela had many questions, but picking one seemed arbitrary.

He looked back toward the hall, as if he expected his mother to appear, and he remained slightly turned away from Adela. Would he be embarrassed to introduce them? From the way he was standing, she knew he'd leave in a moment.

"See you later," she called out preemptively.

"See you later."

Adela turned quickly, nearly tripping on her loungyi.

Back in her room, Adela looked at herself in the only mirror she had, the tiny rectangular one velcroed to her toiletries kit. She could only look at one quadrant of her face at a time: a bluish eye, red in the corners from glare and dust; the freckles that the sun brought out on her cheek; and her teeth, which, while flawed by American standards, certainly revealed the many advantages she'd had compared to most Burmese people.

Was it a face, she wondered, that a Burmese guy would like? Was she exotic to him, as he was to her? Boys at home seemed to find her passable but not worth going out of their way for, the kind of girl they'd start talking to late in the evening when other people were already paired off. That was how she and Greg had gotten together: at a social where she'd been lurking around him all night, speaking ostentatiously about the earthquake in Haiti in hopes of attracting his attention, which, toward ten o'clock, she finally did. Over the years, Adela had accepted her average looks; she even took pride in them. She resented the fact that stunningly attractive women were overrepresented in literature, and she had campaigned for more realistic-looking heroines in her world lit class.

Yet here in Burma, she was anything but average. Her hair, which her mother insisted on calling strawberry blond because of the way it must have looked when she was a child, was now basically brown, although the sun had bleached it to a lighter shade. Still, it was much different from the glossy, inky black hair of Burmese women. And although Adela usually wore a size 8, in Burma she felt like a giant. Bhante—whom she tried to push from her mind as she made these calculations—certainly seemed to find her "big body" noteworthy. It was fortunate that Thiha was tall.

She started composing a description of Thiha for Lena in her mind (long limbs, nice shoulders, the way he tilted his head to the side when he was thinking), then she realized that with the retreat over, she could message Lena that very day. Eager for the satisfaction of a full inbox, she grasped her laptop and rushed over to the office.

After filling in Lena on Thiha's appealing physique, Adela scrolled through the annals of Facebook. Edgerton Fields nostalgia posts from graduating seniors had slowly been replaced with a proliferation of carefully selected references to new lives: photos of sunny college campuses, relationships ended and begun, and notices that so-and-so had checked in on Nantucket or at the MoMA in New York. There were beautiful pictures from Lena's bike ride to Oregon, which had raised more than three-thousand dollars for her organization. She'd made a community page for her trip where she posted updates and information on how to get involved in conservation projects. It was truly impressive.

Adela felt that she had some catching up to do. She'd spent most of her energy writing her blog, and her Facebook page had languished. The last photo she'd posted, of the Secretariat Building, was over a month old. She'd have to photograph the rice fields in the purple dusk, the temple bells against the noon sky. Perhaps she'd even take some pictures of Daw Pancavati or Bhante, if the right moment came up. In the meantime, she linked to her blog and to the MVU page and updated her status: "Having a blast teaching English to monks here at the Yadana Monastery in Yangon, thanks to @MyanmarVolunteersUnited!"

Greg's page was filled with photos of his new intern friends interspersed with articles from *Foreign Policy* and the *Atlantic*. He'd tagged her in one post: "Myanmar's Rohingya Under Attack." It showed he'd been reading her blog, at least. Adela was proud that for once she'd alerted him to an issue of international concern instead of the other way around. Although she was committed to her obsession with Thiha, she quickly checked to see if Greg was still "in a relationship" with the poli sci major; he was.

Then she clicked onward to the article, which reported that thousands of Rohingya people had fled over the border into refugee camps in Bangladesh after the previous month's violence. The Burmese military had fired on one group trying to return to Burma, killing fifty people. A photo showed a dark-skinned young man standing in front of a burning hut. She copied the photo to her desktop and inserted it into a new blog post.

Kala. I first heard that word in Yangon, before the violence in Rakhine State broke out. The prejudice against these people—Muslims, Rohingyas, anyone with dark skin—isn't only in Rakhine State, and it isn't just because of what had happened in June.

In fact, if *Burmese Days* is any indication, discrimination against people with dark skin goes back to the colonial era. The British officials at the club are always going on about "n---s" and "black b---s." Just as the racism described in *Heart of Darkness* had long-lasting impacts on Africa, British attitudes toward people with different skin colors still affects Burma today. Nowadays, even non-Muslim Burmese people seem ashamed of the darkness of their skin; I've had two of my friends here describe themselves as "black," while praising my lighter skin.

That's why I feel partly responsible for the racism that is driving the Buddhist-Muslim conflict. My ancestors convinced Burmese people that white skin was best, and now they're taking out that prejudice on Muslim and Indian people.

Adela did not insert in her blog that she wondered whether her light skin was the source of Thiha's interest in her, if indeed he was interested at all. It was an unfair advantage, but she would've had a hard time giving it up, even if giving it up had been possible.

This is the kind of karma I can understand: white people messed up the world, and it's my job to help fix it. I think it's really time for the international community to get involved. Even Aung San Suu Kyi, who's a hero of the Burmese democracy movement, hasn't stood up for Muslims who are being attacked.

Would Ko Oo be disappointed in Suu Kyi's leadership, she wondered, or would he side with U Nyanika? Adela had been waiting to get in touch with him until she had visited his mother, and now she had another reason to hesitate. What if he hated Muslims, too?

The comments that followed the article Greg had sent were even more disturbing than the facts it contained. Someone who called himself Htet had written, "Even though, Rohingyas were not shot, they are making fake news using the pictures of other events from other countries through the internet and emails. I am sure a lot of you have seen those pictures in which a lot of burnt bodies (it was actually in Africa), a lot of dead bodies with monks around (it was actually in Tibet), a lot of dead bodies on a river bank (the Tsunami pictures) and etc."

Adela remembered the photo of the burned corpse in the *New York Times*. Could it have been fake? It was hard to imagine journalistic fraud on that level. Yet she could not rule it out. And in truth Htet's theory seemed more coherent than the comments of his adversaries. Someone called "Rohingya Re Info Bd" had written, "Thank you very much racist Rakhine Buddhist for your own hands fake or fabricated history against Rohingya Muslims Ethnic. ... Be careful Please for false or own fabricated history against Rohingya Muslims Ethnic, who used to live from very earlier period of 7th century in Rakhine State Myanmar(Burma)." Another commenter insisted the journalist was only taking the Rohingyas' side because she was Muslim herself. Yet another predicted that Western media would not report this crisis because of anti-Muslim bias.

What confused Adela most was that non-Burmese people seemed to have entered the fray. Someone named "Heather," who had better grammar than the others, took the side of the Buddhists, and "Andrew" had written several paragraphs in support of the thesis that Burmese Buddhists were acting "like Nazis." Adela thought of commenting herself, but she was afraid of getting trolled; Htet seemed to be lying in wait for anyone who dared to comment and unleashing a screed of ungrammatical fury.

I guess my meditation retreat kind of complicated my feelings about the conflict. I'm not religious at all, but Buddhism makes sense to me. Life *is* suffering—more for some people than others, of course. Goodwill for all beings is the most amazing thing I've ever experienced (see my previous post "What I Learned on My Meditation Retreat").

But then how can Buddhists hate and kill Muslims just because they aren't citizens, or because they have dark skin, or because some Muslim people committed crimes? I don't know that much about Islam, but I think that like Buddhism, it's a religion of peace. When I think of how Muslim people back home have been discriminated against, it's just sad to realize that it's happening all over the world. Rakhine Buddhists say—

Adela paused. U Nyanika, she realized, was the only Rakhine Buddhist she'd ever met. It wouldn't be credible to base her theory about what his people were like only on him. Maybe he was just a jerk. And she had to admit that some things he'd said were right: she'd checked in *Insurgency and the Politics of Ethnicity*, and Muslim separatists did have an army in Rakhine State before Burma gained independence. But the book also said that in the 1960s these same Muslim separatists had worked together with Rakhine nationalists in fighting the central government. Either of these facts would have complicated what she'd already written in her blog.

She longed to talk through it with someone. But who? The monks were clearly biased. Even U Pyinnya, who seemed the most reasonable, accepted the basic premises of U Nyanika's argument. Daw Pancavati had a good heart, but she wasn't interested in politics—to her, the violence would only provide more proof that life was suffering. Adela hadn't met any Muslims in Burma, and she didn't expect to. She considered asking Bhante, but she couldn't think of a more diplomatic way to phrase the question. What would she ask? "Do you agree with U Nyanika that 99 percent of Muslims are evil?" If he said yes—if he, this man who had guided her toward her little glimpse of paradise—believed something so obviously false, what would she do then? Leave the monastery? Before she'd even kissed Thiha?

She couldn't figure it out by herself, and she couldn't let go of it. The Buddhist-Muslim conflict had started to seem like the thread running through all the experiences she'd had since she'd come to Burma. Somehow, she knew, Thiha would be tied to it as well. The conflict compelled her to stay in Burma, as if it were unfolding in the world for her own enrichment, an experiment in human nature carried out to foster her insight and growth. So Adela refreshed the article and watched, fascinated and repelled by the way the comments multiplied, snaking down the page like the branches of a river flooding its banks.

PATIENCE

When English classes resumed several days later, the monks were eager to hear about Adela's retreat. She described each of her insights as carefully as she could, but there was some debate about their import. U Agga, who was the least skilled in English, concluded from Adela's description that if she kept practicing she could become something called a sotapanna.

"Little more meditation, then you never reborn as animal!" he said.

U Nyanika seemed offended by this suggestion, and he delivered one of his lectures in Burmese, which was as usual eventually silenced by a few words from the brooding U Suriya.

When Adela asked what they were talking about, U Pyinnya gave a thumbs up sign. "Sayama Sabeh do her first retreat—very good!" This summary could not possibly have represented the monks' discussion with any faithfulness, but Adela had learned not to expect any reliable translation of words that were spoken about her in Burmese. Two people would tell her three different things on various occasions, with equal seriousness. She let it go.

Later that day, when she looked up "sotapanna" on Wikipedia, she laughed at the idea that she might qualify. Sotapannas, or Stream Enterers, were meditators who had practiced diligently, breaking the first three fetters to this worldly life: their belief in a self, their doubts about Buddhism, and their clinging to rites and rituals.

Adela realized she must have overstated her progress when she reported her experiences to the monks. She was beset with doubts, and the rituals were the part of Buddhism she liked best. Although she'd promised herself she would meditate regularly, she hadn't done it at all since her retreat ended. However, she did faithfully attend the evening chanting. The sounds had slowly sunk into her mind, and she could even join in on several prayers. Sometimes she heard the words in her dreams. She didn't know what they meant, but she thought, as Bhante had said about karma, that she didn't need to understand. The chanting sounded as mysterious and significant to her as it had from the beginning, and hearing it relaxed her. This attitude did not seem appropriate for a Stream Enterer.

Something else in the Wikipedia entry caught Adela's eye. Stream Enterers were no longer capable of committing the "worst actions": murdering their parents or monks, injuring a Buddha, or "deliberately creating a schism in the monastic community." Why, she wondered, would anyone deliberately create a schism in the monastic community? Or how would one do so by accident?

Adela may not have been a Stream Enterer, but her blog readers were duly impressed by her foray into meditation. "I have to admit your blog is coming together very nicely," Ms. Alvarez noted. Her mother was at first incredulous, then proud, that Adela had remained silent for ten days. "I had my doubts," her mother wrote to her in an email, "but I think Burma is turning out to be a really good experience for you! Just stay healthy, sweetheart." Adela's father recounted being beaten with sticks on a Zen retreat he'd done in his youth, which was his way of telling Adela that she'd done something worthwhile. Adela finally had a chance to compose a long email to Lena explaining the disjointed messages she'd been sending for the past few days, and Lena's response popped up soon enough: "Told you Burma was going to be awesome! Dysentery? Enlightenment? Hot temple helpers? I should have come with you."

Although Adela had, of course, posted nothing about her incipient romance on her blog, she had waxed poetic about Burmese food and her meditation accomplishments. Picking up the thread, a junior from her world lit class commented rather dismissively on her photos of mango trees and Buddha statues: "It's like that movie *Eat Pray Love.*" Just reading the word "love" made Adela blush and look over her shoulder.

❀

The next time Thiha came close enough for Adela to speak to, she was on the Reuters website, reading "Special Report: Plight of Muslim Minority Threatens Myanmar Spring." He was picking mangoes from the tree outside the office. She wondered if he had been assigned this task, or whether he had chosen it because he knew she might be there. The latter possibility emboldened her, and she turned away from her computer to face him. As always, they stared at each other for several moments before either of them could think of anything to say.

"What are you reading?"

"Come see." Adela did not want to shout across the courtyard about Muslims.

He put down his basket of mangoes, came into the office, and pulled up a chair. It was a muggy afternoon. She breathed in carefully: laundry detergent, mango sap, the smell of their sweat mixing in the air between them. Adela tried to note her sensations with equanimity, as she would have if she were meditating. Heart beating. Sweat on upper lip.

Thiha leaned in to look at the screen, and Adela sat back and gulped water from her bottle. She wondered if the two of them looked suspicious, huddled over her laptop. Finally, he sat back.

"What do you think?" he asked.

"It's . . . crazy."

"Yes, crazy."

Not this again, Adela thought. She had to be more direct than she had been with the monks. She took a deep breath.

"Actually, I think that whatever happened in the past, the Rohingya and the Rakhine people should both have human rights."

She waited for him to say, as the spokesperson for Aung San Suu Kyi's party had, that the Rohingya were "not our citizens"; or that they were "dark brown" and "ugly as ogres," as one government official had said; or even to say, as President Thein Sein had, that "vengeance and anarchy" had to be stopped with military force.

Thiha just grunted, as if her point were obvious.

"Why doesn't Suu Kyi speak up?" she asked.

"Thein Sein put her in a difficult position. She defends Rohingya, she lose many vote for our next election. She defends Rakhine, international community criticize her. The military lets this conflict go on purpose. People must be distract from the other mistakes of government."

It was by far the most reasonable analysis Adela had heard.

"But why are people so racist?"

Thiha chuckled. "We are poor. Group above always oppress to the one below. Especially since British time. And . . ." he said, shaking his head, "like you say, we are racism."

He was smart, thought Adela. When he laughed, his face looked younger, almost boyish.

"Your English is good. Where did you learn it?"

"In prison."

Adela nodded, trying not to look surprised.

"I was there three years after Saffron Revolution. I am release in October 2011."

Adela thought of the photos Ko Oo had shown her: thousands of people marching in the streets, monks facing down soldiers with guns, bloodied sandals left behind as people fled from the army. She flipped her laptop shut and pointed to the Saffron Revolution sticker from Ko Oo.

"Yeah, I know about the protests. Were you a monk?"

"No. At that time I was medical student."

Adela wanted to pause the conversation and go over everything she'd learned about him. He did not hate Muslims. He was brilliant. Medical student. Three years in prison.

"Why do you stay at the monastery now?"

As if this question reminded him of his duties, he looked back at his basket of mangoes.

"I tell you another time."

Adela wondered if he was making an excuse to talk to her again, or whether her question was too personal. Maybe he had family problems or couldn't find a job. She hoped his story wasn't as sad as Daw Pancavati's.

"OK."

He stood up.

"Good to talk to you," said Adela, rather formally. She considered putting out her hand to shake his, but her palms were sticky.

"OK. Bye."

She opened the computer again so as not to watch him walk away. The report on Muslims in Myanmar was still there, but the words looked impossibly small. How had she been able to read them? When Adela was sure he was out of sight, she turned around and stared at the mango tree, letting her eyes go blurry as the leaves waved in the breeze.

※

It became their routine. Thiha would find an excuse to stroll by the office in the afternoon, and they'd sit across the table talking, sometimes for a few minutes, once for almost an hour. Adela learned that he was twenty-four years old, he'd been born in Yangon, his father was dead, and his mother was a seamstress. He was the oldest of five siblings, but one brother had died as a baby. He loved his youngest sister most; she was fifteen. He wanted her to be able to attend a good high school, but the fees and bribes were high. He dreamed of continuing his medical studies abroad, perhaps in Australia or the United States.

Given these hopes, Adela didn't understand why he was at the monastery. Shouldn't he be working to support his family, at least? She wanted to ask him directly, but it seemed rude. She was also eager to know what prison had been like, but he avoided that topic.

Instead, he told her stories of his childhood. Adela hung on every detail, as she had with Ko Oo's and Daw Pancavati's stories. But while those two had talked, she'd looked off into the distance, trying to visualize each scene in her mind. While Thiha spoke, she watched him, being sure to move her gaze from his lips to his hands to his eyes so she wouldn't stare at any part of him for too long. It was during these afternoons, listening to his low voice above the hum of the cicadas, that she began to think of him as her own, although they'd never touched. At first they'd both look away when their eyes met, but soon they were indulging in longer glances, during which both of them would forget to speak, and then Thiha would have trouble finding his place in the story he'd been telling.

He'd been just a baby during the 1988 demonstrations, but his father, who was a journalist, had told him about Aung San Suu Kyi's speech to the huge crowd that had gathered at the Shwedagon Pagoda just before the crackdown. Thiha had grown up in tea shops, listening to his father speak in code to other journalists, communicating their dissatisfaction with the system while avoiding words like "democracy" and "human rights." "They" were always the military junta; sometimes his father would describe something as "green," the color of an army uniform, to indicate its association with the government. "She" was always Suu Kyi; sometimes "he" was Suu Kyi's father, Aung San, the leader who'd been assassinated at the Secretariat Building.

Thiha's father died when he was eleven, in a bus accident on a dangerous stretch of road in Mon State. After that Thiha's mother had to take care of the family on her own. Even though his father had never been an outright dissident, the rumors that he associated with members of the opposition made it hard for her to find work. With four kids to take care of, she had to stay up late at night sewing to earn enough money for the family. When the electricity went out, she strained her eyes to work by candlelight. But she kept Thiha in school, as his father had made her promise she would.

"You must miss her, living here at the monastery," Adela said, hoping to unearth his reasons for being here.

"Sometimes yes. But she is with me," he said, touching his chest. "She teach me a lot, when I am a child."

"Like what?"

"She teaches me to be patient."

"Patient how?"

He chuckled. "She do not answer my questions."

"Really?"

"Yes," he said. "Many Burmese parent are like this. The child ask 'Why? Why?' and 'What is this one, what is that one?' The parent, they do not answer."

"Huh."

"At that time, I feel frustrated. Also, she is very different from my father. My father, when I ask a question, he give some answer to me. But my mother never answer me. When my father pass away, I ask her, 'Why they do not fix that road? Many people have died there.' She do not answer, she tell me to pray to the Buddha for the good rebirth for my father."

"It seems like a good question to me."

"No," said Thiha, with conviction that startled Adela. "Not really a good question. How can she answer this one? Why they do not fix the road, this is not for me to know when I am a small boy. Later, what she teach me even save my life," he said.

He paused. She thought he might give her a specific example, but he continued cryptically. "There are some time when we cannot ask the question out loud. We must keep this question in our mind. Slowly, we find the answer by ourself."

"Huh," Adela repeated. Her parents had taken pains to answer all of her outlandish questions when she was growing up. She thought of the faded bumper sticker on her father's car: "Question Authority." Of course, they hadn't been living in a police state.

Thiha didn't ask Adela much about herself, and she was glad. What was there to tell, compared to his life? Still, sometimes she felt like she was interviewing him, or gathering information for her blog. He expressed his views without the hesitance Adela had come to expect from Burmese people, without the "only my opinion" that U Pyinnya often tacked onto his statements. On the other hand, he wasn't close-minded, like U Nyanika. He seemed straightforward and confident, but not egotistical, like Greg. He never offered his opinion unless Adela asked, and he made no attempt to convince her if she disagreed. Adela worked hard to earn his rare, beaming smiles.

Sometimes Thiha was busy around the monastery and they were only able to catch each other's eyes at mealtime. Adela wondered if anyone noticed: Daw Pancavati, for instance, or U Pyinnya, who must have seen them talking in the office. There's nothing wrong with talking, Adela told herself.

But for whatever reason, her standing with the monks was changing. Lighthearted moments in class grew rare, and the monks seemed to be losing focus. U Nyanika didn't do the work Adela assigned any more. Instead, he wrote on any topic he chose, and then demanded that Adela correct his grammar, although he'd argue with her when she did. U Agga often rested his head sleepily on the table, and sometimes he didn't come to class at all. U Pyinnya tried to keep everyone's energy up, and U Suriya was as silent as ever, but as a group they seemed subtly disillusioned with Adela. They stopped calling her Sayama Sabeh and called her Ma Sabeh, or even just Sabeh, which U Pyinnya had insisted at the beginning would be disrespectful.

July was nearly over, and Adela had a little over a month left before her return to the United States. If it hadn't been for Thiha, she would have found a reason to leave the monastery, maybe go to Rakhine State and see for herself how things were there. As it was, she counted down the days reluctantly. What if it was time for her to go, and they'd gotten no further than talking in the office? She didn't want to be patient, she didn't want to be a Stream Enterer. She wanted to kiss Thiha.

AN INVITATION

Adela was loitering in the office one afternoon, scanning her peripheral vision for Thiha, when a man approached with a rake and basket. He stood at the edge of the patio, eyeing the mango leaves the tree had dropped overnight. Adela had seen him before, usually from a distance as he swept the paths in the early morning. She recognized him by the gray cotton scarf that was always wound around his head like a turban. He was one of those people whose status was inscrutable to her. Did he live in the monastery? Was he the official sweeper, or did he pitch in sometimes to earn good karma? From this close, she could see that he was exceptionally thin, as if his skin hung over a skeleton of ropes and wire. He was wearing the most decrepit pair of flip-flops Adela had ever seen. He wanted to rake up the leaves, she concluded, but he didn't want to disturb her.

"It's OK," she said, beckoning him forward. "Ya ba deh." She lifted her feet from the ground to show that he could sweep under them.

He stood by wordlessly for a moment, running a hand over his wispy beard.

Then he called out to her hoarsely from the edge of the patio: "Htamin sa pi bi la?"

Adela had gotten used to the traditional greeting, which had seemed so intrusive to her at first: "Have you eaten rice yet?"

"Sa pi ba bi," she responded. It was polite always to say that one had eaten, or risk obligating the person asking to offer you a meal.

"Nyaza sa pi bi la?"

Adela found it odd that he'd ask her if she'd eaten dinner; it was after four in the afternoon, and no one at the monastery ate dinner. No, she called back, she had not eaten dinner.

He jerked his head to the right, once, then again. Adela stared at him.

He pressed his fingers together and raised them to his lips as if scooping up rice, and again jerked his head toward the other end of the compound. He was inviting her.

The thought of a real dinner, rice and curry, hooked her right in the gut. Sometimes she could smell food cooking at this time in the afternoon, the odors wafting in on the breeze as the neighborhood housewives prepared food for their families: chilies hitting hot oil, spices pounded into a fragrant paste. Adela sniffed. She could almost taste it in the air, something rich and meaty, salty and sour. She shut her laptop.

"Here?" she asked in English, in her confusion. "Where?"

He glanced over his shoulder, then turned and began to walk away, trailing his arm out behind him and clicking his tongue softly as if she were one of the dusty kittens who congregated around the kitchen after mealtimes.

Adela slipped her laptop into her bag and followed him, realizing only as she crossed the patio that she'd miss Thiha that day. She thought of leaving him a note. But what would it say? She scanned around for him one last time, then followed the man in the gray turban.

They walked, a few paces apart, across the courtyard and past Bhante's hall, into the grove of banana trees where Daw Pancavati lived. They crossed paths with no one; the helpers were preparing for teatime, and everyone else rested amidst the sleepy hum of the cicadas. Adela didn't usually walk at this time of day. The heat peaked as the afternoon edged toward evening, as if the sun were trying to sear the earth with its memory. Now, the monastery seemed surreally empty of human life. Adela could feel the sun etching itself onto the back of her neck. Golden light drenched the trees, and she wondered why the green leaves didn't frizzle up and burn.

They arrived at a small gate in the wooden fence that edged the furthest reaches of the compound. Adela's escort pulled it open and waved her through. She squinted into the narrow lane beyond. The man mimed eating rice once again and beckoned insistently. She wasn't even hungry anymore. And she hadn't brought any money, if that was what he wanted. The sun beat against the side of her face, and she held up her hand to block its rays.

"Umm ..." she said, turning back in the direction they'd come.

But the man looked so intent, standing there sweating rivers and motioning her through the gate. Adela saw that his eyes were an odd color, almost golden brown, nearly the same color as his skin. He was good, she thought. He meant no harm.

She squeezed past him and found herself in an alley where mud, dried in the sun and wetted by the rains, had solidified into an uneven pavement. Blossoming shrubs, yellow and pink, lined a tall fence opposite her. A sparsely feathered rooster pecked at a heap of garbage in the shade. On the right, built against the monastery's wall, was a row of shacks cobbled together with corrugated metal. The man ducked into one of them, pulled aside a soiled curtain, and gestured Adela into its dim interior. She was so desperate to get out of the sun that she shouldered her way inside.

Once Adela's eyes adjusted to the darkness, she was startled to see that there were two other people already occupying the small space. A woman crouched in one corner, her face so heavily lined that it looked as if wrinkles had been chiseled in stone. A toddler crawled on the dirt floor, chewing on something wet and ragged—the pit of a mango? The old woman's lips sunk inward over her toothless gums, and her eyes glinted inkily in the dimness.

Adela turned to find the man who had brought her; he was just leaving, and through the doorway she saw him hurrying off down the alley. Her head nearly touched the shack's roof, but there seemed to be no place for her to comfortably sit. She squeezed around a low table, backed into the unoccupied corner, and lowered herself to the ground. A calendar, the only decoration, was opened to March 2011; a pale-skinned woman wearing a strapless yellow dress smiled down on them. It took a moment for Adela to realize that she was no cooler in the hut's shade. The metal walls scorched her through her clothing, and the smells of urine and perfumed soap stung her nostrils.

"Saun ba," the old woman croaked. Wait.

Adela realized she should not have come. She thought yearningly of the office, the fresh air, and of Thiha, who would find their table empty.

No one knew where she was. Her mother's misgivings about her trip came back to her, and Ko Oo's warning: "You cannot know what can happen." The phrase "white slavery" leapt to her mind unbidden, and she laughed out loud, causing the toddler to burst into tears. The woman pulled the child onto her lap, smacked the back of his legs, and then patted him until he fell silent.

It was a ridiculous thought. Adela was in a metal shack not five steps from the monastery's gate, and she could leave whenever she wanted.

Except that she couldn't make herself. The man had invited her. He had insisted. Moreover, every time she stirred as if to go, the old woman patted the air preemptively. Every now and then, a phlegmy cough racked her body. Adela tried not to inhale too deeply, as if her taking shallow breaths would protect her from the spores of respiratory illness all around her. It was surely teatime by now. The only way Adela could know for sure was by opening her laptop, which seemed an incongruous thing to do in a dark metal shack. So she settled herself into a cross-legged position and resigned herself to waiting. She would take the opportunity to meditate.

There was no need to close her eyes. She let them go unfocused, shadows playing across her vision. As she watched her breath go in and out, feeling her belly rise and fall, calm settled over her. Her mind let go of her surroundings, or rather, she felt herself melt into them. In the darkness, she could barely sense the outlines of her body; there was only a pervasive warmth. Her breath caught in her throat, and the old woman coughed, as if they were one body.

She thought, longingly, of Thiha's body. If he were here, they wouldn't have to speak, she wouldn't have to arrange her face into normal expressions. She could just lean into him, let their mouths meet, as they had in her dream. The thought left her strangely drugged, her limbs heavy, as if on the verge of sleep.

It was a feeling like fever, and it took her back to the days of her illness, when she'd lain on the tarp in Daw Pancavati's room. Now, as then, she glimpsed infancy, a time before separateness. The toddler had fallen asleep splayed on the old woman's lap, his taut belly pressed against her soft one, his face deep in her empty breasts. Adela was able to imagine, for moments at a time, that it was she who was locked in that sleepy embrace. Somehow her consciousness slipped in between their bodies, into the warm, sweaty space in which flesh is one. Did she reach out and touch them? When she moved her fingers, she found that her hands were still resting in her lap.

Against the cloth hung over the door, as through the mouth of a cave, Adela saw the silhouette of passersby. The heat had subsided as the light turned from orange to purple. Two men, grunting and panting, struggled to maneuver a two-wheeled cart over the lane's rutted surface. The carcass of some animal, its legs jutting into the air, bumped along inside of it.

Adela realized she'd been clenching her jaw for some time. Why? Her tongue felt thick and dry, impossibly big inside her mouth. She felt for her water bottle and remembered seeing it on the office table when she'd turned to look for Thiha one last time.

With each breath, thirst climbed a little higher in her throat, rising like a panic through her body. Her mouth felt glued shut, her saliva sticky and sour. She hadn't felt so thirsty since that day at the hospital in Yangon when she'd poured water down the throat of the dying Muslim woman. Had that woman's tongue felt this way, like a slab of dough in her mouth? Had Adela herself even been thirsty then, or had she only realized that day for the first time what thirst was? When she turned to look at the woman and child, she saw only a pile of rags. A shudder went through her, and she rubbed her eyes and squinted—their two forms returned. *Metta isn't the opposite of lust,* she told Bhante, imagining him watching the scene from above. *It's the opposite of fear.* I will count to ten, she thought, and then I will get up and leave and find water.

By the time she'd counted to eight, the man with the turban elbowed aside the curtain. In one hand, he held a steaming bowl, which he set on the low table in front of Adela. He thrust a small, ice-cold can into her hand. Adela felt for the tab, popped open the can, and poured its contents down her throat.

The liquid was so cold that at first she couldn't taste it. Only when she swallowed did she feel its choking sweetness, like cough medicine, so sugary that its tinny aftertaste was almost bitter.

Longing for something to take the taste out of her mouth, Adela turned to the bowl in front of her. She could make out the joint of some kind of animal half-submerged in an oily broth. Despite its appearance, it smelled good, musky and rich. She dipped the spoon in the broth, brought it to her lips. It wasn't pork or beef, but something she hadn't had before: mutton, maybe, with cinnamon and pepper.

The man, woman, and child watched Adela intently as she slurped up the broth. She explored the knuckle of meat with her spoon, but it seemed entirely inedible, a mass of cartilage and gristle. Adela thought of the days she'd lain weakened by dysentery, and she felt nausea spiking in her belly. If they hadn't been watching her so carefully, she might have slipped the tangle of sinews into her bag to avoid eating it, even at the risk of getting the greasy mess all over her laptop. With the last sip of broth, she felt a shard of bone clink against her teeth, and then it was gone, pricking her soft throat as it tumbled into her belly.

Adela tasted the iron warmth of her own blood. Even the horrible fizzy drink would have been better, but she'd drunk it all in a few gulps.

"Sa ba, sa ba," the man encouraged her. There was no way she'd get out of the shack without eating the lump of flesh in her bowl. *I will become a vegetarian*, she thought lucidly, *when this is over.*

"Sa kaung la?" the man asked anxiously.

Adela assured him that the food tasted good, then stabbed her spoon into the mass, wrestled off a chunk, and shoved it into her mouth. It was stringy in parts, gelatinous in others, like she imagined a brain might be. With effort, she swallowed. Grease filled her sinuses. Three more bites and she would be free. With a burst of energy, she scarfed down the meat, taking perverse enjoyment in feeling the little tendons pop between her teeth.

"Jayzu beh," she managed. "Sorry, naw, I've got to go." Finally free, she stood to go. But as she tried to rise, something held her down. Commotion, a tangle of limbs, fingers caught in Adela's hair. She heard her own sharp cry of confusion, then the ripping of fabric as she pulled herself free, burst through the curtain, and stumbled out onto the street, her heart hammering in her chest.

Outside, night had come, and a breeze passed over Adela's damp skin. Whatever had happened, she had gotten out. The shrubs loomed above her like swaying masses of hair. Adrenaline coursed through her belly. From inside the shack, hushed voices rose and fell. Adela limped away, realizing she'd twisted her ankle in the turmoil. She felt for her laptop, and looked down to see its rounded white corner in the darkness, poking out of a long rip in her shoulder bag. She stumbled up the alley, groped for the gate, pushed her body through. No one followed her.

As Adela set out toward the dormitory, her heartbeat returned to normal. She giggled in embarrassment. What a ridiculous thing to do, bursting out of the shack that way! She'd have to apologize to the sweeper in the morning, and thank him properly for the meal. He'd probably spent a good deal of money on it. She should have offered to share the food with them.

It was a pleasant evening, and Adela filled her nostrils with the scent of the night-blooming jasmine that grew against the back gate. She was annoyed that she'd twisted her ankle, but other than that, she was unscathed by her strange evening. She would have to tell Thiha, but make it sound like an adventure, and leave out her abrupt departure.

"Thamee!"

Daw Pancavati was standing on the porch of her hut, holding a yellow candle melted onto a tin can.

Adela limped up to the nun's small house.

"Why you do not come to teatime? No one knows where you are!"

"Oh, sorry! Well, it was kind of weird, but the sweeper—you know, the guy who rakes up leaves?"

Daw Pancavati's eyes widened in alarm.

"Yes?"

"He invited me over for dinner."

"He invite you for dinner?" Daw Pancavati looked incredulous. "Where?"

"His . . . house." She pointed toward the back gate.

"That man does not have any house. He stay here in the monastery."

"Oh, well, I don't know whose house it was, then. There was a woman, and a kid?"

The nun sighed, seemingly with relief. "Oh, he take you to his Auntie. You eat food with them?"

Adela sat down on the edge of the porch and cradled her ankle in her hand.

"Yeah. I mean, they didn't eat."

"He buys you food from outside?"

"I guess so."

The intensity of the interrogation was tiresome. Her head hurt and she remembered that she was still very thirsty.

"Could I have some water?"

The nun disappeared inside and returned with a dented aluminum cup filled with cool water.

"Oh my god, that's good," she muttered, draining it in a few gulps. The force of her exclamation embarrassed her. And what a thing to say to a nun. She set the cup aside as delicately as she could.

"You are OK?" asked Daw Pancavati, fingering the torn edge of Adela's bag.

"Of course. He was just being nice. It was nice to, um, get out."

Daw Pancavati popped into her hut again and returned with a needle and thread. She pulled Adela's bag away from her and began repairing the rip by candlelight.

"You should not go out at night," she said, looking down at her work.

"OK."

"This is not like America."

"What do you mean?"

Daw Pancavati sighed. "Thamee, I cannot explain everything for you."

THE SO-CALLED ROHINGYA

When Adela saw Thiha the next day, she didn't mention her excursion. The more she thought about her experience, the more ashamed she felt of her own behavior. She had insulted a man's hospitality, suspected him of evil intentions, for no reason other than her own paranoia. No one had tried to stop her from leaving the shack. She'd stood on the tasseled edge of her bag, she concluded, then tripped over the table. To make it clear that she had no hard feelings, she'd waved and smiled at the sweeper when she'd seen him near the dining hall that morning, but he had not looked up from his work. Maybe Daw Pancavati had scolded him. It was the first time she'd felt anything but admiration for the nun, and it unsettled her.

She decided she would not tell Thiha either. She didn't want him to think she was like the other volunteer in the MVU training, afraid of being attacked by men, prejudiced against Burmese people. He might have the same reaction Daw Pancavati did: she shouldn't have gone in the first place.

Instead, they talked about the Rohingya.

"So when did they come to Burma?" Adela asked, leaning over toward Thiha so that her hair trailed against his shoulder as they clicked through a slideshow on the Radio Free Asia website. "Rohingyas Pushed Back to Sea" was the title. It showed a boat packed with men fleeing persecution in Burma, turned back by Bangladeshi authorities.

Thiha shrugged. "No one can say. Maybe recently, maybe not recently. Our history is very confused. Every group, they say they come to Burma first. Ask the Karen man, ask the Burman man, ask the Mon and Rakhine. All will say they are the first."

"Why does it matter?"

"Really, it does not matter. The British write these histories, to split the blood of our people. British oppress to Burman oppress to Rakhine oppress to Rohingya oppress to someone else. When we fight each other we cannot fight them. Now the army does the same thing, letting Buddhist and Muslim fight."

Adela stared at him.

"What?" he said.

"You're so goddamn smart," she said.

Their eyes met for a moment, and then he turned his face away and looked at the ground, grinning.

"Sorry," she added, but she was not.

❀

This exchange was fresh in Adela's mind the following day when U Nyanika brought in a history of Rakhine State, which he'd written in place of the assignment she'd given them to describe a happy memory from their childhoods. When his turn came to read out loud, he produced this statement:

HISTORY OF THE RAKHINE STATE AND THE SO-CALLED ROHINGYA

We Rakhine lived independently in our own kingdom from the 4th century BC. In 1430 to 1530 AD we had our Golden Age of Mrauk-U. Our Kings at Mrauk-U take tribute from Mon, Burman, Shan, and Bengali rulers. This is why we find some Islam coins in Mrauk-U. In 1600s to 1700s Rakhine has its "Dark Age." Burma kings overtake and destroy Mrauk-U city. They take our Mahi Muni Buddha, most sacred Image, to Mandalay, until today. In 1886, British have overtook all of Myanmar including the Rakhine State. At that time, many people from India and Bengali come to Myanmar. They are some Muslim and some Hindu. We Rakhine become the minority in some place. But only in 1950 do "so-called Rohingya" appear. Quoting Dr. Aye Chan of Kanda University of International Studies, "THEIR CLAIMS OF AN EARLIER HISTORICAL TIE TO BURMA ARE INSUPPORTABLE."

U Nyanika folded his paper and sat down, knitting his bushy eyebrows together.

"Thank you for sharing," said Adela earnestly, not wanting to give him the satisfaction of seeing her roll her eyes. Inwardly, she rebelled against what he'd said. How would this collection of unsupported historical claims justify pushing people out to sea, burning their houses, letting them die?

"Does anyone have any questions or comments for U Nyanika?" she asked the others.

They sat in silence. U Agga furrowed his brow, as if on the verge of saying something, then looked down at the table. Adela realized that if anyone was going to respond to U Nyanika, it would have to be her. She decided to be brave.

"OK. If everything you say is true—"

"Why not true?" interrupted U Nyanika.

"OK, let's say it's true. But so what if these people call themselves Rohingya? How are they hurting you?"

"So-called Rohingya is not Myanmar national race."

"So they're not a national race, they're not citizens, they've only been living here since 1950. Even if all that is true—why can't they stay and live peacefully with the Buddhists? Buddhism is a peaceful religion, right, and so is Islam, so—"

"The Islam is not peace! You see what happen in Sittwe! The rape of our women!" He kept his voice low, but it was filled with passion.

"That was just one incident. The UN even said—"

"UN, NGO, they are bias! They are worse than the British to us. They spread lies, they try to force us, they insult to our culture! So many problem in our country, but the UN, they only care on this one problem—Why?"

U Nyanika's jaw was tense and his eyes looked hard. Adela tried to stop herself from shouting at him.

"Um," she hesitated. "Whose culture? There are many cultures in Burma, as far as I know. I'm not a Myanmar national race, but it's OK for me to be here, right? I'm not hurting anyone."

At this point U Nyanika turned to U Pyinnya and spoke heatedly to him for several minutes. Adela caught her name, but she couldn't read the context. She looked around at the other monks. U Agga grinned anxiously. The others wouldn't meet her eyes.

"What are you guys talking about?" she finally asked. U Pyinnya started to reply, but U Nyanika turned to face her.

"No 'you guys'!" he snarled. "We are monk! You do not understand our country. I say to U Pyinnya long time ago, we should not bring the American lady here to teach us! It is not suitable!"

There was a long silence. Adela's face was hot, and her heart thrummed in her ears. His lip had curled when he spat out the words "American lady," as if he were saying "kala." The boldness she'd felt while they were arguing shrunk away, and suddenly she felt hideous, clumsy, and ignorant. Even afraid. Why had she thought she belonged here? If they didn't want her, she would go. She felt tears coming, and she didn't stop them. She wanted U Nyanika to see that he'd hurt her.

"I'm sorry," she said quietly.

The other monks looked mortified, but on whose behalf it was not clear. Adela's chin quivered, and she longed for a hug or at least a pat on the back, but of course the monks weren't allowed to touch her. She sat there miserably alone, sniffling, while U Nyanika gathered his notebook and pens. His "HISTORY OF THE RAKHINE STATE" drifted to the floor, caught up in the breeze of his robes as he left.

"I'm really sorry," said Adela, wiping her eyes, remembering not to call them "guys" again.

"Sayama does not intend to make a problem," said U Pyinnya glumly.

"No, I really didn't, I just asked him to write about his family!"

"Rakhine people are very hot temper," whispered U Sila, fanning his face with his hands. "This is why, so much problem there," he pronounced.

Although U Sila's theory did accord with Adela's one experience of a Rakhine person, resorting to ethnic stereotypes didn't seem productive. But she did want them to know that she hadn't chosen her position at the monastery.

"I feel bad if you didn't want an American teacher. MVU just put me here, and I didn't even know I'd be teaching monks—"

"No, no," said U Pyinnya. "The MVU does right. There are no male teacher available at this time, they already inform to us."

So the issue was her sex, not her nationality. Apparently her lack of any skill except speaking English had trumped the gender of the pre-med guys who were sent to the clinic. Adela had thought it strange that they'd let a girl teach monks, given the strictly separated dormitories. There were also a host of gender-related rules that Daw Pancavati made sure she followed, such as hanging her underwear on a hidden clothesline to dry, and avoiding certain parts of the pagoda. When Adela asked her friend to justify these practices, the nun had explained that exposure to women could hurt the monks' dignity. It was hard for Adela to believe that monks' dignity would be so fragile, and in principle she objected to double standards. Lena would have said the culture was sexist, plain and simple.

Yet Adela could have argued against her. Many of the richest donors to the monastery were women, and most of the meditators were as well. Moreover, the community had bent the rules for Adela, allowing her to eat fruit in the evening and forgiving her when she forgot the honorific terms that would have made her Burmese speech more polite. Therefore, it had seemed only fair to accept what seemed to her like superstitions.

As Adela analyzed these matters, she felt her pulse return to normal. If U Nyanika didn't want to come to English class, then he could go on writing his grammatically incorrect diatribes by himself.

"No problem for us," U Pyinnya assured her.

"Well, OK, if you say so. I mean, if you want me to do anything differently," she said, looking around at them, "you just have to tell me. I think it's really important that we can be honest with each other."

Everyone nodded.

"Well ... does anyone else want to read what they wrote about their family?"

U Agga had a written an amusing account about the time his brother had left him in charge of the family's water buffalo, and the morning regained some semblance of normalcy. U Nyanika's departure seemed to have reset their relations. The monks began addressing her once again as "Sayama Sabeh." When they left that day, they all stood up in unison, as they'd done in the first few days, and chorused, "Thank you, Sayama!" before leaving for lunch.

Adela was satisfied with the resolution they'd managed. She'd survived a monk mutiny with her dignity intact, and she'd rebutted U Nyanika's racist tirade. If she'd never spoken up, she reasoned, U Nyanika would have continued to dominate the class, bullying them all with his so-called histories. Adela even convinced herself that she had put into words what the other monks thought but were afraid to say.

Yet during lunch, doubt seized her. She saw U Nyanika sitting at Bhante's right hand. What would he say about her? Would they make her leave? She hadn't done anything wrong, she insisted to herself. They had asked for a volunteer English teacher. If anyone was to blame, it was Sarah. She could have waited for a suitable male volunteer to come along. Adela could have gotten a position in Yangon, where she would have been able to walk freely around the city and meet all sorts of interesting people. But as she rewrote the last few months in her mind, she realized she was unwilling to give up what she had gained at Yadana: Daw Pancavati, Bhante, and especially Thiha.

After lunch, she walked Daw Pancavati back to her hut. Adela hadn't seen as much of her since the retreat, and certainly not as much as when she'd been sick. Adela missed her friend, and she wanted reassurance about the incident with U Nyanika. Thus, although Adela sensed that the nun would rather rest, she relayed the morning's events.

As Adela spoke, Daw Pancavati furrowed her brow and let out little grunts of concern.

"U Nyanika leave the class?" she asked when Adela had finished.

"Yeah, but the others stayed, and I think it's going to be fine . . ."

"Thamee, I worry for you."

"Why? Did I do something wrong? You should have heard what U Nyanika was saying. It was so hateful."

"Thamee, he is the monk."

"But even monks can be wrong, right?"

She did not answer.

"U Pyinnya said everything was OK," Adela assured her.

"OK, U Pyinnya say, then it is OK. But please do not talk about those thing again. Sometime it is very—" Daw Pancavati searched for the word. "Very sensitive for us. It is better to forget."

Adela knew her friend was trying to look out for her, but she found herself resentfully composing a blog post in her mind: **Some Burmese people would rather forget what is happening in Rakhine State. But the Rohingya people filling refugee camps don't have that option. The problem won't go away unless regular people start talking about it. Buddhists and Muslims both contribute to the conflict, but Buddhists have so much more power in Burma. The Rohingya have the UN on their side, but the UN doesn't have any real influence here.**

She thought back to the orientation at MVU, where she'd wondered aloud why the UN hadn't intervened to question the election results. She wondered if by now, her understanding had outpaced that of the other volunteers who had chuckled at her naiveté.

Muslims are the majority in some parts of Rakhine State. Rohingyas have to get permission from the authorities if they want to get married or leave their villages, yet they have no recognition as citizens. That means Buddhist control is like apartheid. Some say it is reaching genocidal dimensions.

To be fair, Adela was borrowing this analysis from an op-ed she'd just seen. But she'd seen the results of these policies firsthand. Or at least, close enough.

Adela wanted to leave and write it all down before she forgot. She thanked Daw Pancavati for the advice and rose to go. The nun motioned for Adela to wait, ducked into her house, and returned with some Burmese candies that her friends had brought from the Delta. "Thagya loun," she said. "Jaggery sweets, from the palm tree sugar." Adela recognized the delicious maple-syrup-flavored balls that sometimes appeared at teatime. She accepted the jar and headed back to the office, stopping to grab her copy of *Burmese Days*, a passage from which she wanted to include in her new post.

Soon she'd settled herself at the table, opened the jar of sweets, and thumbed through to the quote she remembered. U Po Kyin, the corrupt Burmese magistrate, had just sent Flory a slanderous letter about the Indian doctor Veraswami. Would Flory defend his only true friend against the mean-spirited attacks of a powerful enemy? Of course not:

> And yet—it was safer to keep out of this business altogether. It is so important (perhaps the most important of all the Ten Precepts of the *pukka sahib*) not to entangle oneself in 'native' quarrels. With Indians there must be no loyalty, no real friendship. Affection, even love—yes ... Even intimacy is allowable, at the right moments. But alliance, partnership, never!

Adela splayed the book on the table and turned to her keyboard. **In one breath, Orwell justifies Flory's relationship with his Burmese concubine and rules out the possibility of true equality between the races. In world lit, we talked a lot about how books are products of their times. Orwell may have been progressive for 1934. Still, Flory's attitude is despicable.**

Would Orwell say I should forget the Rohingya and nod politely when the monks insist Muslims are outsiders? Isn't that insulting in its own way? Shouldn't I pay Burmese people the respect of telling them what I really think? Of course people from anywhere can be friends, can be equals, can—she paused and blushed here—**love each other. If not, my time in Burma has been a waste.**

So absorbed was Adela in this diatribe against Orwell that she didn't even see Thiha approaching. By the time she heard the scrape of a chair, he was already sitting next to her—not in his usual spot across the table.

He chuckled. "So, Ma Sabeh cause some problem."

Adela felt a flush climbing her cheeks. What kind of rumors was U Nyanika spreading? She imagined his claims that she'd insulted the monkhood and stomped on Burmese culture with her corrupting Western female ways. The defensiveness that she had suppressed that morning returned. She turned to face Thiha.

"I didn't do anything wrong. I just told U Nyanika that he was spouting a bunch of racist bullshit."

Thiha raised his eyebrows.

Adela buried her face in her hands, rubbed her eyes, and looked up at him and sighed.

"I didn't say that. I hardly said anything."

He nodded.

"I mean, should I leave? Should I just say this country is none of my business, not my problem, I give up, I'm going home? I don't want to do that. I want to stay here!"

The force of her last statement surprised her.

"Why?" asked Thiha.

Although he spoke quietly, it felt like an accusation. Why would she stay here when people like him were desperate to get out and find opportunities elsewhere? Adela had a choice. She could be anywhere in the world. Why Burma?

She turned and looked out at the mango tree, considering his question. Because I dreamt about the Shwedagon, she thought. Because I like you. Because I'm not just Adela here, I'm Ma Sabeh. Because I found Burma, or Burma found me. Because I do believe, despite my stupid intellectual doubts, that I have been here before, and I did something terrible in my past life to be born in America, and I am lucky to have made my way back home. Because I want to learn to meditate for real. Because the taste of jaggery sweets makes me feel nostalgic for a childhood I can't remember.

Adela felt tears gathering behind her eyes. "I don't know."

They stared out at the compound, not looking at each other. Under the table there was the smallest, lightest, hardly palpable contact between his knee and her knee. Neither of them moved. Adela felt his warmth spread into her body.

So he forgave her. He saw who she was, and he still wanted her.

She pushed the jar of sweets toward him. "They're good."

He smiled. They sat there eating them one by one, until they were gone. Adela took a drink from her water bottle, and then she offered him some. He took a sip. Then he stood up.

"See you later," he said.

That night around ten, there was a knock on her door.

MANGO SEASON

Neither of them spoke. They didn't pretend they were doing anything other than what they were doing. He came in, she put her arms around him, they moved to Adela's bed. She didn't feel cold, but she couldn't stop shivering. He held her against his chest, and Adela felt their hearts beating grotesquely, arhythmically, between them. This is happening, she thought.

They kept their clothes on for a long time. It wasn't until they lay down that their lips brushed together. His mouth tasted savory and sour, like lime and cinnamon, and his lips felt different from Greg's or the other boys she'd kissed. They were more substantial, and up close, the whole architecture of his face was different than she'd expected during her hours of studying it as he spoke. She slid her hands under his shirt and felt his skin warm beneath it, felt the muscles she'd seen by the water tank. She was so completely absorbed by him, and yet the fact of his presence kept surprising her all over again. It was, she thought, like meditating on a person, on body sensations.

They kissed until Adela's mouth was raw. She didn't know what to do next, how to make things progress. Was he just shy? Had he ever done this before? At one point she got up and drank a cup of water, and he motioned for some and drank as well. Then they went back to their strange labor.

Finally, Adela pulled off her shirt. After that it was quick, almost violent. She may have cried; she remembered their faces, wet and close, the smooth skin of his cheek and his eyes like dark pools. That thought came to her again: *Stay here.*

The light in the room changed. He got up and put on his clothes. Still, they didn't speak. Adela let sleep wash over her.

❀

Adela was stabbing someone whose body was covered in a sheet. Her teeth fell out one by one. Her mother was being sucked out to sea by a tidal wave, and Adela couldn't reach her. When she dragged herself to the surface of her dreams, the clock said 9:00. She should be in the office, teaching. She leapt out of bed, dressed, brushed her teeth furiously, and then attempted to walk to the office at a normal pace. The monks were all there.

"Sayama Sabeh is sick?" asked U Pyinnya.

"A little sick," she said, touching her forehead. "A little headache. A little fever. No problem now."

The monks arranged themselves for class.

"Today, let's talk about . . ." she said, faltering, looking around for inspiration, squinting into the sunlight that glared off the tiles outside. "The weather! Maybe some foreigners come here, and they are not used to the weather. How can we help them?"

The monks nodded. Yes, this had happened.

It wasn't until Adela had them engaged in overheated foreigner vs. concerned monk role-plays that she allowed herself to think about what had happened the night before. She felt nauseous with agitation. She had done something irrevocable, unforgivable. She'd had sex in a monastery!

At the same time, she could not stop—*could not stop*—thinking of him. It was fortunate that the monks thought she was ill, because she spent most of the class reclining in her chair like an invalid, with an incongruous smile she couldn't keep off her face. The few hours of sleep she'd gotten had left her dizzy. She couldn't imagine eating, and she couldn't face seeing Thiha from a distance. Yet skipping lunch would be suspicious.

When class ended, she marched to the dining hall, looking straight ahead. Although her body was exhausted, she had an excess of mental energy that tempted her to do something ridiculous, like throw a plate of rice across the room or stand up and scream when everyone was bowing.

Adela made it through lunch without seeing Thiha and then hurried back to her room where she hurled herself onto her bed—the very same bed where they had lain—and stared up at the top bunk, her mind finally blank, until she dozed off.

When she awoke it was dusk, and she felt refreshed. She bounded over to the dining hall and gulped down her juice. Afterward, as she and Daw Pancavati strolled through the banana grove, Adela made conversation by telling her the Burmese words for weather that she'd learned that morning from the monks. The day was aik set set: muggy. It was not as hot as it had been, but the air felt thicker and closer to the earth, like molasses in the lungs. When the sun broke through the clouds, it burned, and when the rain came the earth seemed to steam.

"This weather not good for the mind," said Daw Pancavati.

"I *know*!" Adela agreed, perhaps too heartily.

Daw Pancavati studied her quietly. Adela wondered how much her friend could see of the turmoil in her body. Adela remembered coming home from Edgerton Fields just after meeting Greg; her mother had eyed her suspiciously. "What happened to you?" she'd asked with alarm, as if Adela had shaved her head. "What do you mean?" Adela had asked, unable to stop grinning. Her mother had looked into her daughter's face, and then away. "Oh, you met someone," she'd said, a little embarrassed at how clearly she'd seen it.

In order to avoid something similar happening with Daw Pancavati, Adela was chattier than usual. If she could keep her lips moving, she thought, she'd be fine; staring off into space made her condition obvious. So Adela told the nun about Pomona College, partly to remind herself that her time in Burma was limited, extraneous to her real life. Daw Pancavati listened attentively and asked to know more. Adela described Stanley Quad, with its bubbling fountain, and the sprawling freshman dorm she'd visited as a prospective student. The more she talked about it, the more difficult it was to picture herself there. When she'd first found out she'd gotten in, she'd been ecstatic, even though the thought of leaving the little world of Edgerton Fields intimidated her. Now Pomona seemed almost provincial. If all went as planned, she would be there by September. She would never see the rains yield to the cool blue skies of the dry season, she would never know what could have happened between her and Thiha. She chewed her lip and stared into the distance over Daw Pancavati's shoulder. Everything was happening too fast, or not quickly enough.

※

By seven, Adela was back in her room. She tried to read, then gave up and paced. Thiha would never come to see her again. He had left the monastery. He thought she was an American whore; U Nyanika had sent him to test her, and she had failed. Or he had just lost interest. Bhante would turn up shortly to kick her out of the monastery.

Adela had worked herself up into such a state that when she heard the knock on the door, she froze. She waited, straining her ears, until she heard the slight shuffle of someone turning to go. She ran over and threw open the door. They were both smirking.

Thiha had brought some little oranges and a mango from the tree by the office. That night was different from the first. They talked, and ate, and laughed. They laughed at what they had done the night before, at the silly shyness of it. Again, they spent a great deal of time kissing. Thiha was a messy, surprisingly aggressive kisser, and Adela had to keep scolding him to get him to slow down. After a time, they settled back on her bunk bed and he began peeling the fruit.

"Mango season over. This one is last one."

"What comes next?"

"Thittawthee."

"What's that?"

"Like . . ." he laughed. "Cannot explain."

There were many things he could not explain. For instance, why Adela's feet were so appealing to him.

"So what's the first thing you noticed about me?" she asked.

"Beautiful feet," he said. "I come to the gate, and you are there with your bags. Your feet are very beautiful, very white."

Adela laughed out loud and looked down at her feet, which by now were striped with tan lines from her sandals.

"My feet are white? That's a new one. Why is everyone obsessed with whiteness?"

Although she protested, he had succeeded in making her feel special. No one had ever commented on her feet before.

He shrugged. "I cannot help what I like."

"But you didn't come to the gate. It was U Pyinnya!"

He shook his head. "Not U Pyinnya."

How could their memories have diverged so clearly about their first meeting? Adela vividly remembered U Pyinnya coming to the gate, smiling under his little glasses, and calling her "Miss Ah-deh-la Fa-rost." She and Thiha disputed this point for some time. Adela insisted the first time she'd seen him was when he brought fruit to her table at teatime, which he didn't remember doing at all.

They argued playfully about this, half-wrestling, until their playing became more focused, and then it was some time before they returned to the discussion.

Adela got up and went to the bathroom, and when she came back he had put his clothes on, as if he were preparing to leave.

"What are you doing?" she asked.

"I don't know," he said, laughing at himself.

"Take your clothes off," she demanded, tugging on his shirt. "Don't leave."

When they were both naked again, Adela realized they'd never spoken each other's names.

"Ko Thiha," she tried.

"Just Thiha," he said. "Now we are . . . close."

"What does your name mean?"

"Lion."

"Ooh, sexy."

He smiled, which was his way of blushing. As Adela had observed from afar the day she'd seen him bathing, his body was lean and strong. He could lift bags of rice without effort, and even when he was resting, some tensile strength remained in his muscles. Next to him, Adela felt pale and flabby, but she hoped that she somehow accorded with his ideal of beauty. She remembered what Bhante had said: "Ma Sabeh has big body!" And yet Thiha stared at her so approvingly that she actually liked having her clothes off.

He tried her full name, Adela Camille Frost, but it came out sounding ridiculous and he stuck to Sabeh.

"What do Burmese guys call their girlfriends?" Adela asked, interlacing her fingers with his.

"Sometime chit chit, chit-thu. Like 'Baby, sweetheart.'"

"Have you had many girlfriends?" she asked teasingly.

"Not many."

"Tell me about your first love."

He did not answer. He sat up and looked down at her.

"How many men do you sleep with?"

"Do you really want to know?" Three (well, two and a half, depending on what counted) was not many compared to some girls Adela knew, but she didn't want to shock him. From Daw Pancavati's story, she'd gotten the impression that good Burmese girls didn't have sex before marriage.

"No . . . but . . . you do not get pregnant?"

"No, I'm on the pill." Going off the pill after Greg had broken up with her would have been tantamount to admitting she wasn't going to get another boyfriend. Furthermore, she liked being able to avoid her period by skipping the placebo pills at the end of the month. Burma was not set up well for feminine hygiene.

Thiha nodded. Adela knew she should probably question him about his history—STDs and such—but he was a doctor, she reasoned. Surely he would volunteer any information that was relevant. Instead, since their conversation had turned serious, she gestured to their bodies.

"Is this wrong?"

"Are you married?"

Adela guffawed and shook her head. "Are you?"

"No," he said, frowning.

"What does that mean?"

"We do not marry other people yet, so no problem."

"So, the Third Precept is . . ."

"Do not do something wrong with sex. Do not hurt some person."

"And we aren't doing anything wrong?"

"Some people, they will think so. Some people are very traditional."

"But you don't think it's wrong?"

"Sex is good for health," he said earnestly.

Adela found this claim hilarious. "But we're in a monastery!"

"No one will know." He gestured to the quiet dormitory. "No one come here."

It was true that no one besides Thiha had ever approached the building at night. The arrival of another foreign meditator was a problem Adela was not yet prepared to consider. Still, she doubted him.

"How is it possible that no one will know? People know everywhere I go, everything I say."

"They do not know about me."

"Why not?"

"I am not important man." He smiled, but his eyes were dull.

"But you were in the Saffron Revolution," she said, playing with his fingers. "That was important."

Thiha shook his head. "It is only by accident that I am arrested. At that time, I am giving some health care for monks who have been injured in the demonstration. I stay in one monastery with them. When the soldier come to take the monk, they take me too."

"And they put you in prison just for that?"

"Already they have me. Why let me go?"

"And so you went to prison, and . . ."

He pulled his hand away and began fiddling with the hem of the sheet. If he wouldn't answer at a moment like this, she knew he never would.

"Thiha, why are you here at the monastery?"

He leaned back against the wall and cast his eyes about, as if trapped. Then he spoke haltingly.

"When I get out of prison, I come here for meditation. Many of our guys do this. It is like . . ."

"Like therapy?" Adela suggested.

"Something like this. Good for the mind. In prison the mind can become sick. Here, with Bhante, my mind becomes calm again. I can forgive even my prison guard."

"I know what you mean!" Adela agreed fervently, before realizing that she could not possibly know what he meant. "I mean, I've never had a prison guard. But the meditation I did, I felt like I could forgive anyone."

"Yes, it is good."

"So that's how you came here, but why did you stay?"

Later she would wonder why she dragged these details out of him. Wouldn't he have told her on his own if he wanted to? Or maybe she should have asked more, made him tell her everything, kept asking until it made sense.

He sighed. "After prison, it is difficult to get a job. Now it is change a little, but many employer, they do not want to give the ex-political prisoner a job. I do not have my medical degree. At home, my mother have to feed me. All the time I am in prison, she visits to me. Sometime she have to travel a long way. Now I cannot help my family. I am only . . ." he shook his head.

Adela could see then the years that separated them, not only the six-year difference in their ages but also his prison sentence, which stretched like black water between them. The skin on his back was puckered with scars that he didn't like her to touch. She snuck a glance at them now, as he craned his neck toward the window, as if he were expecting someone to appear.

Adela took his hand and pulled him back to her.

"I understand. But, so what you're doing now is like . . ."

"Waya wutsa. I help around the monastery, I give some medical care for the monks and visitors."

Adela smiled. "Like me."

"Most are not like you," he said, allowing a smile to return to his face.

"OK, not like me," she giggled, "but—can't you finish your degree and become a doctor? Then you could help your mom and your little sister."

"Yes, I want to do like this. Last year, I apply for the scholarship to Singapore. There I can get good training. You know our hospitals in Myanmar, they are not good. I can come back with knowledge to help people."

"So, when will you find out if you got it?"

"I find out recently, that I get this scholarship."

"Really? When will you leave?

"September."

"September! It's so soon!" Any reference to time upset Adela. She was scheduled to leave at the end of August, but still she felt abandoned. And why hadn't he mentioned the scholarship? Didn't he feel he could confide in her?

"That's great."

He nodded. "It is good for me."

They lay there for a while. Adela rested her head on his chest and listened to his heartbeat: ka-thunk, ka-thunk, ka-thunk. Did hearts make a different sound in Burmese? Lately she'd been indulging in poetic thoughts like this. She wanted to expand on her blog, write something more personal about her experiences: poems, or even a novel. Three months ago, she'd been reading about the real world in the library's basement. Now she was immersed in it. That gave her some truth to reveal, didn't it? Still, she felt shy to tell Thiha about her ambitions, which seemed trivial next to his own.

Some time later, he sat up and looked at Adela's watch.

"I will go," he said. Adela rolled over, half-awake, trying to remember what they'd been talking about that had upset her. He put his cheek against hers for a moment, inhaled her scent, and then he was gone.

❀

The next day Thiha let Adela know with a quick shake of his head in the dining hall that he couldn't come that night. It was for the best; Adela needed time to rest and think. She retired early, but she lay in bed thinking for a long while.

How could she justify their relationship? She wanted to be with him, and he lived in the monastery. She had agreed to stay at Yadana until the end of August. They weren't hurting anyone. They were adults. Neither of them was married. (Adela worried for a moment on this point, thinking of Ko Oo and his sometimes absent, sometimes dead wife.) The idea of leaving the monastery together, and living somewhere else, was even more scandalous than staying. And they could not, she knew, both stay there as if nothing had happened. If literature were any measure, no one could stop something like that once it had begun. Their affair would run its course, unless one of them left the monastery. He didn't seem to be able to, and Adela couldn't make herself.

Thiha couldn't come the following night either. Adela didn't want to arouse any suspicion, and she trusted his judgment. Yet it was early August, and they had less than a month together. In her room alone once again, she sunk into malaise. Finally, they had gotten past all the obstacles between them, and they couldn't even spend time together. She went out and walked slowly around the compound, wanting to be seen doing something innocent, all the while reliving the past few nights in her mind.

THE KIDS

Fortunately, something happened shortly thereafter to distract Adela from Thiha's absence. When she showed up to teach one morning, she found only U Pyinnya.

"Today you teach the children," he said, gesturing to the other side of the compound.

Adela had practically forgotten the children were there; the layer of noise they created by chanting their lessons had become part of the landscape, like the cicadas buzzing.

"Good opportunity for them," he said, "to learn English!"

Adela looked down at the newspaper article she'd printed out on Burma's role in the Association of Southeast Asian Nations—as benign a newsworthy topic as she could find. She felt fairly sure that the children did not have a sudden, desperate need for an English teacher. Rather, the monks didn't want to study with her anymore, whether because of her altercation with U Nyanika, because they didn't like being taught by a girl, or because they'd simply lost interest in her classes. Adela didn't let herself entertain the possibility that they knew about her and Thiha.

Adela had no idea how to teach children. Yet if she refused, she wouldn't have any reason to stay at the monastery.

"OK!" she said, tucking the article back into her bag. "Let's go!"

They walked over to the school, where lessons were already in progress. Only bamboo partitions separated the classrooms, so the cacophony inside the building was overwhelming. The headmistress, wearing a white shirt and green loungyi, mimed a greeting; Adela could not hear her when she spoke her name. U Pyinnya gave Adela a thumbs up sign and turned to go.

The teacher led Adela to a room where dozens of children were clambering over small benches, hitting each other, chattering away, and singing songs. When they saw their headmistress, they fell silent and arranged themselves on the floor. Some took little slates out of their shoulder bags. Adela stepped over and around them to get to the front of the room, where a blackboard hung on the bamboo scaffold that made up the wall.

"Sayama Sabeh," the headmistress shouted over the din, inclining her hand politely toward Adela.

The students stood up. In unison, they shouted, "MIN-GA-LA-BA SA-YA-MA!"

The headmistress motioned for them to sit down. She indicated a sweating glass of water and a stub of chalk on the small table in front of Adela. Then she retreated.

The children stared up at their new teacher. For a few moments Adela had their complete attention. What would the foreigner do next? She considered some possibilities. Teach them the alphabet. Ignore them. Leave. By the time she had ruled out all of these, many of the students had turned back to their own pursuits, prodding each other and giggling. Adela reached for the glass of water and drained it in a few gulps. This was *not* going to work. Even for Thiha, she couldn't stay in this room for two hours every morning. Already, her shirt was soaked in sweat and her ears were ringing. She realized how fortunate she'd been to teach the monks, no matter how hostile U Nyanika had been.

The first thing Adela had to do was get out of that room. She made her way to the door, motioned for the kids to follow her, and led them Pied Piper–style onto the dusty expanse in front of the school. A tamarind tree stood there, and she gathered them under it. The other classes shrieking their lessons inside were still audible, but muffled. A breeze swept through the feathery leaves above them. One enterprising student mimed something to sit on, pulled a friend off to help him, and returned with one of the classroom's wooden benches. Soon the children were arrayed on the benches beneath the tree's canopy, looking up at Adela.

"Tree!" she said, pointing to the tree.

"TEE!" they shouted back.

"Bama lo bah leh?" she asked: "What is it called in Burmese?"

"THIT PIN!" they shouted back.

"Ingaleik lo . . ."

"TEE!" they hollered, catching on.

"Thit pin," Adela shouted back.

They howled with laughter.

She pointed to the sky.

"SA-KAI!" they repeated. And so on. It had limited pedagogical value, but the children found it hilarious, and it passed the time. At one point Adela saw the headmistress watching the spectacle from the school's threshold. Adela wondered if she would tell U Pyinnya that the foreigner was unsuitable even as an instructor for children. But the headmistress didn't seem perturbed, and when the period ended she brought out another batch of kids. Apparently, Adela's behavior fit into a category of strange things foreigners did: sit in the sun until their skin turned brown, avoid spicy food, and hold English classes outside.

❀

When Adela arrived at school the following day, there was a little chalk-board hanging from a nail that had been pounded into the tamarind tree, and the benches were already set up. With time to think overnight, she had formulated a plan. Ko Oo had been a battalion commander. What would he do, she asked herself, confronted with a group of unruly children?

She divided them into battalions of six, naming the most energetic ones "battalion commanders," responsible for keeping their troops in line. It was a questionable thing to do in a country with a history of military rule, but the kids loved it. Within their battalions, each child had a partner with whom to shout English and Burmese words back and forth. The battalions then competed in vocabulary bees.

They soon ran out of things to point at under the tree, and so the lessons became more abstract. One day, one of the boldest boys asked Adela, "Ba lu myo leh?" literally, "What kind of person are you?"

"Amerikan lu myo ba!" replied Adela.

Like everything she said in Burmese, this answer produced a flurry of laughter. But suddenly, she was curious. Who were these kids? The question was hard to translate into English. "Where are you from?" would have been a more common question, but "What is your ethnicity?" was a better translation. Adela settled on the Burglish "What is your ethnic?" for ease of pronunciation. It wasn't quite correct, but any English speaker would understand what they meant. Soon they were shouting this question back and forth with their partners. After several minutes, she had one pair from each battalion demonstrate.

"What iss you eth-a-nic?" yelled one boy at his partner, who was only six inches away.

"Karen eth-a-nic!" replied his partner.

In this manner, Adela learned that about two-thirds of the kids called themselves "myanma ethnic" or "bama ethnic"—Burman, the majority group—and the rest were something else, often a mix of several ethnicities. Most notably, three of the kids—Sanda, Razak, and Pho Cho—were "*mu-sa-lin*" ethnic: Muslims. Sanda, a sweet girl with dark curls, actually called herself "kala" at first. Several kids hooted with laughter, and Razak prodded her to change her answer.

"What is *kala*?" Adela asked, hoping to get a more honest response from kids than she had from adults. But they just laughed, and Sanda looked like she might start crying. Adela named the little girl "helper for the day," a coveted role that involved erasing the chalkboard and fetching glasses of water. Sanda's chin was still trembling, so Adela sat the girl on her lap while the other kids reported their answers. Sanda snuggled into Adela's sweaty armpit and Adela patted her back. The girl's ribs stuck out like tiny bird-bones, and Adela could feel her heart pounding inside its little cage.

The whole incident was so interesting that Adela decided to write it up in her blog:

As the students continued the exercise, I thought about what I'd just learned. First, the kids saw ethnicity and religion as basically the same thing, or at least there was no word other than *kala* for the ethnicity of Muslim people. I never thought anyone would call themselves kala. Did Sanda call herself kala because that was the way other people referred to her, or did her family actually embrace this word?

More importantly, why were Muslim kids attending a school in a Buddhist monastery? I assumed only Buddhists would be admitted. Their education does have a strong religious element, and the children chant suttas daily. But before I brought up the issue of ethnicity, I hadn't

noticed the Buddhist students discriminating against the Muslim kids. Razak is one of the most popular kids in class; I'd made him a battalion commander. The fact that Muslim children can get an education at a monastery school is the first heartening example of Buddhist-Muslim cooperation I've seen in Burma.

❀

That night, Thiha was finally able to visit her again.

"I missed you!" she muttered into his chest as they lay entwined on her bed, their bodies exhausted and sticky with sweat. She kissed his neck thoughtfully, tasting the salt of his skin.

"Hey, did I tell you I started teaching the children?" She sat up and leaned against the wall.

"No more monks," he said sleepily, as if it were common knowledge around the monastery.

"I was going to ask you, is it normal for Muslim kids to attend monastery schools?"

Thiha propped up his head on his elbow. "Not a lot, maybe some. Their parents cannot pay the government school fee, they can come to here for free."

"And no one minds?"

"No . . . it is not like this. What people say about the politics, it is different to what they do in their life."

She was tempted to pull out her laptop and take notes as he talked, but instead she just tried to formulate what she'd write later.

Inter-marriage between Buddhists and Muslims is fairly common. Sometimes Buddhist women convert to Islam, and the children are considered Muslim as well, which is one of the main fears of Buddhist nationalists.

"Wait, what?"

Something Thiha said had startled her.

"Yes. In fact there are other Muslim in this monastery."

"Really? Who?"

"Kyaw Kyaw, the guy who sweep . . ."

"The skinny one?" Adela gasped. "The one who invited me for dinner?"

Thiha chuckled in disbelief. "Kyaw Kyaw invites you for dinner?"

"Yes! He took me to his hut, or his mother's hut, or something. But I never told you because—it's a long story, but Daw Pancavati acted really weird about it. Like I shouldn't be associating with him, which was odd, because usually she's so nice to everyone. Do you think it's because he's Muslim?"

"I don't know. It can be."

Adela remembered the metal shack, the sickly old woman, the meal she'd forced herself to eat. They had offered her hospitality when they had so little. The fact that they were Muslim made her feel even worse. They probably thought she'd left so abruptly because she was scared of Muslims, disgusted by them. Kyaw Kyaw had never acknowledged her again, and he kept his eyes averted when she passed by.

Thiha went on. "There are others, too . . . the lady I give some food after the meal . . ."

"Oh, the one who begs with the kid?"

"Yes. She come after Nargis. She is pregnant at that time."

"That's *her* baby? She looks like she's about seventy years old!"

He nodded. "She has seen a lot of dukkha."

"So it's OK for them to stay here?"

"Why not?"

Adela tried to keep up with what Thiha was telling her, weaving into a post in her mind.

Although many Buddhists say prejudiced things about Muslims, in daily life, they are often able to coexist without much communal conflict. Yadana may be different from other monasteries, in that it became a sanctuary for monks who'd participated in the Saffron Revolution. Bhante is apparently more tolerant than most abbots. Yet he's able to secure donations from influential people who support his work. This is despite the growing power of the 969 movement, a group of Buddhist nationalists who practically advocate violence against Muslims.

Thiha interrupted her summary of his points.

"What is this word, communal conflict?"

"I don't know, it's like a way of talking about the conflict without blaming anyone?" She'd read it in a newspaper article, and it had sounded like the kind of term Greg would use.

"Also . . ." he continued. "969 does not say people should do violence. They just spread some message, like prejudice against Muslims."

"But that's messed up—monks are behind all of this? It's so hateful. When I was in the hospital in Yangon, and I was trying to help this woman who was dying, someone told me not to because she was a kala!"

Thiha looked confused. "Who tell you not to help her? What are you doing at that time?"

"Well, they didn't exactly tell me not to help her. But they definitely called her kala. I was giving her water."

He grunted, examining his fingernails. Adela wondered if the conversation bored him. But her mind was overflowing. She grabbed her laptop. "Hey, would you mind if I wrote some of this stuff down?"

Thiha eyed her suspiciously. "Why?"

"It's for my blog. What you're telling me is amazing. People don't know this stuff. I saw 969 mentioned in news articles, but I had no idea they had so many followers."

"Yes. Even my mother, she follow this 969 movement."

"Really? But you're—I mean, your dad was a journalist, he was in the democracy movement."

He chuckled. "My mother is not journalist. She is seamstress. Anyway, many people in the democracy movement, they follow 969."

969 even has a presence on social media, and their leaders have gained thousands of followers on Facebook since the recent outbreak of violence. Although Internet connections are inconsistent, Facebook is popular in Burma. Unfortunately, it can be used as a platform for racist views, even among people who support democracy. Aung San Suu Kyi has been criticized by the international community for not condemning 969 or the violence against Muslims.

Adela looked up from her computer.

"Are *you* on Facebook?" she asked. She would have been embarrassed to have Thiha scroll through her timeline and see the person she'd been back at Edgerton Fields. She wasn't even quite ready to have him read her blog. He'd realize how much of what she'd written was based on what he'd said. And what if he thought she'd gotten it all wrong?

He shook his head. "I have no chance."

She turned back to her screen. "But I thought people wanted change, wanted democracy—especially monks. That was the whole point of the Saffron Revolution, right?"

"Maybe some want the democracy. Maybe some don't want the army rule. But what monk protest the first time in Saffron Revolution, it is the high gasoline price."

Ko Oo had never mentioned that.

"Why did they care about gasoline prices?"

"Government policy change, gasoline price goes up overnight. People suffer a lot. Also they cannot donate to the monk."

"So it was just about . . . money?" Adela tried not to sound disappointed.

"No, no." He started to say something, then stopped. "Cannot explain."

"Try," she urged, somewhat breathlessly. She was possessed by the urge to know, to fit together all the pieces he was giving her.

"Maybe people do not know, 'This is what I want,' or 'That is what I want.' They know their situation is not good. Like 969 is also connected with our economic situation. Many people, they worry for their country. They worry for their children. They look around for what is the cause of their problem. Then some people, some politician or some monk, can give them an answer for their problem. Like my mother say for 969, 'Myanma yinkyayhmu go saunt shauk ya aung.' Let us protect the Myanma culture. And they say, 'Bama lu myo, buddha batha.'"

"You mean, 'Burmese is Buddhist,'" Adela translated, with some pride. Thiha usually didn't speak Burmese with her, and she wanted to show him that she understood.

"Houk," he said, confirming her interpretation.

"Hey, how come you never speak to me in Burmese?" She wondered if it pained him to hear her butcher his language.

"Is good for me to practice my English."

"Is that all I am for you, an English teacher?" she teased.

"No," he said, closing her computer and pulling her toward him.

In fact, Adela would have liked to keep talking about 969. But she let him kiss her. Somehow the Buddhist-Muslim conflict and her relationship with Thiha had become entangled in her mind, both gripping, both slightly dangerous, both just beyond her comprehension.

For instance, the sex confused her. After the thrill of their first encounters had worn off, she realized that Thiha was not overly attentive to her needs. In fact, sometimes it seemed that he didn't even know she was there. In those weeks, Adela saw how solitary sex could be. It reminded her of dreams, in which other people were present, but not real. There was nothing casual about it—how could there be when they were going to such lengths to conceal their meetings—but it was not as romantic as Adela had expected it would be. American guys had always made some pretense of intimacy, saying her name or caressing her tenderly. It was in such moments that she and Greg had first used the word "love." But she and Thiha didn't speak at all. He never closed his eyes, but he never really looked at her, either.

Before, they talked and joked, but there was always a break at some point, when Thiha seemed to leave his body. Adela wondered if it was because of his traumas in prison, if Burmese men were usually like that, or if it was just his particular personality. She'd never dated an older guy before. Maybe age was the difference. It was liberating, in a way; once she realized he was unreachable, she stopped searching for his eyes and simply took what she needed. It made the sex she'd had before seem childish, burdened by teenage expectations.

Sometimes after sex he didn't want her to touch him. A few times he left right away, but mostly he'd stare quietly into space until she fell asleep. In contrast to the way he'd plied her with stories about his family during their courtship, he stopped volunteering much information at all. Adela started to wonder what he really thought about her—about her crusade for religious tolerance, about her large, unwieldy body. Clearly there was something that kept him coming to her room, but it could have been anything, including boredom.

Several times, though, he did things that made Adela wonder if he was, in his own way, attached to her. Once he wrote down the title of an American pop song—"Someone Like You," by Adele—and he insisted that she should watch the video on her computer. Adela didn't know where he'd heard it, but it was a sappy song, full of melancholy and longing. She put it on her iPod and listened to it over and over.

And there was the time he told her about yay zet. One night they were lying in bed, and Adela asked him if he thought he would ever come to the United States. She was just curious, but he seemed to take it as an invitation.

"Or Sabeh will come back to Myanmar," he said with certainty.

Adela was surprised. She thought it was understood that their relationship was precious exactly because it had no future.

"Yay zet pa lo, tway ya deh."

"We had to meet . . . because of what?"

"Because of yay zet. Karma from previous life. We know each other already in the past."

Adela hadn't thought he was particularly religious; he had mocked the army generals who made huge donations to monasteries in order to work off their bad karma before they died.

"How can you tell?"

He nodded firmly. "When I see you I know."

Part of her wanted to act incredulous and tease him, but she knew what he meant. She *had* known something when she saw him—really saw him— for the first time. Ever since her dream about Thiha, she'd had a feeling that it didn't matter what happened between them. Something already was, or had been, or would be. Actually being together was extra.

"When I see you the first time," he said, pointing at his chest, "Seit htay hma, thi ya deh"—I knew in my seit.

Seit was a word Adela loved. It meant something like "mind," but Burmese people always pointed to their chests when they said it, as if there were a way of knowing that had more to do with the body than the brain: a mind/heart.

They looked at each other a long time.

"I love you," she blurted out, without thinking about whether she meant it, or how he would interpret it, just wanting to reciprocate in the only way she knew how.

He didn't say anything back.

THE IDEA ONLY

Teaching the children, at first a distraction, began to engage much of Adela's energy. After she ran out of things to point at under the tree, she led them on little walks around the compound. The rain usually held off until the afternoon, but when it was wet outside she brought them to the office, dragged the tables out of the way, and sat them down on the floor. Then she could show them photos on her computer from her life back home. The students gathered reverently, battalion by battalion, to view snapshots of Adela's father at the library where he worked, of her mother in front of the Hirshhorn, and of the campus at Edgerton Fields. In the photos she had from when she was their age, she was usually engaged in something they'd never had a chance to do, such as going to a "SA-WIMMING POOL" or "SA-KEE-ING," a mysterious pursuit that required an explanation of snow and elementary physics, and several diagrams on the whiteboard.

Adela asked the students to bring in photos of themselves, but none of them had any. She was so saddened by their lack of mementos that she resolved to take a picture of each one of them, which she planned to print and deliver back to them before she left the country. She did not want to forget their faces.

To this end, one cloudy morning in August the kids took turns writing their names on the blackboard hanging on the tamarind tree. Against this backdrop, Adela photographed each one. It was Razak who suggested that they add their ages and ethnicities below their names. Adela also took some candid shots of the kids practicing English together for her blog. Maybe she'd get a selfie with one of them to use as her Facebook profile picture.

When she clicked through the photos after class, tears prickled her eyes. The children had worn clean shirts and plastered their hair to their heads with water. Each one had an expression filled with a unique mix of earnestness, bravado, terror, and glee. Adela's favorite was the one of Sanda: her black hair neatly tied back, her tentative smile showing her dimples, her long-lashed brown eyes so hopeful, so trusting.

It was then, as Adela looked into Sanda's eyes on her camera screen, that the idea came to her. It was an idea that seemed to start in her "seit" rather than her brain and then blossomed through her entire body with the obviousness of fate. As the plan took shape in her mind, she marveled at how everything that had happened to her in Burma had propelled her toward it. She could make a difference. It would be a small thing, or maybe it wouldn't be so small.

Adela returned to the three photos in question, admiring the way the kids had printed their names so carefully on the blackboard: SANDA, 7 YEAR OLD, MUSLIM; PHO CHO, 7 YEARS OLD, MUSLIM; and RAZAK, 8 YEAR OLD, MUSALIM. They were perfect: Razak's mischievous grin, Pho Cho's proud stance, and Sanda's adorable curls.

Adela transferred the pictures to her computer, then she rushed over to the corner of the compound where she knew she would find Kyaw Kyaw. Sure enough, she saw him sweeping leaves into a woven basket.

They'd shared no words since he'd invited her for dinner. It would be strange to break the silence now, for this. Plus, she wanted to capture him in action. When Burmese adults posed, they always looked so formal, handing envelopes of money to Bhante with frozen expressions or standing solemnly before the pagoda. In any case, her Burmese wasn't good enough to explain why she needed his photo. Therefore, while Adela did not disguise what she was doing, she was nonchalant, first training her camera on a spray of brilliant yellow flowers before aiming it at Kyaw Kyaw.

After lunch, she positioned herself behind the dining hall, where the Muslim lady always came to beg for her meal. It wasn't Thiha who served her leftovers that day, and Adela was glad. She still had to think about how she wanted to explain her idea to him. When the lady saw Adela's camera, she raised her palms to her forehead as if she were posing. She even held her child up in the air—quite an effort for her, though he was scrawny as a chicken—so that he could be in a picture as well. The waya wutsa fellow with the pot of leftovers positioned himself courteously outside of the photo's frame.

Afterward, Adela rushed to the office and uploaded the new pictures. She composed the following captions: "Muslim kids study at the monastery school"; "Muslim man helps out at the monastery"; and "Muslim woman and child accept food leftover from monks' alms."

Adela had never created a "community" page on Facebook before, but it only took a few minutes. She checked to see if Sarah's women's project had a page. It didn't, but the page Lena had made for her fund-raising bike ride provided a useful model. Adela used a shot she'd taken of the pagoda spire at sunset as the banner photo, and for the profile picture she chose a logo she'd seen on bumper stickers back home, made up of all the world's religious symbols juxtaposed to spell "COEXIST." She titled her page BUDDHIST AND MUSLIM COEXISTENCE IN BURMA: YADANA MONASTERY. She embedded a link to her blog, which would provide context for the photos. The photos themselves were her evidence of the claim she made in the title: despite the current violence, Buddhists and Muslims could live alongside each other peacefully—even in a monastery. Her page would educate her friends back home, inspire people here who were already working for peace, and challenge those like U Nyanika, who saw Muslims in a negative light. It was, she thought, at once proactive and positive.

As the cursor hovered over the "Make Page Public" button, Adela hesitated. Although she feared that she would lose her nerve if she didn't publish the page soon, she knew it would reach more people if she could translate it into Burmese. There was only one person she could ask.

Adela found Thiha washing dishes, and she walked by him several times in silence to signal that she wanted to see him. It was early afternoon, hours before he would be able to get away. Adela paced the monastery's perimeter, adding to the page in her mind. She'd need to add links so people could donate to organizations that worked for peace. And she'd need to broaden her network to reach as many people as possible. Lena had accumulated quite a cadre of Facebook friends through her bike trip fund-raiser; they might be interested in Adela's cause, as well. If the page had caught on by the time she got to Pomona, maybe Adela could give a talk on campus, or Skype into Ms. Alvarez's classes.

She needed to talk to Thiha first. His Burmese captions would allow her to reach people here, who could see their own country through fresh eyes. MVU volunteers could continue the project, adding their pictures and stories after Adela left. It wasn't about her. She was just the catalyst, someone who saw the possibility.

❀

By the time Thiha knocked on her door the following night, Adela had the page prepared for launch. At the office earlier that day, she'd added a "Donate" button with a link to Human Rights Watch, which had reported on the struggles that Rohingyas were facing, and to Doctors Without Borders, which provided medical aid to them.

She led Thiha inside, kissing him quickly and pulling him down to where she'd set up her laptop. He was soaking wet; the rain was pounding on the roof so hard it sounded like they were in the shower, and she had to shout over the noise.

"So I had this idea!"

He scanned the page. She watched impatiently as his eyes flicked back and forth in the screen's glow.

"What is the point?"

"What?" She thought she'd heard him wrong.

"What is the point?"

"The point? It's to make people see that actually some Buddhists are tolerant of Muslims, and vice versa. If we can get people to see what is around them, instead of listening to 969 or whatever they're fed on the news, it might help. I mean, you should see these Muslim kids at school, they're great students, and you said yourself that poor kids like them have no other opportunities, maybe more of them could attend monastery schools . . ."

He grunted, scrolling down the page.

"You use this monastery's name."

"Well, yeah, it has to be specific. Otherwise people could just say, 'These photos are from anywhere, they're not real.'"

"You ask Bhante already."

Adela sighed. She hadn't spoken to Bhante since the end of her retreat. She saw him around, and he waved at her. To request an audience with him and tell him about the page seemed awkward. More monks and meditators were starting to arrive for the beginning of the rainy season retreat. Daw Pancavati had told her Bhante was busy every day, and even that his health was suffering.

"I don't want to bother him."

"Not a good idea to use this monastery name."

"Well, OK, if you insist, I'll take out the name. But will you translate the captions into Burmese?"

He looked off into the distance, or he would have if they hadn't been in an eight-by-eight-foot-square room. Adela had taken for granted that he would do her this favor, but he seemed to be weighing the question in his mind.

"What, do you think it's a bad idea?"

"No, not bad idea."

"Do you think it could help?"

"It is possible."

Adela had been expecting a more enthusiastic reaction. But then, Thiha wasn't an especially enthusiastic person. Even when he believed deeply in a cause—the Saffron Revolution, for example—he was rather muted. Except for U Nyanika, Burmese people didn't seem prone to drama. And Thiha hadn't said it was a bad idea. They were, as he'd said, "close." He would tell her if he had serious doubts. Perhaps he was just scared. Of course, he would be. He'd spent three years in prison. But only Adela's name would be on the page. Thiha didn't even have a Facebook account. No one would know he had anything to do with it.

"I know, it's a little scary. It's—" she paused, searching for the word Daw Pancavati had used. "It's sensitive, and it's hard to know the right thing to do. But if we don't do anything, it's like saying that what's happening is OK."

"People will know this page is made by you."

"Yeah, but what do I care? I'm leaving. It's not like anyone's going to come after me." She spoke with conviction, yet the idea that she was taking a risk was exhilarating. "No one would know you were involved."

"Some people will not like this."

"Some people didn't like the Saffron Revolution. Some people don't like democracy and human rights. But we still have to stand up for them. That-ti shi ba. We have to have courage."

Thiha was still scanning the page. Adela reached out and turned his face toward hers. His eyes were the way they'd been that first day they talked in Daw Pancavati's room: calm, attentive, wise. She tried to hold his eyes with her own, the way she had then. She was ready to beg.

"Thiha."

He looked away. "OK, I will write in Burmese for you."

"Thank you. Thank you!"

He nodded toward the door.

"Sabeh, I cannot stay tonight."

"Not even for a little while?"

He shook his head.

Adela felt bad she'd used up their time. Now that he'd agreed, she wanted him. Although she didn't formulate the equation so clearly in her mind, she felt she owed him something for his help.

He stood up. "I will come to office tomorrow."

"Wait." Adela rose and kissed him. It was a real kiss, the kind she'd had to teach him: languorous and soft. He held her for a minute, pressing her into the wall with his body, and Adela thought he might stay after all. But he let her go and turned toward the door.

Adela lay down in bed, but she couldn't sleep. After an hour of lying awake, she wrapped herself in a blanket and pulled a chair under the eaves of the dormitory. The sky was dark blue above her, swirling with clouds. Thiha's words came back to her: "What is the point?"

But it wasn't Thiha she wanted to debate with. Instead, she found herself imagining a conversation with Greg.

It's just a little . . . simplistic," he'd say.

"Like the KONY2012 video that got millions of views?"

"I'm just saying."

"So what would you do to stop the genocide of Rohingya people?"

Imaginary Greg had no response. Adela stared up at the full moon, the third she'd seen in Burma. "Hey, didn't you say I couldn't do anything worthwhile in three months?" she couldn't help adding.

Adela let herself doze, half-dreaming and half-thinking, until the moon thinned to an iridescent wafer in the dawn sky.

❀

The next day, the page was up, complete with Burmese captions. She invited all her friends to like the page, and over the next few hours, many of them did. Ko Oo liked it immediately, perhaps without understanding what it was, because his post on the wall read, "Have A Good Time, Ma Adela!" In any case, many of his Burmese friends joined him in liking the page. Once Lena and Greg were on board, other people from Edgerton Fields caught on too. Her mother wasn't on Facebook, nor was Ms. Alvarez. Her father only had fifteen friends, but nonetheless she appreciated his post on the wall: "Great idea, Sweetheart!"

As Adela packed up her computer for the night, she felt a twinge of anxiety. She hadn't used the monastery's name; she called it Y————a. Like Orwell writing n———r, she was saying it without saying it. It seemed a good compromise between her feeling that the full name was necessary, and Thiha's hesitance to use it. Still, it gnawed at her a little.

If she had the patience, she thought, she'd write a beautiful novel that subtly revealed the hypocrisy of racism while documenting the universal human failings that led people toward hatred and violence. But Adela knew she was no Joseph Conrad. And in the meantime, more people would die, little girls like Sanda would be denied an education, and the world wouldn't notice.

Instead, she told herself as she curled up in bed, she could at least do this—make people aware. She snuggled down under her blanket, mapping out the rest of her time in Burma. She had a little over two weeks left at the monastery, then she'd go back to Yangon for a debrief with Sarah and Kip. She wanted to return to Yadana with gifts and photos for the children, and she'd decided to give a larger donation to the monastery as well, even if it meant borrowing money from her mother.

She wanted to spend more time with Thiha, too. She should ask him about his plans for Singapore. She had to reconnect with Daw Pancavati as well—lately she'd been rushing off after every meal to a rendezvous with Thiha or with her computer. Adela toyed with the idea of getting the monks together and showing them the Facebook page; even U Nyanika couldn't object to photos of smiling children. And she needed to thank Bhante. Perhaps she'd do a little meditating before she left. She'd definitely go to evening chanting more often.

Glancing around the familiar room, Adela thought of all she'd miss about Burma: the sound of the temple bells in the early morning, when the sky was just turning from black to dark blue; the way the bats wheeled in the purple dusk over the rice fields; the eye-watering sting of frying spices; tea leaf salad, jaggery sweets, and mangoes; the way her skin had browned under the sun. Burma had become a part of her, sunk into her cells, even if they were, as Bhante would have reminded her, impermanent.

COEXIST

The next morning, another "lady meditator" arrived, this time from Sweden. She was lurking outside the better shower room when Adela emerged, clutching a basket of toiletries. The woman seemed to stand nearly seven feet tall, and if Burmese people found Adela's skin appealingly light, they would surely admire this woman even more; she was practically translucent.

This Swedish meditator lacked the concentration of the woman from Taiwan, which made her unpredictable. Adela realized immediately that it would be dangerous for Thiha to visit at night. The woman's room was a few doors down from Adela's. If Thiha were to startle her, she might scream, summoning the whole monastery. When Adela and Thiha saw each other at lunch that day, they exchanged glum expressions that acknowledged the intractability of their situation. Adela certainly couldn't visit him—he shared a building with the other Waya wutsa men. Their physical relationship seemed impossible to carry on.

As soon as Thiha was out of reach, Adela longed to touch him, to smell him, to take his picture. She framed the shot in her mind: he would lean back against the wall in her room, looking down and to the side as he did when he was concentrating on something she'd said. The obsession with his presence and his body's distance from hers, which she hadn't felt for several weeks, returned.

Maybe she *would* come back to Burma. Why not? She could come back next summer and start an NGO, as Sarah had. After she and Thiha both graduated they could get an apartment in Yangon, in one of those beautiful old colonial buildings, and he could start a new hospital with all he'd learned in Singapore.

But first she needed to check on her page. There were huge thunderstorms again that afternoon, and the electricity was on and off. Every time Adela tried to get on the Internet, there was some interruption—the power cut out, or Facebook wouldn't load.

On one occasion, just as she was about to open her laptop, U Pyinnya came into the office with a set of meditation instructions he wanted her to help translate into English for the Swedish lady.

"Can I help you with something today?" he asked brightly, which alerted Adela that he was about to ask for her assistance.

"No, I'm good," she smiled. She hadn't talked to U Pyinnya recently, and she missed his jolly sincerity.

"And you teach the children, it is OK?" he asked, his brow furrowed with concern.

"I love it," Adela assured him, glad she could say so honestly.

"We monks do not study anymore," lamented U Pyinnya, acknowledging the obvious.

Adela sensed that whatever transpired to end their classes had not been his doing, and she was eager to show him she didn't hold a grudge.

"It's fine, really!" she said.

She decided to do something humble and very Burmese.

"Hpaya," she said, using the respectful term for addressing a monk, "I must apologize for my weakness as a teacher." She looked down at her hands and shook her head. "Please forgive me."

"No, no!" U Pyinnya protested. "Sayama Sabeh is very good! No, it is our weakness as students!"

"No, no! You are all excellent students! If students cannot make progress, it is the surely the fault of the teacher!"

Their exchange went on in this fashion, with each of them pointing out their own flaws and praising the other. Adela noticed the way she had changed her patterns of speech to make it more likely that she'd be understood by non-native speakers: she avoided using contractions, and she looked her interlocutors in the eyes as they spoke, nodding her head with exaggerated encouragement. She would have to unlearn to talk that way when she returned to the United States.

Adela ended this segment of their conversation feeling satisfied and virtuous, and U Pyinnya broached the subject of the translation. She gave up on checking on her page and happily devoted the rest of the afternoon to his project.

Finally, she reflected, she had assimilated to Burmese culture. Or at least she knew how *she* was supposed to act: apologize at every opportunity, strive to be helpful. None of it had come naturally, but after nearly three months, these behaviors had become reflexes. She wondered how—or whether—they'd carry over into her life back home. Just as she'd have to stop enunciating each word, would she have to get back in the habit of self-promotion? Greg, the king of resumé-finessing, would probably consider her Facebook project a good first step in that direction, better by far than Bhante's lessons in humility.

She and Greg would stay just friends, she had decided, but she would enjoy explaining Burma to him. She sensed that there were parts of her experience that would only become real to her in telling them to someone else, someone who knew her from before. With Thiha she had to leave so much unsaid. She wanted to hear Greg struggle to point out the ideological flaws in her (wildly successful) Facebook page; she wanted to plot next steps for the project with Lena in long phone calls. And then there was the prospect of arriving at Pomona, casually mentioning to her new friends that she'd spent her summer doing work around the Buddhist-Muslim conflict.

❁

That night it rained clamorously from dusk until midnight—the electricity had been off since the afternoon. Adela sat up in her candle-lit room, unable to fall asleep. Outside her windows was only slick blackness. The gutters roiled with water and thunder rattled the frame of her bunk bed. Now and then she'd open her laptop, draining its batteries to re-read the days-old comments against Facebook's friendly blue-and-white backdrop.

She was dozing upright when the door burst open, no knock. Adela upset her cup of water, startled, and when she looked up, Thiha was standing before her, dripping.

"What are you—" she started to say, standing up, but he shook his head quickly to silence her. No one would hear them through the storm anyway, Adela realized. She went to him, pulling his soaked body toward her, tasting the rain on his lips.

But instead of pressing himself into her, he shuddered. She pulled back to look at his face, but he reached over and extinguished the candle between two fingers. A strange sound came from his throat, and Adela realized he was crying.

"Are you—what's—Thiha?" She put her arms around him, and his ribs shook with each breath.

"Thiha?" she asked again, stroking his back. The only thing she could imagine was that his mother had died.

"Thiha—" she started, but he put his hand over her mouth, and he whispered the only words he said that night: "Don't say my name."

Adela pulled his wet T-shirt over his head and unzipped his pants. He let himself be undressed, almost like a child, and he did not resist when she kissed the scars on his back, or when she lay down on top of him. The room was their cave, damp and dark, and Adela told herself that they were safe there, that no one would find them, that she would fix whatever had gone wrong.

When lightning thrust them into an eerie moment of daylight, Adela saw that he was looking at her. But his eyes said nothing she could understand.

He dressed in the dark before the rain tapered off, and then he was gone.

❀

The next morning the clouds had cleared, and Adela squinted into the sunlight as she walked across the muddy courtyard. In the dining hall, the fans spun slowly on the ceiling. The electricity was back on. Thiha stood at the front table dishing out the rice, his face calm. He looked straight into her eyes as he greeted her.

"Good morning, Ma Sabeh," he said.

It was Adela who shuddered then. Who was this person? What had she done to him? She looked searchingly at him, but he had turned to speak to another helper, resting his hand casually on the man's shoulder.

Adela was mystified. Her mind tacked back and forth between his strange behavior the previous night and his nonchalance this morning.

Whatever was wrong, she would talk to him later. Now that the power was back on, she'd finally be able to check on her page. It had been three days since it had gone live, and she couldn't wait to see the reaction.

Adela rushed through her lessons with the children, scarfed down her lunch, and ran over to the office to plug in her laptop, her insides flooding with adrenaline. She felt like she had when she'd been waiting to get back tests at Edgerton Fields: sure she'd done well—she always did—but anxious all the same, luxuriating in uncertainty.

The first thing Adela noticed was that the number of Likes had plateaued at around a hundred. The comments, however, stretched down the right side of the page—ten in the past few hours. The most recent one read: "Doctorwithout Border oppress to our Rakhine People. Western neo-colonialist media is bias, like, this foreign lady who does not understand our Myanmar country."

Adela snorted. It was amazing how extremists could twist something totally innocent into a global plot. But she'd expected that kind of response from the U Nyanikas of the world.

She had not expected that the comments would continue in this manner, another one popping up before she could fully process the first: "TERRORIST KALA make this page NOT american lady." Then, a moment later: "Islam take-over must be stop!"

No, it was not an extremist minority who had misinterpreted Adela's project. Everyone had. Or at least, every person with a Burmese name—the only people, at this point, who seemed to be commenting. One person had posted a lengthy explanation of the history of Rakhine State, nearly word for word what U Nyanika had written in class. There were links to Rakhine nationalist websites, as well as to the 969 movement, and even conspiracy theories about 9/11.

But the comment that hurt the most didn't come from a Rakhine person at all. "We Rohingyas do not need charity from monk at Yadana. This photos lie do NOT believe!" Even Muslims, whom she had been trying to help, seemed to have taken offense at her efforts.

Once Adela realized what was happening, her first reaction was denial. There had been a misunderstanding. She refreshed the page. Another comment appeared: "ONly traitor Myanmar people donate to Yadana." A cold weight settled in her guts. The silly, bright purple COEXIST logo stared back at her, against the background of Yadana's disturbingly recognizable spire.

Then she got angry. They had defaced her page! It must be against Face-book's rules. She started deleting the comments, but there were so many, and as she deleted them she was forced to read each one. It was too much to bear.

She let herself entertain a childish hope: if she closed her laptop and opened it again, the comments would disappear.

She closed her computer. Its hum fell into silence, and all around, the noise of the monastery encroached, reminding her of the terrible realness of the physical world. After counting to ten, she reopened the laptop, lis-tened to its comforting wake-up sounds, waited for her browser to open, and chewed her tongue as Facebook loaded.

Of course, the comments were still there, multiplying by the minute. But how had her effort gone so wrong? A Burmese person must have found the page—maybe a friend of Ko Oo?—and reposted it somewhere, and it had caught the attention of an extended network of Buddhist supremacists. Maybe U Nyanika had been secretly monitoring her Facebook page all along. Had he posted the history of Rakhine State, or was it just a well-worn history that every Rakhine person repeated? Maybe the vicious com-ments were coming from a small group of people with many Facebook accounts.

Adela clicked on "Rakhine Rakhine," the person who'd said only traitors donated to Yadana. There were no photos of him/her, but Adela assumed it was a man. His profile picture was a red-and-white flag with a blue seal in the middle, and his cover photo was a wallpapered image of a three-headed lion with Burmese numbers over it: 969. Sure enough, he had Liked 969's page.

Rakhine Rakhine had an odd assortment of posts. Photos of kittens and stock images of chubby white babies appeared alongside pictures of bloodied corpses. The captions were not in English, but Adela assumed they were presented as evidence of the violence of Muslims or Rohingyas against Rakhine people. There were also many images of Buddha statues, and cartoons she didn't understand. In Rakhine Rakhine's "About" sec-tion, there was only a quote from Winston Churchill: "You have enemies? Good. That means you've stood up for something, some time in your life."

The quote gave her a little prick of hope. She had stood up for something, and now she was hated. Being hated by a fanatic like Rakhine Rakhine was almost a compliment. She tried to channel Lena: *At least you did something.*

Yet being hated felt worse than Adela would have thought. It was hard to shield herself from the intrusive idea that she had made a mistake. As she scrolled through the comments, her mind oscillated between outrage and panic. Equanimity was out of reach.

Adela closed her laptop and stared out at the compound. The daily life of the monastery seemed to go on undisturbed. In the distance, Kyaw Kyaw swept the temple steps. The Swedish lady meditator walked slowly back and forth in front of their dormitory. It was only inside the slim, dangerous box folded in front of Adela that havoc had broken loose.

❁

Adela was so shocked by the page's dramatic failure that it took her several hours to realize that she needed to take it down. Once she'd come to that conclusion, it took her another day to work up the nerve to open her computer again. In the meantime, she skulked around in a daze, trying not to draw attention to herself. She skipped teatime. She avoided Thiha, not ready to explain what had happened.

By the time she reached the office the following afternoon, dozens more sickening comments had appeared. Someone had posted a picture of a dead body with the caption "THIS is what we do to traitor, Beware." She winced as she thought of the smiling photos of Razak, Sanda, and Pho Cho. Kyaw Kyaw sweeping the leaves, the poor Muslim lady. How could innocent people inspire such venom? How could Adela have subjected them to it? Far from increasing tolerance, the page had turned into a venue for hate speech.

Through a blur of tears, she deleted BUDDHIST AND MUSLIM COEXISTENCE IN BURMA: Y———A MONASTERY, YANGON. Then she deactivated her personal account. She'd linked the community page to her own, which was public despite the fact that her mother (who hardly knew what Facebook was) had often nagged her to change her security settings. She couldn't close her blog, because it was hosted on the Edgerton Fields website, but luckily the trolls hadn't posted many comments there—maybe they were confused by her literary ramblings.

The commenters had, however, bombed Adela's personal page, posting rude remarks on her photos and adding messages to her wall. "American kamyinma insult to Myanmar culture" was the most recent. She didn't know exactly what the word meant, but the implication was clear.

Adela thought of her flamer, Rakhine Rakhine. She couldn't even discern that person's gender. Yet how much of herself she'd revealed on this page! Her father's name, her Edgerton Fields email address (thankfully now defunct), her date of birth, the silly photos of her and Lena in their pajamas, wearing beauty masks made of oatmeal and honey. She was not naked in any photos, but she was not modestly dressed by Burmese standards. No wonder they called her an American kamyinma. Adela thought of how casually she'd dismissed Thiha's concern that people would know who she was. Why had she been so certain she wouldn't face any danger?

Once Adela had deleted the page, she told herself that the worst was over. A handful of fanatics had gotten out of control, but they were far away, scattered across the world, and they didn't know her. No one at the monastery was even Internet-literate. The page had been an experiment, and it had worked out poorly. Failure, she'd heard over and over, was a learning experience. She imagined laughing about this one day, even referring to it ruefully in an interview, once she'd succeeded at something else.

To pull her mind from its spiral of despair, she imagined sitting in a studio with Terry Gross, the host of her father's favorite program on NPR.

"So how was it for you, Adela, when your first Facebook page created such a hostile response?"

"Well, I'll be honest, Terry, it was pretty rough."

Adela let her mind prattle on this way, filling in the details of her little radio play, Terry nodding sympathetically, Adela giving frank and insightful answers.

Still, paranoia gripped her. That afternoon Bhante didn't wave to her. Daw Pancavati said she wasn't feeling well after lunch and went back to her hut before they could make their usual small talk. Thiha was nowhere to be found. Adela sat outside the office, her computer folded shut in front of her. This time when she saw Kyaw Kyaw sweeping up leaves near the gate, she fled to her room, where she remained all evening.

Now Adela's desperation to talk to someone overwhelmed her shame, and she longed to see Thiha. But the weather was clear, and she knew he couldn't come. What could she say to him, anyway? He had tried to warn her, she realized now, although his advice not to use the monastery's name probably wouldn't have made any difference. She'd mentioned Yadana on her own page and in her blog, so anyone could have found out where she was. With horror, Adela remembered her chipper post about MVU. Slowly the tentacles of disaster spread through everything she'd done in Burma.

But Thiha hadn't only told her not to use the monastery's name, she remembered. He'd also told her to ask Bhante's permission. Of course, Bhante would have forbidden it. He'd have said she'd been "thinking, thinking," and she should meditate instead of wasting time on the kun-pyu-taa.

But would he have been right? Did he even listen to the news? Did he know what was going on in Rakhine State? Adela clung to the hope that her page had been productive in some way. At least she had proved a point to the extremists: outsiders cared about this conflict. Maybe the racist comments would help the more moderate Buddhists realize how dangerous the situation had become. Adela's mind cycled through these small points in her own defense, but none of them stuck. If she couldn't convince herself, who else would believe her?

HAVE COURAGE

The next day, the three Muslim kids were not in school. Adela knew it could not possibly be a coincidence. As she stumbled through her lesson, she saw the headmistress watching from the school door. There was no denying it: people knew. Had the kids' parents taken them out of school, or had they been expelled? Either way, what Adela had done had reached the monastery.

The rest of the kids acted as if there was nothing wrong, but their cacophony irritated her. She needed to think. She shouted at them to be quiet and told them to practice the alphabet on their slates, even though there wasn't enough chalk to go around. Sensing her mood, they fell silent and did their best to comply. She stared off at the pagoda spire, getting angrier by the minute. If a mistake had been made, it was hers. Sanda, Razak, and Pho Cho shouldn't be denied an education because of it.

When the hour ended, Adela marched up to the headmistress. The woman saw her coming and started to duck inside the building, so Adela had to call out from a few feet away.

"Sayama, where are the Muslim children?"

The woman raised her eyebrows.

"Sanda, Razak, and Pho Cho. The Muslim children. They're not here."

"Not here today," the headmistress replied in a sing-songy voice. She seemed to be blocking the door to the school with her body, and Adela craned around her to see if they might be inside.

"But where are they?"

Adela wanted a confrontation. She wanted someone to yell at her, to tell her what she had done wrong. She wanted a chance to explain herself.

The poor woman just shook her head. "I do not know."

Adela could tell she was being honest.

The students had gathered around them and stared with mouths agape. The headmistress shooed them inside with a few sharp words. Her hair was coming loose from its bun, and Adela felt a momentary pang of sympathy for her.

"Please," the headmistress said. "You ..." and she gestured vaguely across the compound, which was the closest she could bring herself to asking Adela to leave.

"I'm going to find them," Adela announced, backing away. "I'm going to find them!"

The headmistress's face twisted with some bitter emotion—disgust, distaste, regret?—and she darted back into the school as Adela stomped away.

Adela knew it was useless. How would she find the kids? She thought of the row of corrugated metal shacks where Kyaw Kyaw's auntie lived. What would she do if she found them? Bring them back to school and insist that they be readmitted? Maybe their parents had removed them. Maybe their parents wouldn't welcome Adela's intervention. Maybe they would be upset that she hadn't asked their permission to post the photos and names of their children online, to be exposed to racist vitriol.

❁

Adela never learned how everyone at the monastery found out about the page. Perhaps one of Bhante's donors had come to him, or U Nyanika had stumbled upon it. Most people would never have had a chance to see the page before she took it down, and so they probably imagined something worse than the truth—that Adela had blatantly insulted Buddhism, called Myanmar culture barbaric, posted photos of herself having sex with Muslim men, or done something equally far-fetched that confirmed their stereotypes of American girls. In the end, it didn't matter how it happened, who saw the page and who didn't. As Bhante had said about karma: "Ma Sabeh does not understand how kan work. Still, kan work."

Adela skipped lunch and cornered Thiha behind the dining hall. The Swedish meditator was passing with excruciating slowness a dozen yards away, and Adela pretended to be fixing her sandal until a tree blocked her from view.

"We need to talk," she mouthed.

He shook his head helplessly.

"Meet me in the office," she whispered. "At midnight."

Someone came and they rushed off in opposite directions.

There was no way Adela could pretend anymore that everything would be fine. Thiha was scared, she could see it. Now she recognized the look on his face from the other night during the rainstorm, the same look he'd had the first time he came to her room: it was fear. Maybe he'd already known what had happened with the page, or maybe he'd just had a premonition. A chill ran through Adela's core when she thought of his blank, unreachable eyes. But her own fear seemed silly next to his. Even as she imagined the police coming to carry her off to a Burmese prison, she knew it wouldn't happen. Thiha didn't have to imagine; he'd been there.

❀

Adela was at the office well before midnight. Instead of sitting in a chair, where her silhouette could be seen from a distance, she crouched on the floor in a shadowy corner.

After half an hour, Thiha emerged from the darkness. He squatted down beside her. She got up and started pacing.

"This is fucked up."

He was silent.

"How could this happen?"

"This country . . ." he began. Then he shook his head, trailing off.

"Did you know this was going to happen?"

"No. I think no one notice."

So he'd thought it would be pointless, a little exercise in vanity. And he'd gone along with it to be nice.

"Does everyone know about us?"

In the dark, she saw him nod.

Of course they'd found out.

"Why did you help me do this?"

"Sabeh," he said reaching out his hand, whether because he wanted to be close to her or because he was afraid she was speaking too loudly.

She sat down heavily beside him, slumping against his chest and listening to the familiar sound of his heart beating through his T-shirt. The smell of his skin made her want to cry. Soon they were kissing, groping at each other, there on the floor of the office.

The touch of his fingers on her skin seemed to itch. She wanted him but she wanted it to be over with. There was some kind of anger in their bodies that was relieved by pressing them together. As they rolled about on the dirty floor, Adela felt how impersonal it was, how their lust had nothing to do with either of them. They were just bodies, sealed bags of skin filled with unattractive things.

At the moment she had this thought, Thiha pulled away from her. They sat up and disentangled themselves.

"When I am in prison," he said, "all I want is someone to touch me."

He left the second part unsaid. Now you're touching me, and it's not enough. Now you're touching me, and it's not you that I want.

They were quiet for a long while. He rested his head on his knees, and she thought he might have gone to sleep.

"What's going to happen?" she finally asked.

He shook his head, not looking at her.

"Nothing's going to happen," she said, answering for him, trying to convince both of them. "I'm going back to America and you're going to Singapore, and Buddhists and Muslims are going to keep killing each other."

It was a slim comfort, but in fact it was the best she could have hoped for.

❀

The next morning Thiha was gone. Adela knew he was gone because he wasn't in his usual spot at breakfast, dishing out the rice. On its own, that wouldn't have meant anything; sometimes the other men let him sleep in, or he had a patient to take care of. But when Adela saw another person in his place, it hit her in the chest. Thiha was gone and she would not see him again in this lifetime.

She never determined whether he had known he'd have to leave the night before, or whether someone had asked or forced him to leave that morning. Of course it would have been clear who had helped Adela translate the page. Maybe he had a chance to say goodbye to her and he didn't take it. She wouldn't have blamed him. Everything was so clearly her fault, or so she thought most of the time. For isolated instants, she still felt totally blameless, as if she were actually the victim.

Either way, Adela had lost Thiha, and she was close to friendless. She began to fantasize about leaving the monastery. She could pack her bag, let herself out of the gate, and flag down a passing taxi. She could go to the MVU office and find Kip. He would take her out to dinner and convince her that she had only been trying to help. She could go swimming in a fancy hotel pool, get a massage, and buy souvenirs for her parents as if nothing had happened.

Yet she stayed, because remaining in the monastery as she'd planned felt like part of her punishment. She stuck to her normal routine, as if any deviation would cause everything to fall apart. No one spoke to her. Daw Pancavati, like Thiha, was missing from breakfast. Adela wondered if someone would stop her from going to the school that morning, but no one did.

She taught the children colors that day. Green for tamarind leaves, blue for the sky, yellow for the flowers that climbed the gate. Black for the sky at night, although like most things that are called black, it wasn't really. She left out white, for fear the children would point to her skin. The Muslim kids did not return. The headmistress watched her from the door, but they did not speak again.

After the lesson, Adela made herself walk to the dining hall. *Lifting, moving, placing*, she thought, looking down at her feet. She could still walk. She could still breathe.

Halfway there, a shadow crossed her path. When she looked up, U Nyanika stood in front of her, his arms folded into his robes. He looked a little off to the side of her head as he spoke.

"You bring shame to this monastery. You do not eat anymore in our hall with the monk."

It was the first time he'd addressed Adela since he'd left the class. What had it been, a few weeks? It seemed like longer. The last time they'd spoken, she had still been innocent—just another American girl whose opinions were her only crime. From U Nyanika's perspective, which was worst? That Adela had put up the page, that she'd hurt the monastery's reputation, that she'd had a relationship with Thiha, or just that she didn't agree with him? Whatever the case, Adela was sure he had something to do with getting the Muslim kids kicked out of school.

"You're wrong!" she shouted. Caught in his cold stare, she struggled to control her voice. "You're wrong." She may not have acted wisely, but she knew U Nyanika's prejudice against Muslims was unfair.

He remained impassive. Adela searched for an insult that would preserve her dignity. "What you say about Muslims is not what the Buddha taught."

If he was surprised or offended by what she'd said, he didn't let on. His expression stayed the same, his eyebrows knitted together in the middle. Adela realized she was going to cry, and before he could see her face crumple, she turned and walked away from the dining hall.

⚘

Adela was sobbing in her room when she heard a knock on the door. She hoped it was Thiha and she knew it was not. She did not get up, but she stopped crying and listened.

The door creaked as Daw Pancavati entered. She was carrying a plate of food. She knelt beside Adela's bed but didn't touch her.

"Thamee," she said, and Adela was so glad to hear the word that she started sobbing all over again.

"I'm so sorry! I never meant to hurt anyone! I was only trying to help!" Snot streamed down her chin. "It was just a stupid Facebook page!"

Daw Pancavati laid a hand on her back. Adela cried for a while, and then she started to fear that Daw Pancavati would leave, so she wiped her face and sat up.

"Where is Thiha?"

"Ko Thiha decide to leave. And this is right."

"But it wasn't his fault! He didn't do anything!"

"You do not . . . do anything with him?" the nun asked uncertainly.

"No, I mean, we did, but—"

"Dukkha yauk nay deh," she sighed. Suffering has arrived.

In Daw Pancavati's mind, Adela knew, it was all the same: desire for Thiha, desire to make the Facebook page, desire for admiration, desire to come to Burma in the first place. Of course suffering had arrived. It always did.

"Why did people get so mad about the Facebook page?"

"I do not know about the face book. Donors do not like this face book."

Why did it bother Adela so much that everything came down to money?

"A lot of people depend on Bhante," continued Daw Pancavati.

The children at the school. The lady who begged for leftovers. Adela herself, gobbling up the food that had been donated for the monks each day.

"Donor do not give, how Bhante can share the dhamma this way?"

The donations, the monks, even Bhante, all of it was just infrastructure for bringing the Buddha's teachings to as many people as possible. Adela had disrupted the balance.

"I am really, really, really sorry."

"Thamee does not want to do something bad, I know. This is kan."

Adela was relieved that Daw Pancavati blamed karma, rather than holding her personally responsible. She wondered if there was some karmic way to make things right, a Buddhist equivalent to confession and Hail Marys.

"What should I do?"

"More meditation is good for you."

Adela could not disagree. When she remembered the tranquility she'd felt during her retreat, she felt a physical longing.

"Here at the monastery?"

"I do not think here. I think you find a teacher in your home."

Adela had known she would have to leave. Still, she felt like she was being exiled.

"But what should I do before I go? Should I apologize to Bhante?"

"I am not sure."

The nun looked tired. Adela wondered what Daw Pancavati been doing the past few days. Had people tried to blame her for Adela's behavior? That would be too unfair to imagine. She hated to ask for more. Nonetheless, Daw Pancavati was the only person in a position to help her.

"Can you try to find out?"

"I try to find a way for you. Eat a little," she said, gesturing to the food. "I come back later."

Adela remembered reading that eating alone was a punishment in many cultures, a way of marking off people who had been expelled from the group for breaking some taboo. It was humiliating to sit there, shoveling food into her mouth, staring at the wall. Solitary confinement.

She thought of the years Thiha had spent in prison. He was twenty when he was arrested, just a couple of years older than she was. Could she imagine spending the next few years in a room like this? That prospect was bad enough, and the conditions he faced must have been worse—rotten food, no window, not even a bed. Had he avoided telling her about prison because it pained him to remember it, or because he didn't think she deserved to know? Had he sensed how she would have latched on to each detail, repeated his words to Lena later, even included them in her blog? Would she have been any more careful with his stories than she had been with the photos she'd posted on her page?

She'd been so foolish, so self-important, it made her sick. The story Bhante had told during her retreat came back to her, about the giant who thought he was so majestic until he found himself groveling at the Buddha's feet. She was ready to grovel, she was ready to beg. But most of the people whose forgiveness she longed for were unreachable.

❀

A few hours later, Adela decided to venture out of her room. She had to get in touch with someone—her parents, Lena, Ms. Alvarez, even Greg. Besides her mother and Ms. Alvarez, who weren't on Facebook, they must have seen what had happened. They were probably worried. Adela straightened her clothing, put her laptop into her bag, and prepared for the long walk across the courtyard.

U Agga was on the ancient office computer when she arrived, but he scurried away when he saw her coming. Adela didn't even try to talk to him.

She plugged in her computer and opened her email, thankful she'd never listed her Gmail address on her Facebook page. As it was, there were only a few messages, all ominous in their brevity. The most recent was from her father.

Adela,
Is everything OK?
love,
Dad

Adela wrote back a quick, reassuring email making light of the dramatic response to her page and implying that this sort of thing happened all the time on Facebook. Another email, from two days ago, was from MVU.

Adela,
Please get in touch as soon as you can. We need to talk in person.
Sarah

All that Adela feared had come to pass. The fanatics had connected her to MVU, and Sarah had watched it all transpire. Sarah, who had suspected her weaknesses from the beginning, had been right all along. Adela told herself she'd reply to Sarah's email later, then signed into Gchat. Lena messaged her immediately.

what is going ON, dellies??

Seeing her old nickname made her throat clog up. To some people, she was still a loveable creature, not a traitor to a religion and a country that wasn't even her own.

aaaahhhh i really messed up.
those people are insane!
i know. i'm like a pariah!
but why? you were doing something good!
yeah, i dont know.
what about that guy
OMG that is another story
one for the old folks home ;)

They had always joked that they'd share a room in a nursing home some-day, and that they'd relive each exciting moment of their lives, classifying love affairs into best and worst, making charts that compared this boy to that one. Especially now, it was a comforting prospect. Someday I will be old, Adela thought, and Thiha will be old, and Bhante and U Nyanika will have died, and none of this will matter. Sickness, aging, and death would find them all. It was, as Daw Pancavati had promised, strangely reassuring.

Lena distracted Adela by telling her about the guy she'd met in Oregon: he chewed tobacco, but the sex was intriguing. Adela couldn't bring herself to talk about Thiha that way, or even to think of their last two meetings. Still, chatting with Lena emboldened her. Outside the world of the monastery, outside Burma, she would still be considered a normal person. So she had slept with a Burmese guy, and she had started a Facebook page that had gone awry. People made mistakes.

Lena ended with something they used to say to each other when they were facing a long night of writing papers: *courage!* They'd always pronounced it with a French accent, but seeing the word on-screen reminded Adela of the Saffron Revolution. In fact, it was not the best note on which to end, launching Adela back into the world where people needed courage to endure long prison terms, not write term papers.

Adela clung to Lena's friendly words as long as she could. They lasted about halfway through the walk back to her room, when she saw U Pyinnya and U Nyanika from across the courtyard. They were deep in conversation, but Adela could feel U Nyanika's eyes following her like the unforgiving sun.

THE AMULET

Back in her room, with nothing else to do, Adela picked up *Burmese Days*, desperate for distraction. It was the scene where the Orwell stand-in character, Flory, renounces his Burmese concubine, Ma Hla May, in the hopes of getting the shallow English girl to marry him. Ma Hla May throws herself at Flory's feet and bows down to him, calls him master, and begs for forgiveness.

Adela felt like begging for forgiveness as well, but before whom could she bow down? Thiha was gone. Bhante wouldn't see her. She wouldn't be able to find the kids from school or their families. She wanted to lay her misdeeds at someone's feet, to explain that she'd meant no harm. Yet the only person she could speak to was Daw Pancavati, and the nun had never really blamed her in the first place.

Just as Adela thought of her friend, there was a knock at the door. Daw Pancavati came in and knelt by Adela's bed.

"Thamee, Bhante want to bless your amulet again." She gestured toward the sitting Buddha figure that rested against Adela's chest.

"What? You talked to him?"

Daw Pancavati nodded.

"What did he say?"

"He say . . . he want to bless your amulet again. That is all."

Adela's hand went to Ko Oo's amulet, which hung around her neck as it had for the past three months.

"Why?"

The nun looked delicately to one side.

"We Buddhist believe that some thing can take away the amulet's power."

"Like what?"

Daw Pancavati was silent for a moment, waiting for Adela to guess, but Adela was too confused to think.

"Men and women, when they . . ." the nun began.

"Oh."

"We are not supposed to wear the amulet when we . . ."

Adela held up her hand to stop her friend from proceeding. "Uh, in that case . . . yeah, he'd better re-bless it."

My god, Adela thought. Bhante knew. He and Daw Pancavati had discussed her sex life. Adela untied the cord and deposited the amulet in her friend's hand, hoping it wouldn't contaminate her, too.

"No one told me that, about amulets. My friend who gave it to me didn't mention that. I mean why would he. And Thiha—anyway, I'm sorry."

"No need for sorry. We will fix." She put the amulet in her bag.

"But Bhante won't see me?"

"No need, he says."

"But *I* need to see *him*." Adela had no plan for what she'd say to Bhante, nor any clear reason for meeting him. Nonetheless, being prohibited from doing so was upsetting.

"Thamee, Bhante does this gift for you, he will chant some prayer over your amulet. Make it new again. For your new life."

"That's nice of him," Adela said, unable to keep the sarcasm out of her voice. "I mean, I'm very grateful," she added, remembering how much her apologetic words had pleased U Pyinnya.

Daw Pancavati stood up.

"You need something else, thamee?"

"I guess not . . . but . . . no, never mind, I'm fine."

Adela waited for her friend to inquire further, but the nun turned quietly away. Next door, Adela heard the Swedish lady thumping about in what sounded like a calisthenics routine. Apparently, isolation could drive anyone a bit crazy.

Adela felt the spot on her neck where the amulet had rested. Perhaps all of her misfortunes had occurred because she'd drained the amulet's potency by wearing it with Thiha. Had he noticed or cared? Had he thought it was just a trinket she'd picked up in a souvenir market in Yangon? The amulet Ko Oo's mother had given him had seen him safely through police lines, between Burmese army bullets in the jungle, and finally to the United States. Adela had destroyed its power in just a few months.

It was so quick, what she'd done. Adela remembered hearing that dreams, no matter how long they seem to be, take only a few seconds to dream. Three months: just a few seconds in the eons of time stretching backward into all the past good karma she'd done to be born human, in this big body, and to get herself to Burma. Three months in time, extending toward her next existence as a cockroach or mos-quee-to or whatever one ends up as after wearing an amulet during sex. Like everything else she'd done, she hadn't even known it was wrong at the time. Rather, she had known something was wrong, but not what.

❀

Adela assumed the day that Thiha left, the day that U Nyanika banished her from the dining hall, would be the worst day of her life. She woke up the next morning with a sense of relief. It reminded her of the time in sixth grade when some boys in her class found a secret letter to her best friend, in which she described her crush on a popular kid who would never have looked at a scraggly-haired know-it-all like Adela. The boys had photocopied the letter and posted it around the school, in a kind of proto-Facebook shaming. As the eleven-year-old Adela had walked into school the next day, she'd felt detached from her body, as if she were watching the scene from afar. Perhaps it was her first experience of not-self. She remembered realizing for herself something adults had often told her: it is not possible to die of embarrassment. Having nothing more to hide had been strangely empowering.

Adela felt similarly exposed by this debacle. All of her crimes were known. She had been punished and she was contrite. She resolved to do whatever she could in her remaining days to make amends.

It was thus with a lightened heart that Adela tidied her room that morning. She had decided not to return to the school; she couldn't bring herself to say goodbye to the children, and she didn't want them to see her forcibly led away if someone decided she'd done them enough harm. Her only consolation was that they would never understand her transgressions. If their parents were anything like Thiha's mother, their questions would go unanswered, and Adela had to admit that was for the best. She would be glad to be remembered only as the eccentric American lady who let them run around outside shouting English words.

Eager to start her new, irreproachable life, Adela washed the plate, crusted with food, that Daw Pancavati had brought her the previous day. She put on her longest skirt and most unflattering top, and swept the grit from under her bed with the little broom that stood in the hallway, the one she'd walked past dozens of times without seeing. Inspired to clean the whole corridor, she opened the main door to sweep out the dust.

Adela was busying herself with this virtuous task when she heard an unaccountably loud voice coming from outdoors. There was a woman standing in front of the dining hall, yelling at Daw Pancavati in Burmese. She was heavy-set, wearing a light purple loungyi and a lace blouse, and her long hair was elaborately looped atop her head.

The courtyard was otherwise empty. It was nine in the morning, and everyone was immersed in their routines. The sun was just starting to burn the dew off everything, so that the earth seemed to smolder from within.

"Kamyinma beh hma leh?" demanded the lady in purple.

Where is the kamyinma? Adela recognized the word from the post on her Facebook page. *American kamyinma insult to Myanmar culture.*

Daw Pancavati laid a hand on the woman's arm and spoke to her softly. Adela had never heard a Burmese adult yell before. U Nyanika had raised his voice, but not even very much—it had only seemed loud in comparison to the gentle way the other monks spoke. This woman's voice sounded wrong. Adela felt queasy, the way she had as a child when her parents fought.

Adela ducked back into the dormitory and watched from the doorway. She was sure the disturbance had something to do with her.

Daw Pancavati took the woman's arm and led her across the courtyard. When they were a few paces away, Adela realized there was no possible destination but the doorway in which she was standing. She thought of darting into her room, but she didn't want to make Daw Pancavati come and drag her out. So she came out of the building and took a seat, in the most dignified manner she could, in one of the chairs under the eaves.

The woman had stopped talking, and her mouth was set in a firm, lip-sticked line. Her large eyeglasses glinted in the morning sun, and her hair seemed too black, almost blue.

When the lady caught sight of Adela, she started yelling again. Adela squinted against the sun, peering into the woman's face. She appeared to be about fifty years old. Her eyebrows arched delicately, and her full lips were somehow familiar, although Adela was sure they'd never met.

Adela looked up at Daw Pancavati to ask who this woman was, but before the words left her mouth, she knew what her friend would say.

"Ko Thiha's mother."

Adela thought of the contradictory things Thiha had told her. His mother was a martyr who had sacrificed her eyesight to keep her son in school and visited him dutifully in prison. She was a follower of 969, and she hadn't answered any of her young son's questions about his father's death. Yet the only description Adela could apply to her at this moment was that she was really mad.

"What is she saying?" Adela asked Daw Pancavati.

Daw Pancavati paused, either listening or figuring out how to summarize.

"She is very angry with you."

"Yeah, I can see that."

"She say that Ko Thiha promise to marry with another girl."

"What? He's engaged?"

"A long time ago already."

Adela thought of Thiha's reluctance to talk about certain parts of his life, his vague reasons for staying at the monastery. She wasn't hurt that he'd been involved with someone else, but rather that he'd hidden it from her.

"He never told me that," she said, shouting to be heard over the woman's ongoing tirade. "Tell her he never told me that. In fact, he specifically told me ..."

She trailed off. All he'd said was that he wasn't married. She hadn't asked anything else.

Daw Pancavati waited until the woman paused for breath, and then gently inserted Adela's point.

Thiha's mother shook her head, whether in disbelief or disgust. She had stopped looking at Daw Pancavati and was instead yelling directly into Adela's face. She kept talking about someone named Htun Lin.

"Who is Htun Lin?"

"Oh, Ngwe Htun Lin." Daw Pancavati had to lean down so Adela could hear her. "This is Ko Thiha other name."

Don't say my name.

It is common for Burmese people to have several different names that they use in various circumstances.

She'd written that in her blog months ago. Still, hearing Thiha's mother pronounce the name she had given him disoriented Adela. She tried to match up Thiha's face with that name, and she couldn't. She hadn't known Ngwe Htun Lin at all.

It was as lonely a feeling as Adela had known. The mother's monologue went on, and Adela looked out at the banana grove in the distance and thought, unaccountably, of her first day in Yangon, when she'd seen the woman selling boiled beans slap her child in the street. She could almost feel it on her cheek: the slap her own parents had never given her, the one Thiha's mother was giving her now.

Thiha's mother paused to wipe her forehead with a handkerchief. It was hot, and she'd been talking nonstop for several minutes. Adela had the urge to fan her, to shield her from the sun, which had edged above the dining hall and was making its inevitable progress across the sky. This day, too, will end, Adela promised herself. Things could not stay as bad as they were at that moment.

"And," Daw Pancavati said, turning to Adela, "he lose his scholarship in Singapore."

"What?" Adela felt something crumple inside of her. "*What?*" she repeated, wanting to repeat the word endlessly, as if asking could postpone knowing. "But why?"

"I do not know this," said Daw Pancavati. "She say they contact him at home, they know he has left our monastery."

"But what did they say? Did it have something to do with—"

Thiha's mother and Daw Pancavati went on talking, but their voices only stabbed vaguely at Adela's consciousness without penetrating the certainty that was forming in her mind. She leaned forward, feeling bile rise in her throat.

"That's impossible," she said, staring at the ground.

But it wasn't. Adela had let herself believe Thiha when he told her no one at the monastery would find out about them. He'd let himself believe her that no one would know who translated the Facebook page. Somehow, word had gotten back to whoever had awarded him the scholarship: this Ngwe Htun Lin had insulted the nation, consorted with an American girl, spread lies about Buddhism, dishonored Bhante Panditabhivamsa's monastery. He already had a criminal record. Adela didn't know which organization had offered him the scholarship, but surely it was not immune from pressure. And Thiha was just one person. As he'd said, not an important man.

Just then, Adela saw the Swedish lady standing a short distance away, gaping at the three of them as if at a cluster of mad dogs on the street. Listen carefully, Adela wanted to say to her. This is what happens outside of the meditation hall. Become a nun and stay here forever. Anything else is just dukkha.

As if she'd received Adela's message, the Swedish lady began backing slowly away from the trio. Adela turned to Thiha's mother, who had stopped yelling and was staring down at her handbag, taking thick, shaky breaths. Her scalp glistened under her hair, and drips of sweat furrowed their way through her makeup. This was the woman who had raised Thiha, who had tried to protect him from things he hadn't been ready to understand.

Adela felt nauseous with remorse. But how could she make Thiha's mother understand? Burmese people often used the English word "sorry," but it would sound hopelessly casual in this case. No language was enough.

She remembered Daw Pancavati's story about how her employer had made her bow down to him every day. She thought of Ma Hla May from *Burmese Days*, begging for Flory's forgiveness by throwing herself on the ground at his feet. She thought of the giant in Bhante's story prostrating himself before the Buddha.

Adela rose from her chair and kneeled in the dirt beside where Thiha's mother stood. As she stared at the mud that caked the tips of the woman's high-heeled sandals, she pushed from her mind the memory of Thiha praising her own pale feet. She raised her palms to her chest and bowed three times, smelling the moist earth.

Without looking down, Thiha's mother turned and walked across the compound toward Bhante's hall. So Bhante would hear about this, too. The American girl had corrupted Thiha, derailed his engagement, ruined his career.

Adela raised herself with effort and sat heavily in the chair, wiping grit from her face. Daw Pancavati, who had been standing the whole time, remained so.

"I am sorry," said the nun.

"*You're* sorry?" Laughter burst from Adela unbidden, racking her body like a sob. "Are you kidding?"

"Are you kidding," Daw Pancavati repeated, puzzled.

Adela remembered how U Pyinnya had repeated her words that first day: "I am good?" he'd said, so perplexed. Adela had not turned out to be very good at all.

"I mean that it is my fault," Adela explained. "This—" she said, gesturing toward Thiha's mother's retreating figure, and then to their surroundings. "It's all my fault."

Daw Pancavati shook her head. "Maybe some thing your fault. Not all that she say. Some thing she also do not know. When Thiha comes here first time, he try to become a monk. Bhante will not allow this, because he is engage. This is like a debt that he must pay, he is not free."

"Why didn't he just marry the girl?"

"Maybe he do not want her. Their families arrange it a long time ago, before he go to prison. I am not sure, this girl want to marry him or not."

"Does he love her?" Adela asked in a small voice, the word *love* seeming somehow obscene. Who talked about love in monasteries? Who would carry on a romance in a place like this?

"I do not know, thamee."

As with all the most important things, there was no one to ask. Adela wasn't sure if Thiha himself could have explained it. Was this the first love he had declined to tell her about? Or was she just a girl his mother had chosen? Either way, he had concealed her from Adela. He hadn't told her he was staying in the monastery to avoid getting married.

She had to admit she probably would have pursued him anyway. Nonetheless, she had been honest with him. There was nothing she wouldn't have told him, if he'd been interested to know. Not that her commitment to transparency had done him much good. If she had made the page without telling him, without his Burmese captions, he might still be at the monastery, and he might still have his scholarship.

Adela realized that while she had been honest with Thiha, she hadn't even given the others a chance to object: the kids, and the Muslim lady, and Kyaw Kyaw, the sweeper. She hadn't lied to them, she just hadn't considered that she had any obligation to tell them the truth.

"Did Kyaw Kyaw have to leave too?"

Daw Pancavati nodded. "He will go."

Adela felt tears choke her again. Her face ached with the strain of holding back her sadness and rage.

"You hate him, don't you?" she snapped. Suddenly she was so angry she could hardly speak. "Because he's Muslim. Because he's a kala. That night I went to his house to eat, you told me I shouldn't have gone. You acted like he did something wrong." The words came out in a torrent. It was as if Thiha's mother had handed her a hot coal, and she had to pass it to someone else before it burned through her skin.

"He does not do wrong," the nun responded calmly. "You do wrong by accepting him."

"You say all this stuff about goodwill, and you don't even mean it! You don't even care what happens to them!" She knew she was being childish and unfair, but it felt good to yell at someone.

"I care. But I cannot change this."

"Well, isn't it convenient for you to think so?" spat Adela. She couldn't believe she was talking to her friend this way. "Just keep chanting the metta sutta, right?"

A touch, and Adela would have crumbled. But Daw Pancavati did not touch Adela. She looked at her without malice.

"I chant this for you now, thamee," she said, and she closed her eyes. Adela heard the words she'd heard in the Edgerton Fields cafetorium from Ko Oo's mouth. This time, she knew what they meant. *May you be free from danger. May you be free from mental suffering. May you be free from physical suffering. May you live in comfort.*

Adela slumped in her chair. She let the sound flow over, and she felt her throat relax. She let herself rest for a moment, sitting in front of the dormitory, her face streaked with mud and tears. When the chanting stopped and she opened her eyes, Daw Pancavati's face welcomed her.

"I'm sorry," Adela muttered. "I know it's not your fault."

The nun shook her head. "It is good to feel this, to know anger. Then you can know where it lead."

"But does Kyaw Kyaw have to leave?" Adela continued in a meeker tone. "My god, how many people's lives can I ruin? And the Muslim lady who begs for food?"

Daw Pancavati furrowed her brow. "She is here. This lady is not Muslim. She come from my village after Nargis."

Adela groaned. She hadn't even gotten her facts right.

"I'm such an idiot," she said, burying her face in her hands.

"Thamee, you are not like this."

"But I did so many stupid things."

"Everyone do the stupid thing. We are not the Buddha."

"Is there anything else? Just tell me now."

Daw Pancavati hesitated before she spoke. "U Pyinnya and U Suriya, they will leave the monastery, too, after rains retreat."

"Why?"

"U Pyinnya and U Suriya, a long time they have some disagreement with U Nyanika. They go to a place that is better for them."

"And Bhante agrees to this? He's not angry with them?"

"It is best."

U Agga had been wrong. Adela couldn't be a Stream Enterer. She had created a schism in the monastic community.

"But what was their disagreement about? Did U Pyinnya and U Suriya agree with what I was trying to do?"

That seemed impossible; the only comment of substance she'd ever heard U Suriya make was, "Monk should not involve in politics." She couldn't see him standing up in defense of her Facebook page.

"No, not like this. But they do not agree what U Nyanika does."

"Like kicking me out of the dining hall."

"This and many other thing."

"Do *you* agree with U Nyanika? That I should just . . . stay away from everyone?"

"Thamee, this is not my place to agree, to disagree. No one ask me. But you are my daughter, I feel metta for you. I chant for you every time."

It was not the ringing defense that Adela wanted to hear, but Daw Pancavati was trying so hard to make her feel better. And what had Adela done for her friend? She had shat all over her room and brought her dukkha. She had given her nothing.

"Amay, how can I repay you for everything you've done for me?"

"Do not repay. I have no children. Take care of me when I am old."

"Of course," said Adela. Then she turned her face away, because it was the only thing Daw Pancavati ever asked her for, and they both knew she wouldn't do it.

"I've got to pack," Adela said abruptly. "I'm leaving tomorrow."

She would have several nights in Yangon before her flight. She was not looking forward to her debrief with MVU, but there was no way to avoid it. She had never responded to Sarah's email asking her to get in touch right away.

Adela went back to her room, took her clothes down from their hangers, and put them in her suitcase. She gathered up her toiletries and put them back in her kit. In half an hour the room looked just as it had when she'd entered it three months before. A bunk bed. A cord with a few hangers dangling from it. A small table and a jug of water with a plastic cup overturned on the top. It had seemed like so little then. Now each object was suffused with meaning. She and Thiha had drunk from that cup. They had rested their heads on that musty pillow.

She took out her camera and photographed each object in the room, lovingly, from various angles. At the time, she felt like she was preserving evidence, building some kind of case for herself. But when she looked at the pictures later, they were so dim, so lacking compared to the images in her mind: just an unhinged girl's obsessive catalog of her months in a foreign country, which no one else would ever care to see.

THE HORROR, THE HORROR!

An hour later, Daw Pancavati was sent to summon Adela once again. Apparently, the nun was considered the only person whom Adela could not insult or degrade or corrupt. Or maybe the others just didn't care what Adela did to her.

Daw Pancavati escorted Adela to the office, where Sarah was waiting.

Sarah was dressed as always in a loungyi and white blouse, her braid trailing over her shoulder. Adela wondered what secret Sarah had learned, living in this country so many years, that allowed her to appear freshly showered throughout the hot days. Daw Pancavati left them, probably glad she didn't have to translate this conversation as well.

"Hello, Adela."

Adela almost corrected her. No one had called her anything but Sabeh in months. She took a seat across the table.

"I don't think I need to tell you," said Sarah, looking at her directly, "that this has been very bad for MVU."

Adela thought remorsefully of the link to MVU that she'd posted. She would have to say she was sorry, again. But her apology caught in her throat, and a sudden hostility came over her.

"No, you don't need to tell me. If that's what you came here for, consider it done," she snapped.

How strange it was to speak English naturally, with no concern that she wouldn't be understood. It was like having a weight taken off her tongue. She wanted to be sarcastic, she wanted to curse.

"No, that's not why I came," Sarah said, unperturbed by Adela's outburst. "Actually I came here to tell you that in an hour, the immigration police are coming to pick you up. You're being deported."

The word felt like a door closing on her fingers. "Deported?"

"I think it's symbolic, since you were supposed to leave in two days anyway. They're just reminding everyone who's in charge."

"What does that mean, 'deported'? Who's 'they'?"

Sarah smiled wryly. "They is they. And being deported means you get a free plane trip to Bangkok."

Adela tried to put Sarah's words together. Bangkok? Why would she go to Bangkok?

"Then what?"

"Then you can do what you like. You can stay there a few days, or you can reschedule your ticket home and leave right away."

Adela could hardly imagine standing up from the table without help. The idea that she was supposed to make her way home by herself was unbelievable, overwhelming.

"And . . . you probably can't come back to Myanmar any time soon."

Adela cleared her throat to cover the strangled sound that came from her mouth. Just days ago, she'd been fantasizing that she and Thiha would live in Yangon together in a few years' time. It had never been likely, but now it would be impossible.

"OK."

They sat in silence. Adela saw a drop of mango juice that had dried on the table, and she began scraping at it with her fingernail. How had it gotten there? Had she and Thiha eaten mangoes here? She wondered about the other traces of her presence around the monastery. She'd dripped candle wax on the table by her bed and broken one of the floor tiles in the bathroom throwing a bottle of shampoo at a rat. There must be more personal things, too: little patches of bacteria, saliva on the rim of the cup in her room. All the cells of not-self she was constantly shedding.

"Adela, are you alright?"

Adela looked up from the table, shivering suddenly despite the afternoon's heat.

"I'll be fine," she croaked. "Sorry about MVU."

"No need to apologize to me. I'm not MVU."

"But you helped to found it, right?"

"Yeah . . . I mean, MVU is fine. People come, they do their three months, they leave."

"Or they destroy a few people's lives," Adela added with undisguised self-pity.

Sarah raised her eyebrows. "You might be overestimating your impact."

Of course Sarah had to bring her down a notch. But Adela hoped she might be right.

"Sarah, do you know anything about my, um—this guy who helped me? So, his mother came here this morning and said he'd lost his scholarship, and I was just wondering, does that sound credible to you?" Adela asked, her voice getting high and squeaky at the end.

"Oh, the guy who translated the page." Sarah squinted. "Yeah, I suppose it's possible."

"He was an ex-political prisoner, and I'm worried that—I don't know . . ."

Sarah shook her head. "I doubt he'd go to prison again. These days they tend to punish people in other ways."

"What do you mean?"

"You know, hard to get a job, hard to rent an apartment, hard to do anything bureaucratic, which in this country means everything . . . it's not necessarily an organized thing. Rumors and a bad reputation are a pretty effective punishment."

Adela thought of Thiha's little sister and her school fees. She thought of his dreams of opening a real hospital. How could Sarah be so nonchalant? Anger swept over Adela again. She wanted to know what Sarah thought of her, she wanted to hear the worst.

"So what did you think of the page?" she demanded.

Sarah shrugged. "It's actually not a bad idea, but you probably weren't the right person to do it."

"Who is?"

"Someone with credibility. Someone who checked their sources and built connections first."

"Someone like you, you mean."

Sarah scoffed. "Definitely not someone like me. Adela, you don't seem to understand that our role here is very limited. And that's the way it should be."

"Our role?"

"You and me, Adela," she said, gesturing back and forth between their faces. "People like you and me."

"But you have your women's income generation project," Adela protested. "What do you do with them?"

"As little as possible."

"What do you mean?"

"I just try to create the space for the women to collaborate."

"Is it . . . working out?" Adela asked, somewhat accusatorily.

Sarah sighed. "Honestly, there are a lot of problems. Between the Rakhine Women's Development Association and the Women's Muslim Leadership Council, for instance. As you can imagine, there's a—lack of trust."

"Yeah. But how can they collaborate if they hate each other?"

"Well, they can't. But that part isn't my job. I can't make them not hate each other."

"I guess not," Adela replied sulkily.

Sarah pushed her chair back from the table. "Listen, I'm in Myanmar because I want to be. And I try to do my job as best I can. But there will always be things I can't understand."

Adela felt herself perking up. An argument seemed like a nice distraction. "Maybe some things aren't worth understanding. Like racism, or hating someone because of their religion."

Sarah shook her head emphatically. "Those are the things that are *most* worth understanding. I try to keep relationships with people even when I think they're wrong."

"Like, how wrong? Hitler? Ne Win? People who torture political prisoners?"

"Like . . . immigration police, for instance. Would you rather they'd dragged you from your bed at night?"

"No. Is that what they were going to do?"

"It would not have been pleasant. They let me come here first because I have a relationship with them."

"Isn't that kind of unethical?"

"There's no way MVU could function otherwise. So many volunteers coming and going? Things are bound to come up. It's not like every person in the immigration police is evil."

"Just 99 percent of them," said Adela, cackling grimly. It was her private joke with U Nyanika.

Sarah looked quizzically at her. "Well, I imagine you have some packing to do."

"Actually, no."

"In any case, I've got to be going."

Adela was too proud to ask Sarah to stay and keep her company. In some parallel universe, where Adela hadn't just damaged Sarah's organization and trampled on the principles she held dear, they could have been friends.

"Thanks for coming," Adela sighed.

"Yeah," she said, standing up.

"So I have an hour?"

"More or less."

"Should I, like, wait by the gate, or do they want to come and drag me out of my room?"

"In theory, you're not supposed to know about it."

"But Bhante knows."

"The people in the monastery? Sure, they know."

"So that's why they didn't just kick me out. They wanted this to happen."

"I guess so. Cooperating with the authorities, having you leave in such a public way, it's a pretty clear way for the monastery's leadership to distance themselves from what you did."

"But why is this such a big deal? Don't the immigration police have dangerous criminals to catch?"

"To tell the truth, I was surprised, too. Other foreigners have certainly had more of an impact and gotten away with it, but I guess you stepped on someone's toes. Probably just bad luck. Sometimes their decisions seem quite random."

Adela would have liked to think she'd been specially selected as an enemy of the state, but in a way it seemed more fitting that her deportation was a haphazard mistake, pushed through the bureaucracy by some distant cousin of U Nyanika or Thiha's mother. She would leave, balance would be restored, and everything would go back to normal—for everyone except Thiha, Kyaw Kyaw, and the Muslim kids and their families.

Sarah glanced at her watch. "Bye, Adela."

Adela waved her off weakly. Sarah strode toward the gate, her shoulder bag swinging against her hip and her braid falling neatly down her back.

Since Adela had already packed her suitcase, she decided to walk around the compound one last time. From a distance, she said her goodbyes. School was in session, and the lessons had reached a hysterical pitch. Did the kids miss Razak and Pho Cho and Sanda? As adults, would any of them remember, foggily, the kala kids who had disappeared? What kind of place would Burma be by the time they reached adulthood?

Adela gave a wide berth to the dining hall, but as she did so she thought of U Pyinnya and U Suriya, who would leave partly because of what she'd set in motion. In her mind she wished them well, and U Nyanika, too. Adela despised him, and she knew he felt the same about her. Yet there was a strange intimacy to their hatred. He had told her what he really thought, and for that she was grateful.

It was harder to let go of the chance to explain herself to the people she'd hardly spoken to—Kyaw Kyaw, who was as inscrutable to her as he'd been the day he invited her for dinner. And the waya wutsa men and women who cooked and cleaned and made it possible for the monastery to run. She tried to recall their faces so she could send them metta, but Thiha was the only one she could picture.

As Adela passed Bhante's hall, she thought of his face: sometimes smiling, sometimes calm, but never angry. She couldn't believe that he wished her any harm. If he shared U Nyanika's views of Muslims, wouldn't he have punished her more severely? She was tempted to go in and try to talk to him, but she knew it would reflect poorly on Daw Pancavati if she did, so she headed for the nun's hut instead.

When Adela entered, Daw Pancavati was sitting cross-legged in the middle of the room. Next to her was a woven plastic bag about the size of her body. The light in the room was different, harsher; the pink curtains were gone. The mattress was bare, and the small table that usually held medicines and books had been wiped clean. The room had been prepared for someone else's use.

Daw Pancavati smiled and held out Adela's amulet. Adela knelt beside her friend on the floor, tears already blurring her vision.

"They're making you leaving because of me, aren't they? They blame you for what I did."

Daw Pancavati fastened the amulet around Adela's neck. "This one keep you safe now. I am sorry I cannot do more for you, thamee."

"But where will you go?"

"I will go to my village. I still have one sister. There is a monastery in the next village also."

"But Yadana is where you wanted to stay, where you wanted to die!"

The nun smiled and touched the center of her chest. "I take my refuge with me. Do not worry for me, thamee. The Buddha does not mind, I am here or I am there."

For the second time that day, Adela bowed down. As her forehead touched the floor, the nun began chanting a prayer over her. Adela rested there, wishing she never had to lift her face again. When the prayer ended, Daw Pancavati laid a hand on Adela's bowed shoulder, and spoke in English:

"May you have the good life in America. Be careful and do right. Please find the meditation teacher for you. Send metta to all beings. Come back someday."

Adela lifted her tear-stained face. "You won't come out and say goodbye to me when I go?"

Daw Pancavati shook her head. "I do not want to see this."

Adela looped her arms around the nun's waist, breathing in her smell of camphor and milky tea.

"I love you, amay." She looked one more time into Daw Pancavati's dear face, and around at the bare walls that had sheltered her in her sickness.

For the last time, Adela walked back to the dormitory. In her room, with all of her things packed up, there was nothing left to do. So she sat down and meditated. She didn't know when the police would arrive, but she wanted to greet them this way: calm, ready, without any anger in her heart. At first her breath felt hot in her chest, and each inhale harbored a sob. Slowly her breath cooled, and she felt it expand into the space around her, into this room where she'd slept and dreamed a hundred nights. With the amulet's familiar weight on her chest, she felt herself returning to that state of concentration that she'd had while on retreat. Each breath was enough. She stopped thinking of what she'd done, and she stopped thinking about going home. She stopped thinking, and she breathed.

❀

When the knock on the door came, minutes or hours later, it was surprisingly timid. Adela opened her eyes. The second knock was more forceful.

She stood slowly and she lifted, moved, and placed her feet until she reached the door.

Two men stood outside. Neither of them wore uniforms. Both had on slacks, white shirts, and mirrored sunglasses.

"Ah-deh-la Fa-rost?" mumbled one of them, as if he were shy about mispronouncing her name. He was holding her open passport in his hand, which she hadn't seen since she'd handed it over to Daw Pancavati for safe-keeping when she'd arrived.

"Yes."

"We take you to airport now."

"OK. I'm ready."

She slung her backpack over her shoulder and reached for her suitcase, but the silent officer stepped around her and grabbed it, whether because he thought it was his duty, or because he worried she would slow them down by struggling with it. Adela suppressed the urge to laugh out loud at the irony: even while being deported, the white girl gets her luggage carried.

They made their way across the courtyard in a ridiculous procession, one of them on each side of her as if she were going to run away. A small crowd of assorted monastery dwellers had gathered and was milling around the gate. Adela didn't know whether she should look them in the eye, smile, or even wave. She searched their faces for disapproval or vindi-cation, but their eyes were placid, their foreheads uncreased. They looked as if they were accepting a delivery of water jugs, which often came at this time of day, and which required several people's labor to distribute through the compound.

There was no one among the crowd whom Adela had known espe-cially, so she lowered her eyes and walked toward the green truck that was apparently their destination. The gate had been pushed all the way open to let it in. It was really too large a vehicle for the task at hand, and Adela wondered if there'd be anyone else inside. The silent policeman shoved her suitcase up, climbed in himself, and then extended a hand so that she could climb up. He really was polite, and Adela wondered how much he knew about what she'd done.

The other fellow got in the driver's seat. The sides of the truck were open, covered with green slats only up to the level of her neck, and so she could see Bhante emerge and stand on the steps of the main hall. He was far enough away that Adela couldn't see the expression on his face, but she knew it would be as it usually was: beaming with equanimity. He raised his hand and gave her one of his signature waves, spreading his fingers and rotating his hand slowly. She stuck her arm out of the truck to be sure he'd see her, and she waved back.

The truck reversed noisily onto the street, and all the people in the neighborhood poked their heads out of shops and out from under umbrellas to watch. The noodle seller looked up from slicing cabbage, squinted at her, then looked away. The waya wutsa guys slid the iron gate back into place as if they were closing the eye of a giant. Just like that, all Adela had seen was closed off from her, to be visited only through the veil of memory.

Across the road, a small girl with curly black hair picked through a pile of garbage. Beside her was a wooden cart into which she sorted bottles and bits of metal. As the truck pulled slowly away, it passed dangerously close to her, and she lifted her face just in time for Adela to see that it was Sanda, Sanda who had smiled so bravely for her photograph, Sanda who had pressed herself into Adela's chest like a little bird the day she learned she should not call herself kala.

The horror! The horror! Was that what Kurtz had seen on his deathbed in *Heart of Darkness*? The faces of the people whose lives he'd broken in the service of his own dreams? In that split second Adela knew she'd seen Sanda, but later she'd tell herself it was a mirage, or a different child altogether. What were the chances Adela would see the consequences of her actions laid bare like that? Adela never told anyone about seeing Sanda leap back as the truck roared past her, even later when she confessed everything else to Greg and Lena.

Adela watched the trees slide past, and she felt Burma slipping away from her, along with all the promises she'd broken. She hadn't visited Ko Oo's mother; the photograph of him standing in front of the library was still in her suitcase. She squeezed her eyes shut with remorse. She hadn't visited the Bridge on the River Kwai for Grandpa Douglas. She hadn't donated to the monastery, or bowed down at the Shwedagon Pagoda.

This last one made her the saddest. All she'd ever see was that glimpse from a taxicab window at night, nothing more than she'd dreamed before she'd come. She'd been in Burma two months and twenty-eight days. Had anything she'd seen been more real than that dream?

❀

Adela cried all through the flight from Yangon to Bangkok. It was not her usual sort of crying, with sobbing and tears, but rather a noise that came from her throat every time she breathed: *eeuh, eeuh, eeuh.* The sound filled the small plane, drawing stares from the passengers around her: All of the events of the past months seemed to occupy her body at once: her illness, her meditation retreat, sex with Thiha, the page and its horrible consequences. Her body's only response was this keening sound, some attempt to exorcise the images that flashed before her eyes: the charred corpse in the green field; Thiha splashing his chest with glittering water; a knuckle of meat in a bowl of greasy broth; Daw Pancavati wiping vomit from the corner's of Adela's mouth; U Nyanika silhouetted against the noonday sun as he blocked her way into the dining hall; Sanda scavenging in the garbage. Adela heard Bhante's voice like a curse: "*Seeing.* You must note, '*Seeing, seeing.*'" It was as if her eyes were stuck open, even—especially—when she closed them. She saw, but each image seemed empty of meaning or, rather, vulnerable to many meanings.

After her long flight to Tokyo, Adela felt a change. The airport was bright and orderly. Travelers browsed through the newsstands and toted their luggage in and out of the bathrooms. Just as she'd done on her way into Burma, she got herself some sushi.

A man in a gray suit had left a *Wall Street Journal* behind, and Adela scanned the front page. No headline mentioned her exploits, and as she swallowed down her sushi with a glass of water, she laughed a little. The world had gone on without her. Most people hadn't heard about, and wouldn't care about, "communal conflict" in Myanmar. Her mother's Volkswagen would be waiting at the airport. Adela would sleep in a soft bed with clean sheets, and she would wake up back in the world that she knew.

Adela dozed dreamlessly most of the way from Tokyo to DC. When she woke up, the flight attendant was offering bitter, bright green tea. Back at the monastery, where it was already the morning of the following day, Daw Pancavati would be pouring out a cup of Laphet yay. Then Adela remembered: Daw Pancavati wouldn't be there. She was probably in the back of a truck on some dusty road leading south to the Irrawaddy Delta, her plastic bag of belongings beside her.

As the captain announced their descent into Dulles, the evening sky burned pink and smoggy above the clouds. Adela felt in the pit of her belly that she was sinking irreversibly nearer to the earth, and she did as Daw Pancavati had told her to: she sent metta. As Bhante had instructed, she started with herself, her throat raw from crying and the salt of dried tears prickling the skin on her neck. Adela continued around the plane: Chinese man wearing a paper hospital mask; flight attendant who had refilled her water bottle twice; pregnant lady holding an airsick bag to her face; the pilot, unseen, who guided them all downward. It was enough, for the time being. She couldn't bear to confront, even in prayer, all the people she'd hurt.

THE NEXT LIFE

It shocked me how easy it was to leave Burma behind. A week after I left, I was at Pomona, going to ice cream socials and touring the library. There were deep shadows under my eyes and I had trouble putting words together, but I was standing. "Oh, that's so cool you went to Burma!" was the universal response when I said what I'd done that summer. I'd spent so much time rehearsing how I'd describe what had happened, and it turned out that most people weren't even curious.

There were a few hard weeks in September. My mother, Lena, and even Greg were calling me all the time, trying to make sure I was OK. I usually ignored them. If I started talking about Burma again, I'd never stop. I was crying a lot, but I had to do it where no one could hear me, which was in the shower. My days were filled with acting normal, going to class and making new friends, then before bed I'd take a long, hysterical shower and crawl under the covers with my passport, staring in disbelief at the girl who smirked out at me from the photograph.

By October I was doing a little better. I made myself go to a lecture called "Engaged Buddhism: Walking the Middle Path," by a religion professor who also led the campus meditation group. Her name was Martha— that's what she made us call her, instead of Professor Schwartz. I sat in the front row, so close that I could see the sunspots on her face and the jeweled pins holding up her coil of white hair. The person who introduced her mentioned some monasteries where she'd studied in Burma and Thailand, but Yadana wasn't among them.

I couldn't concentrate on her lecture. I had been trying to meditate since I got back from Burma, but something was wrong. After a few minutes of sitting and watching the breath, I'd hyperventilate and my heart would beat too fast. It felt like drowning.

As the crowd filed out after the question-and-answer period, I approached the podium. Martha put down her bag and gazed patiently at me.

"When I meditate, I can't breathe," I said, and it started happening to me right then, I was gasping for air in the hall emptying of people. She motioned me to a chair.

"This summer I spent three months in Burma," I said, and then I started to cry.

It was such a relief to look through my tears into Martha's eyes. They were like Daw Pancavati's—not judging or condemning or saving me, just seeing me. I confessed everything. It took nearly an hour.

"The monks were right, you can become a Stream Enterer," she said when I finished. "You found the Buddha's teachings very young, from across the world. And this amulet came to you," she said, gesturing to my neck. "This is not by accident."

Just as I started to feel puffed up with pride again, she said, "There is also an important role for remorse in our lives that is often overlooked in the West. It's remorse about what you've done, not shame about who you are."

She laid a hand on my arm to see how I was digesting these points. My eyes were full of tears, but I held her gaze.

"It is remorse that makes us fear hurting people again. If we knew how much each moment mattered, we would take every opportunity to be generous. We would keep the Precepts."

"I do feel remorse," I said. "I am so sorry."

"What are you sorry for?"

I paused. I'd gotten used to trying to forget about it.

"I don't know."

"I think you do," she said. "I think you do know. Make a list. And come to my meditation group on Thursday nights. Will you?"

"I will," I said, blowing my nose. She didn't hug me, but she held me with her eyes. I sensed the edges of a great refuge of calmness, like the one I'd known during my retreat.

"Do," she said.

So I started going to Martha's group. We do half an hour of sitting meditation and then Martha gives a dharma talk, with time for questions afterward. Her talks aren't like Bhante's; she doesn't quote suttas or make us answer rhetorical questions. Instead she speaks about things she heard on the radio, or a disagreement she had with her neighbor. But Martha is wise: at the end of every story there is a little kernel of insight.

The first time I went, Martha told us about her daughter, who'd died of a drug overdose as a teenager. For a year afterward, Martha carried a lock of her daughter's hair with her, and she would show it to strangers and tell them what had happened. Each person she showed it to shared in return a story of losing someone—maybe a child, maybe a parent or lover or friend. When the year was over, she put the lock of hair on the altar in her bedroom, and she told us that each time she sees it she remembers that, sooner or later, everyone loses the people they love. It's not right or wrong, she said, it's just the way this world works. The reality of death and suffering is comforting because it's the truth. When we stop avoiding it, that reality becomes our refuge.

The story was somehow familiar, and it made me think of Daw Pancavati and the son she lost in Cyclone Nargis. I realized then that Martha had given us her own version of the Buddhist parable Daw Pancavati told me—the one where the woman carries her dead baby around trying to find a mustard seed from a house where no one has died.

A couple of kids cried at the end of Martha's talk that night. Everyone has their own reasons for being there—anxiety, depression, some kind of emptiness. It's kind of like group therapy.

I never say much. How would I explain? Because of karma from my past lives, I had an affair with a guy in a monastery in Burma, and then I caused a schism in the monastic community and was deported for starting a Facebook page? Chloe and Hunter and Kayla are nice, but I don't think they even believe in karma. The way people practice Buddhism here is so different—there is a lot of thinking, as Bhante would say. Everyone wants the wisdom and tranquility without anything even vaguely superstitious.

I miss the chanting, the bowing, all the rituals I'm not supposed to be attached to.

But the group is the closest thing I have to Burma. It was there that I was able to start meditating again. Surrounded by the breathing of others, panic didn't clench my chest. I could go back to those three months with a calmer mind. Finally, one night in November after coming home from meditation, I made the list of what I was sorry for.

First Precept: Refrain from harming living beings. I hurt Thiha and his family, Bhante and the monastery, Kyaw Kyaw, the Muslim kids, MVU, Daw Pancavati, and myself. I did not have the intention to harm anyone, but I didn't use wisdom or skill to avoid it.

Second Precept: Refrain from taking what is not freely given. I took people's photos and used them without their consent for my own purposes. Sarah had warned me against that in the MVU orientation, on my first day in Yangon.

Third Precept: Refrain from sexual misconduct. I had sex—in a monastery—with a man who was engaged to someone else. I didn't know he was engaged, but I knew something was not right. Something *was* right about it. We were meant to know each other. Just not that way, not at that time.

Fourth Precept: Refrain from harmful speech. I ignored Daw Pancavati's advice not to talk about the Buddhist-Muslim conflict anymore. It wasn't wrong to talk about it—it was the way I talked about it. It was how I spoke and when and with whom.

Fifth Precept: Refrain from taking intoxicants which dull the mind. I put up the Facebook page drunk on vanity and pride. What spell was I under that I thought I should carry out this grand plan without the advice of the people I was supposedly trying to help?

When I showed Martha the list, she told me I should try to make amends. It sounded kind of like Twelve Steps—Martha is also a substance abuse counselor—but I trust her.

Still, it was hard to think of what I could do. I had no way to get in touch with Thiha, and it seemed the best way I could make amends to him was to stay far, far away.

Daw Pancavati was also unreachable, short of going to the Irrawaddy Delta, which I couldn't do since I was banned from returning to Burma. So I emailed Sarah, and I asked her to help me make donations to the monastery, to MVU, and to her women's income generation project. She wrote back:

> Adela,
> What a surprise to hear from you. The donations are a good idea. Actually, I don't work at MVU anymore—my women's project got funding from a foundation in Germany, so I'm doing that fulltime now. The Buddhist-Muslim issue is getting a lot of attention from NGOs these days. Maybe too much. Anyway, I can arrange the donations if you transfer the money to my US bank account; see details below.
> Sarah

I wondered what she meant by the Buddhist-Muslim issue getting "too much" attention. In any case, I was glad that her organization had gotten support. It was comforting that Sarah was still Sarah, not going out of her way to make me feel better.

Martha recommended that I donate whatever extra spending money I had at the end of each month. I decided to get a job in the library so I could donate more. When I told my mother, she said I was nuts. "Adela, you're just swinging from one extreme to another! Let it go! You have your whole life ahead of you," she said.

Lives, I wanted to correct her. I have lifetimes and lifetimes ahead of me. But I knew that wouldn't convince her, so I just silently sent her metta.

Lena didn't really understand either. We've talked on the phone a couple of times, but our conversations have been strained. She couldn't get over the fact that I blamed myself for what happened. "What are you going to do, hide in your room and meditate for the rest of your life?" she asked. "That doesn't help anyone. You were trying to do the right thing. You made a difference."

I hate that phrase. Everyone makes a difference, whether they like it or not.

With Greg it was the same. "Voluntourism is inherently problematic," he admitted. "But all things said and done, it doesn't seem like that many people even noticed the page. It was no KONY2012. So don't beat yourself up."

Martha warns me about that too, whenever I get too dramatic. "The self is a delusion, whether you're praising it or blaming it," she likes to say.

Every time I think I have things figured out, someone I respect says something that surprises me. A few days after I transferred my first month's donations to Sarah's account, my mom forwarded a thick envelope that had arrived from Edgerton Fields months ago: my senior essay. As far as Ms. Alvarez knew, my trip and my blog had been a success—I never explained those few odd comments that appeared late in the summer. On the last page of my paper, she'd written "A-," and beneath it:

> Adela,
> You make a convincing case that the narration in Heart of Darkness is unreliable, although other scholars have demonstrated this previously. But you take for granted Conrad's own anti-colonial sentiments. Remember that Chinua Achebe accused Conrad himself of perpetuating racist stereotypes of Africans. Perhaps what you read as Marlow's unreliability as a narrator stems at least in part from Conrad's own blind spots, rather than from his ability to see his characters and his own historical moment clearly. Conrad may have been prescient, but by equating his position with present-day anti-racism, you dehistoricize his perspective. As Conrad himself wrote: "The most you can hope for is some knowledge of yourself—that comes too late—a crop of inextinguishable regrets." It doesn't sound good in a graduation card, but I believe it.
> Best,
> Amy Alvarez

It seemed like a lifetime ago that I had written that paper, and I could hardly remember my main argument, so it took me a minute to understand what she was saying. Conrad was a misguided racist who had written a book that revealed the horror of racism, or at least one that had meanings beyond what he'd intended. Could my page have been similar?

I wonder, because two people got in touch with me just after that. One was Ma Soe, Sarah's assistant, whom I remembered only as the woman who'd driven the van and brought us lunch during the orientation. She wanted to thank me for my donations to MVU. She also said that she was sorry for what happened with my Facebook page. "I am ashamed when I see what someone write to you, and I really apologize," she wrote. "We Myanmar people have some weakness with this issue. When I see your page at first, I feel inspire. Thank you for your metta for us."

The other person who contacted me was a kid from Edgerton Fields who I vaguely remembered from phys ed class. He was a year behind me, and he'd decided to do his senior essay on the Buddhist-Muslim conflict, or as he called it, "the genocide of the Rohingya." He'd seen what happened with my page—as Lena told me, it caused a bit of a furor among the kids at Edgerton Fields. He plans to interview Burmese refugees living in Massachusetts about their feelings on the 969 movement. I told him where to find Ko Oo, and I asked him to say hi for me.

I gave the kid the same advice Greg had inscribed in my copy of *Insurgency and the Politics of Ethnicity*: "Burma is complicated." I left off "Have fun."

Regardless of what my mom and Lena and Greg thought, Martha was right. After I started making donations, I felt better. Even alone in my room, I could meditate without panicking. I got a regular practice going, half an hour every morning and evening. All through California's strange non-winter, I watched the air going in and out of my lungs, comforting myself with the thought that each mindful breath weighed against what I'd done and built up good karma for the next life.

I was feeling so good, in fact, that this spring, when I saw the poster for the roundtable on "Communal Conflict in Myanmar" that the International Relations Program was hosting, I decided to go. The first part was beautiful: a monk video-conferenced in from Burma, and told the story of how he and his monastery had sheltered hundreds of Muslims during the latest outbreak of violence, in Meikhtila. It was the version of Buddhism I recognized from my own experience. But the panel discussion afterward was awful. I watched a Rakhine activist and a Rohingya cleric, both equally irate, lay into each other with questionable statistics and sweeping historical accounts. The audience just seemed confused.

It was the photographic negative of the discussion at the MVU training a year earlier, where I'd asked why the UN hadn't intervened in the elections. Instead of feeling like the least-informed person in the room, I felt like I knew more than I wanted to. I knew that neither of the men was telling the whole truth. Whatever facts they used, they were only attacking each other, neither of them acknowledging the human suffering on the other side. That's one thing that's changed in the past year: I can't idealize one position or another. There's no denying that Muslims in Burma are suffering. Disproportionately. And they're not the only ones. But these figureheads who claim to speak for their communities, and the well-intentioned Westerners who try to intervene—I wonder if their reactions to that suffering make the situation even worse.

As for me, I'm happy with my novels. My favorite class is called The Colonial Encounter in Literature. I signed up for it because *Burmese Days* was on the syllabus. But the book struck me so much differently than it had when I read it in Burma. This time, I felt sympathy for everyone: Flory, with his self-hatred; his Burmese lover, terrified of being abandoned; even the scheming U Po Kyin—how he suffers because of his greed, dying before he can build his pagodas and redeem his karma! It's a catalogue of human failings, and I couldn't help but see my own.

And then I realized that Orwell wasn't trying to describe the way things should be. He wasn't even describing the way things were. He was just describing what he saw. Like Joseph Conrad, he was writing the only book he could write. That was what I got wrong about analyzing literature in high school: I was always complaining that authors weren't providing clear examples of social justice or gender equality. But authors write books because they don't know how the world should be. If they knew, they'd be politicians, they'd be journalists. They'd be interning at the New America Foundation, like Greg.

I don't know how the world works, but still the world works, and not the way I want it to. If I had my way, I'd still be in Burma. I'd have seen the rains taper off, and the dry season yield to the heat of March. Thiha and I would have had a chance to really know each other. I would have taken care of Daw Pancavati, like she asked me to. I would be doing some slow and worthwhile work, like Sarah. I would have stayed.

Stay here, my dream told me. As much as I wanted to stay, it was bad advice. You can't stay anywhere. Bhante would call it anicca, impermanence. My dream of the Shwedagon Pagoda wasn't a message from the universe, it was just my mind clinging to desire, from this life or another. If I dream of Burma again, if I dream of Thiha again, I'll remember to say goodbye.

Author's Note

This novel comes out of my experiences as a researcher focusing on Burma/Myanmar over the past eighteen years. That is not to say that it contains "the truth" about the Buddhist-Muslim conflict. Although I reference actual events, this book is a work of fiction. Also, while I share a home country with the main character, this is not an autobiography; I have not done the things Adela did (except meditation retreats). My goal is to draw attention not only to the Buddhist-Muslim conflict in all of its complexity, but also to the challenges of representation across cultural divides and power discrepancies.

As I wrote and revised this book, many people gave me advice. Some were intimately familiar with Burma, and others gave suggestions from a literary perspective. I do not mention their names here because of the politically sensitive nature of the topics covered, but I am grateful for their help.

I also want to express my gratitude to family and friends who encouraged me, to the staff of Northern Illinois University Press who took a chance on this novel, and to two anonymous reviewers whose comments helped me improve the manuscript.

Brief Outline of Historical Events Mentioned in This Novel

Early history: Many kinds of power structures exist within the territory now known as Burma/Myanmar, including kingdoms led by Burman Buddhists and by other ethnic and religious groups.

1885: Britain's piecemeal conquest of what is now Burma is completed; the area becomes a province of British India. The "Frontier Areas" (Shan, Kachin, Chin, and Karenni States) are allowed more autonomy in comparison to the central area where Burmans are a majority, in what many historians describe as "Divide and Rule" policy. The British designate 135 ethnic groups within Burma.

1947: General Aung San, who helped to negotiate Burma's independence, is assassinated.

1948: British decolonization proceeds, followed by civil war between the central government and ethnic, political, and religious groups seeking autonomy or change. The new country designates eight "National Races" (Burman, Karen, Karenni, Kachin, Shan, Mon, Rakhine, and Chin) and recognizes the same 135 ethnic subgroups that the British did.

1962: A military junta led by General Ne Win and a "Revolutionary Council" of army leaders takes over the country, claiming that their rule will prevent the disintegration of the country into ethnic and political factions.

1974: The Burmese Socialist Programme Party (BSPP), or MaSaLa, also led by General Ne Win, institutes one-party rule.

1988: Pro-democracy protests, during which Daw Aung San Suu Kyi emerges as a leader, end with a crackdown and a reestablishment of military rule.

1990: The junta holds multi-party elections but does not hand over power to the winning National League for Democracy, led by Daw Aung San Suu Kyi; she is placed under house arrest.

2007: "Saffron Revolution": after the government cancels fuel subsidies and the price of gasoline increases overnight, monks (in their saffron-colored robes) take to the streets to protest government policy and ask for change. People from many walks of life join the protests or support the monks, but the demonstrations do not bring about immediate political change.

2008: Cyclone Nargis kills nearly a hundred thousand people and displaces hundreds of thousands; the junta turns away international aid and is criticized in the West for its slow response to the disaster.

2010: Elections are held for the first time since 1990; military-backed parties win a majority of votes, but some opposition parties win seats in parliament.

2012: Violent conflicts occur between Buddhists and Muslims, first in Rakhine State and then in other areas across the country.

Glossary of Terms, Public Figures, and Events

In this book I do not italicize Burmese words. I hope that Burmese readers will find terms they know easy to recognize, while those unfamiliar with the language will be able to absorb their meanings. I sacrifice accuracy for comprehension when there is a commonly used English transliteration of a word (*sayama* instead of *hsayama*, for instance). I render terms from Pali language without diacritical marks and without trying to replicate the distinctive ways that Burmese speakers pronounce these terms.

969: A Buddhist nationalist movement.

Anicca: Impermanence.

Anatta: Non-self or not-self.

Aung San: Leader who fought for independence from the British, assassinated in 1947, father of Aung San Suu Kyi.

Aung San Suu Kyi: Sometimes called Suu Kyi in Western media, or Daw Suu by Burmese people, a leader the National League for Democracy, daughter of Aung San.

Amay: Mother; affectionate title for a woman older than oneself.

Bama: Majority ethnic group in Burma; also known as Burman or Myanma.

Bama lu myo, buddha batha: To be Burmese/Burman is to be Buddhist.

Bhante: Polite title that can be used to address monks; Venerable Sir.

Buddham saranam gacchami, Dhammam saranam gacchami, Sangham saranam gacchami: I take refuge in the Buddha, I take refuge in the Dhamma [Buddha's teachings], I take refuge in the Sangha [the disciples of the

Buddha]. These phrases are traditionally recited out loud or silently when one bows down before a monk or Buddha image.

Buddho yo sabbapaninam saranam khemamuttamam: The Buddha, who is the safe, secure refuge of all beings.

Burma: English name of the country assigned by British colonizers in the nineteenth century. This has also been, since ancient times, similar to the name of the country in spoken Burmese language; it was preferred by some exiles or pro-democracy groups who do not recognize the legitimacy of the military junta's change of the country's English name to Myanmar in 1989.

Burmese: Adjective referring to Burman, or to someone of any native ethnic group in Burma, or to the language.

Burman: Majority ethnic group in Burma; also known as bama or myanma.

Chin: An ethnic minority group in Burma.

Daw: Aunt; polite title for a woman older than oneself.

Dhamma, dharma: The teachings of the Buddha; the Truth; Universal Laws.

Dana: Offerings for monks; the virtue of generosity.

Dukkha: Suffering; the unsatisfactoriness inherent in the experience of living beings.

Hman ba: Correct; a polite way to respond to a comment from a monk or respected person.

Hpaya: A polite title with which to address a monk.

Ingaleik lo . . .: [What is it called] in English?

KIO: Kachin Independence Organization, a political group with an armed struggle wing, founded to support the rights of Kachin people.

KNU: Karen National Union, a political group with an armed struggle wing, founded to support the rights of Karen people.

Kachin: An ethnic minority group in Burma.

Kala: Foreigner; dark-skinned person; Indian; Muslim; widely regarded as a derogatory term.

Kamyinma: Slut.

Kamyinma beh hma leh?: Where is the slut?

Kan, karma: The law of cause and effect; the result of past actions that accumulates over many lifetimes.

Karen: An ethnic minority group in Burma.

Karenni: An ethnic minority group in Burma.

Ko: Brother; polite title for a man the same age or older than oneself.

KONY2012: A campaign launched by the nongovernmental organization Invisible Children in 2012 in order to bring to justice the African warlord Joseph Kony.

Laphet yay: Green tea brewed with milk in Burmese style.

Laphet yay thauk ma la?: Would you like some tea?

Loungyi: Sarong worn by men or women.

MVU: Myanmar Volunteers United, a fictional nongovernmental organization.

Ma: Sister; polite title for a woman the same age or older than oneself.

Manahpyan: Tomorrow.

MaSaLa: Burmese Socialist Programme Party (BSPP), associated with a military dictatorship in power from 1962 to 1988.

Mingalaba: Greeting used by students for their teachers.

Metta: A feeling of non-attached goodwill to be directed toward all beings.

Myanma: Majority ethnic group in Burma; also known as bama or Burman; can also refer to all of the ethnic groups or to the culture in Burma more generally.

Myanma Lanzin youth: Youth wing of the Burmese Socialist Programme Party (BSPP).

Myanmar: English name of the country assigned by the military junta in 1989. Since ancient times, this was similar to the name of the country in the written Burmese language; it is preferred over "Burma" by the current government and by many people living inside the country who do not recognize the legitimacy of the English name that the British gave the country in the nineteenth century.

National League for Democracy: An opposition party (in 2012, when the events of the novel take place).

Nat: A spirit; nat-worship, or animism, is a traditional religion in many parts of Southeast Asia and has been mixed to some extent with more recently arrived religions such as Buddhism and Christianity.

Naw?: Isn't that right? (usually added to the end of a statement).

Neibbana, nirvana: Enlightenment, ultimate liberation from the cycle of birth and death.

Yadana Yeiktha: Jewel Retreat Center; a fictional monastery outside Yangon.

Pali: Ancient language in which the Buddhist scriptures are written.

Panatipata veramani sikkhapadam samadiyami. / Adinnadana veramani sikkhapadam samadiyami. / Abramacariya veramani sikkhapadam samadiyami.:
I undertake the precept to refrain from harming living beings; I
undertake the precept to refrain from taking what is not freely given;
I undertake the precept to refrain from any kind of sexual activity.
[The first three of the Eight Precepts followed by those on meditation
retreats.].

Paticcasamuppada: Dependent origination; the universal law explaining
how all phenomena arise and pass away dependent on multiple
causes and conditions.

Peh byouk: Boiled beans.

Rakhine: An ethnic minority group in Burma.

Rohingya: A name some people use for an ethnic minority group of Muslim people living mostly in Rakhine State.

SSA: Shan State Army, an armed struggle group, founded to support the
rights of Shan people.

Sabbe Buddha assmasama, sabbe Buddha mahiddhika, sabbe dasabalupeta
vesarajjehupagata: All the Buddhas together, all of mighty power, All
endowed with the Ten Powers, attained to highest knowledge.

Sabeh: Jasmine flower; woman's name.

Sangha: The disciples of the Buddha; the monastic community.

Saffron Revolution: a protest of government policy led by Buddhist monks
in Burma in 2007, named for the dark red color of the monks' robes.

Sayama: Female teacher; polite title for a learned woman or teacher.

Shan: An ethnic minority group in Burma.

Seit: Mind/heart.

Seit htay hma, thi ya deh: I know in my mind/heart.

Sotapanna: Stream Enterer, a person who has attained the first of four stages
of enlightenment.

Sutta: Sayings of the Buddha, from scriptures.

Thagya loun: A candy made from palm sugar or jaggery.

Thadi: Mindfulness.

Thadi shi ya meh: You must practice mindfulness.

Thadi ya nay meh: I will remember you / think of you.

Thanaka: A kind of sunscreen made from tree bark.

Thamee: Daughter; affectionate title for a woman younger than oneself.

That-ti: Courage.

That-ti shi ba: Have courage.

Thein Sein: President of Burma, 2011–2016.

Thila shin: Buddhist nun.

Thittawthee: Asian pear.

Thway wun: Dysentery.

Ti nyein deh: To be stable.

U: Polite title for a man or a monk.

Uppekha: Equanimity.

Waya wutsa: Work done by people who stay in a monastery to help meditators and monks.

Yay zet: To have a romantic or strong personal connection to someone because of karma from past lives.

Yay zet pa lo, tway ya deh: We were destined to meet because of our connection from past lives.